CHILDREN OF APIS

BOOK 1: Rebel Blood

JOHN RAPOSA

Children of Apis

Copyright © 2017 by John Raposa

Printed in the United States of America

First Printing, 2017

ISBN 978-0998573175

1

www.ChildrenofApis@gmail.com

www.ChildrenofApis.com

This book is dedicated to my family, whose support made this book possible.

To my wife, Ruth, who was the first to come up with this crazy idea.

To my step-children, Baylee and Ian.

To my daughters, Shannon, Shaelyn, and my angel Kayleigh who read and critiqued each word over my shoulder.

1

DENNIS

"WELL, IT GOES without saying, that was the tastiest meal I've ever had. It was a little undercooked though."

All I can do is roll my eyes and shake my head, as I finish urinating behind a tree. I zip up my fly and then turn toward Thomas, who is flashing an innocent smile. It's tough to stay mad at him, even though he and his friends really screwed up tonight. It was bad enough that they caught the rabbit, but to start the fire while I was down by the stream collecting water was reckless.

"We are close to Ring Road. You guys are lucky your fire wasn't spotted by a patrol."

"Come on Dennis, stop being such a worry wart. There's nobody around for miles. We picked the perfect time to leave. Nobody will know we've escaped until tomorrow morning. By then, we'll be long gone."

"How about if we don't take any chances? Don't forget, you guys all agreed I would be in charge of this escape. After all, I arranged for everything and found out where to go. All we need to do is enter the coordinates into this handheld monitor."

I reach into my coat pocket, but the slip of paper isn't there. I start frantically checking the other pockets, but they just contain random supplies. Thomas must sense my anxiety because he starts chuckling.

"If you're looking for the piece of paper with the all-important numbers, I saw Rudy with it before we left."

I immediately halt my search and look up at Thomas. My heart is hammering, and I've broken out into a sweat. My nerves are already frayed, and we have only been gone for a few hours.

"Let's grab the other two and get out of here. The sooner we get away from here the better for my health."

The two of us start making the short walk back when we immediately hear strange voices. I quickly slip behind a tree, at the edge of the small clearing, where the guys built their small fire. Only a few embers remain lit from when I kicked dirt on the flames. Lonnie and Rudy have their backs to us, and they currently have their hands in the air. Three soldiers are standing on the opposite side of the fire with their rifles drawn. The taller of the three soldiers takes command of the situation and starts yelling at our friends.

"It looks like you two were enjoying a little unlawful food. By the looks of these backpacks, it appears you were planning more than one night."

"Hey Joe, there are two more backpacks over here!"

The tall soldier glances over in the direction of his companion. This situation is going from bad to worse. Pretty soon the soldiers are going to start searching around the clearing. Thomas and I need to get away from here immediately. While the head soldier is distracted, I notice Lonnie reaching behind his back to grab something. My heart sinks when I realize it's the gun he was showing off a few hours ago. He attempts to quickly bring the gun around, but the soldier on the right reacts to the movement and opens fire. Lonnie's body thrashes back and forth like a ragdoll before flopping to the ground. Rudy instinctively lunges to his right, only to be cut down by two well-placed rounds from the leader.

The exchange is over in seconds, but my body is frozen in place as I stare at the two prone bodies of my friends. My trance is broken by the soft whimper of Thomas a few feet away. I slowly back away from the tree and move toward Thomas. I place my hand on his shoulder and turn him toward me while placing a finger to my lips. He slowly nods, but the shocked expression remains on his face. I gradually pull him away, praying that neither of us steps on a twig or a branch. As we retreat from the clearing, I can hear the leader barking out orders.

"The others can't be far from here. Get some lights going on the surrounding area. I will radio in for some support."

It takes every ounce of discipline to continue our controlled withdrawal from the clearing. I increase our pace, occasionally looking back over my shoulder to see the lights scanning the woods. It doesn't take long before Thomas, and I are fleeing through the woods. Branches and vines tear at our exposed flesh and briars claw at our clothing, as we flee back to our community. I have no idea what I will do when I get back. My only immediate concern is to somehow get myself and Thomas back home safely.

2

COWAN/DENNIS

"WOW DID YOU see that one Bree? It was just off to the right."

As I turn my head, Bree's eyes suddenly pop open.

"Why can't these meteor showers happen earlier in the night?"

After voicing her complaint, Bree sits up and stretches her arms causing her long, blonde hair to pull loose from its elastic. Her brown eyes look up at the sky and I realize, not for the first time, she is no longer the skinny tomboy with the freckles and the bony knees. She has grown up to be a beautiful woman. Our friends always wonder why we haven't tried dating, but for some reason, we don't see each other in that way. We have been close friends for as long as I can remember. There just seems to be a special bond between us that's tough to explain. It's just comfortable when we're together, as we can go hours just sitting down without saying a word. My friendship with Marcus is different. While I enjoy hanging out with him, we spend most of the time joking and horsing around. Even though I consider him my best friend, there are some things I hesitate to talk to him about. Bree and I have always shared our deepest secrets and innermost feelings. I slowly realize that she is staring at me with a quizzical look on her face.

"Why are you looking at me like that?"

"Never mind, I'll just sit here and talk to the stars. I guess you're allowed to ignore me after I fell asleep on you." Bree gives me her patented smirk, causing her nose to crinkle, before laying back down.

I turn to look back up and silently enjoy the occasional meteor streaking across the sky. Our blanket is laid out in a small field out behind the old Bellows Falls High School, which is not far from our house on Green Street. Bree made sure we stayed well away from the section containing the crumbling stones with names and dates on them. I can't help but smile, remembering how she freaked out when Kenji told us they were markers for old burial sites. She wouldn't stop talking about how we had been lying on ground containing dead bodies. At first, we thought Kenji was having a little fun at our expense because we just assumed bodies have always been incinerated. When Bree was shown proof, in an old history book, she had nightmares for the better part of a week. It took me a while to convince her to even come near the place she called the Dead Stones. Now she forces me to walk a little further north for our meteor viewing.

Tonight, even though we selected one of the few spots with grass, I can feel rocks and coarse weeds digging into my back. The barren landscape does provide an unobstructed view of the show.

"The meteors definitely seem to be brighter than the last few times we were out here. Kenji was worried the light of the moon might interfere with the viewing since it will be full on Tuesday."

When Bree doesn't immediately answer, I assume she fell back asleep. A short while later, I hear her voice off to my right.

"How does he know this stuff?"

"He's constantly smuggling books and reading everything he can get his hands on. My eyes glaze over if I read too much. It's nice having him around because he's like a walking library." It's also nice laying here next to Bree, just staring up into the sky. This has become somewhat of a tradition over the past few years. I must admit it's much better being outside in the middle of August than during the winter.

"Imagine these are the same stars people have been looking up at for thousands of years."

"You are starting to get a little deep Bree."

"Seriously, the stars just hang out up there looking down on the earth. They just move across the sky and never seem to change at all. It's the earth that has drastically changed."

She's right about the earth, or at least our little corner here in what used to be the northeastern United States. It's totally different than it was twenty-seven years ago. We still don't know what happened back then. Everything is kept secret, and people are hesitant to talk about why a lucky few were selected to escape underground. It's just referred to as the Grounding and continues to be one big mystery. Of course, there are a number of people who know what occurred, since they planned way ahead of time for the Grounding. I can't imagine how much time and money it took to build the underground facility near the river, which was used to house all the survivors. How many other facilities were built around the country? Were the same people who built the facilities responsible for what happened? If so, what was their motivation? Our gang has tried discussing this topic over the years, but we haven't made much headway. Perhaps, I should bring this subject up again.

"Hey did I lose you? I've been babbling over here about stars and stuff, and all I hear are crickets."

"Sorry Bree, I was daydreaming about what you said. Can you daydream at night? Anyway, I was just thinking that we know very little about what took place twenty-seven years ago. How do we know that whatever occurred won't happen again?"

"I believe we would sense if we are in imminent danger. Everyone appears to be going about their normal daily routines. I haven't spotted anything peculiar or out of the ordinary. Although, how would we know what is peculiar? After everything we've been through, what is normal to us would probably be considered shocking to people years ago."

We proceed to lay in silence, staring up at the sky and contemplating our situation. I start to think about how different the land is compared to some of the pictures I've seen. Kenji has some geography books with pictures of the United States before the disaster. He pointed out our present location, which lies in a town formerly known as Bellows Falls, Vermont. This town is located in southeastern Vermont along the Connecticut River. The land used to be surrounded by fields and lush, green forests. When we first surfaced, from our underground facility, the land was barren with very few plants and only a few short trees. Patches of snow were still visible in shady areas between the collapsed buildings. At the time, we didn't realize snow in late July was extremely uncommon in this part of the country. Now we barely see any snow in May, since the temperatures have been getting steadily warmer over the past twelve years.

I can hear Bree's heavy breathing on my right, indicating she once again lost her battle with sleep. We probably should head back home and get some rest before having to get up for work tomorrow, but it's so peaceful just lying here. A rustle in the neighboring grass distracts my attention from the celestial display. The noise is probably just a small critter hunting for some food. I'm glad for the intrusion because it's a sign the animals are slowly increasing in numbers. This is a stark contrast to when we first surfaced. The numbers were so few, we would go days without sighting any wildlife. We assumed the lack of human survivors also meant the entire wildlife population must have also perished. While underground, rumors spread concerning animals also being brought underground prior to the event. There were a number of separate, secure areas in the facility which we assumed were set aside to care for the animals. The areas of the facility we inhabited were immense, so it's tough to imagine the space required to house the wildlife for such a long period of time.

The rustling sounds like it's getting closer. I sit up and try to locate my little friend. The disturbance seems to be coming from a small cluster of bushes about twenty feet from our blanket. I stand up and feel both knees pop. The sound feels loud enough to wake the neighborhood, let alone frighten my intruder. My entire body is stiff and sore from lying down so long. I slowly make my way over to the bushes. Even though my eyes have become accustomed to the dark, it's tough to make out anything clearly. The rustling has stopped as my little friend becomes aware of my presence. Standing motionless, I try to slow my breathing as I attempt to outwit my worthy adversary. After a few moments, I begin to move closer. My right foot lands on a hidden twig and an audible snap guarantees the outcome. My opponent jumps out from the grass, way off to my left, and scurries away into the darkness. Bowing my head in defeat, I turn and walk back to my sleeping companion. It's time to wake her up and head back home for a few hours of sleep. Tomorrow promises to be a rough day.

"Are they gone yet? What are we going to do Dennis?"

"Would you be quiet? I'm not even sure if the person is a soldier. Just give me a minute to think."

The individual appears to be heading back to their initial position. He's bending over and jostling someone. It's tough to see through the bushes, but it seems that his partner was previously asleep. Thomas has started to whimper again and is muttering under his breath.

"They're gonna kill us just like they did to Rudy and Lonnie. He's probably telling his friends to surround us. We need to get out of here."

"Thomas, you need to be quiet, or you're going to get us killed. I don't think they are soldiers. It looks like they're picking up a blanket and folding it."

The second figure is much shorter than the first. After folding the blanket, I hear a few mumbled words, and then the two figures start walking away in the opposite direction. I take a few deep breaths to calm my nerves and look over at Thomas. He is kneeling beside me crying with his head down. The poor kid has seen his close friends shot and now he's running for his life. I feel guilty about getting them involved. I just wanted to show them a better life, away from this place.

"Hey, little buddy. Let's get out of here and head back home."

Thomas' head snaps up, and his eyes glare at me.

"It's all your fault. If it weren't for you, Lonnie and Rudy would still be alive. We were doing fine until you convinced them to leave. I never want to see you again!"

Thomas springs to his feet and charges off into the darkness. I begin to call after him but wisely remain quiet in case soldiers are in the vicinity. Running after him would be pointless and would only endanger the two of us. It's probably best to give him time to cool down.

I wait for another fifteen minutes to make certain I'm alone and to review my predicament. It appears the best option is to return home and act like I wasn't involved. I'll probably get questioned about Lonnie and Rudy, but I just have to say that they worked in my unit and they were good kids. With my immediate plans decided, I get up and begin heading home. I began the night with dreams of freedom, but would gratefully settle for my earlier life.

3

MITCH

WHAT A MORNING it has been already, and it's only 10:05. I am late for my own staff meeting. At least they can't start without me. Throughout history people have dreaded Monday mornings, so why should 2084 be any different? I head down the hallway of the Apis Corporation building. It's located just north of the Headquarters building for the Northeast Territory, where our town is located. Both buildings were built, just downriver of the hydroelectric plant, in preparation for the imminent eruption. Their walls and roofs were reinforced to withstand the weight of snow and ice that would accumulate during our anticipated stay underground. These structures, along with a few factories, are just a handful of modern buildings left standing in our community.

The Apis Corporation building is home to our Apis Pill research and manufacturing facility, in addition to our Artificial Womb and Neonatal Care

Centers. As I walk down the hallway, I glance at some of the framed photographs of honey bees in different natural settings. Since the honey bee is a member of the genus Apis, the building has numerous displays which pay tribute to the insect responsible for the company's success.

At the end of the hallway is the door to the private room primarily used for our staff meetings. To the left of the door is a small mirror. I take the opportunity to stop and straighten my tie. The reflection staring back causes my hands to pause. The previous flecks of gray, just over my ears, are beginning to win battles higher up. I try to dismiss my apprehension by reminding myself I am fifty-five with a full head of hair. "Better gray than nay" my father used to say. My face still looks youthful although the distinguished wrinkles, around my green eyes, are getting deeper. I suddenly realize how silly I must look, staring at myself in the mirror, and quickly turn to open the door.

The room is located in the northeast corner of the building on the second floor. The windows, on the eastern side of the room, overlook the Connecticut River. This river served as the primary source of power during our required stay underground. The rectangular space is dominated by a large oak table surrounded by eight black, cushioned chairs. A number of chairs are scattered around the outside of the room to accommodate extra guests. A large whiteboard is mounted to the wall on my right as I enter the room. Four of the chairs are occupied by my long-time staff members.

Abby Chen is in charge of Apis Pill research and production. She is a petite, Asian scientist who has been working with me for over twenty years. James Moeller heads up Apis Pill and water administration. He is stocky, with blonde hair, dark eyes, and chiseled German features. My close friend Stuart Barnes performs population monitoring, and he looks like your typical accountant. He is tall and thin with a pale complexion behind his thick glasses. To Stuart's left is Michele Timms who runs the Artificial Womb and Neonatal Facilities. She's a brilliant African-American researcher with green eyes and a beautiful mane of black hair.

As I take the seat at the end of the table, conversations cease, and everyone turns in my direction.

"Good morning everyone, I apologize for being late. I was getting some additional guidance for the upcoming monthly territory meeting I will be attending later next week." Scattered greetings are uttered from the group.

"Please tell me that we have more encouraging news to present this month?" A number of concerned faces stare back at me as I look around the table. "Okay then, how about we go clockwise around the table this week."

I turn to my left to look at Abby who is wearing a traditional white lab coat with the ever-present honey bee logo on the pocket. Her dark hair is pulled back in a tight ponytail. Abby begins to nervously arrange a stack of papers in front of her. She adjusts her black framed glasses while taking a deep breath.

"As you know Mitch, we have been struggling to produce the Apis Pill in larger quantities for quite some time. The weather is finally warming over the past number of years, which is benefitting the honey bee population. Since the pill is comprised primarily of honey, it is critical we increase our total bee population. We are still maintaining healthy amounts of bees in our underground facility, but they will soon be insufficient to support our increasing needs. It is imperative we supplement with additional bees in our open-air facilities above ground."

Abby is a tireless worker, but she can rattle easily in a meeting. I try to choose my next words carefully, so she doesn't get too anxious. "Well, that's more encouraging than some of our recent updates. What have you learned thus far from your open-air facilities?" Abby flips through the stack of papers in front of her and finally selects one.

"Honey bees are a very hardy species when acting as a group. They can adjust the temperature in their colony regardless of the outside temperature. In extreme cold, well below zero degrees Fahrenheit, they cluster together to generate and conserve heat. When the outside temperatures are well above 100 degrees Fahrenheit, they can lower the inside colony temperature by evaporating moisture and producing air currents. Thus, they have adapted fairly well to the climate. Our main issue remains the lack of plant growth around our community. The worker bees are required to travel long distances to pollinate and collect nectar. This essentially wears them out and shortens their lifespan. As a result, we are having difficulty maintaining our worker bee numbers, which has caused our honey production to suffer. The average monthly temperatures have been steadily increasing over the past few years. This, coupled with the ash enriched soil, has resulted in rejuvenated plant growth. So, our worker bees should start reaping the benefits if you'll pardon the pun."

Abby looks up and gives me a shy smile before looking back down at her notes. It's too bad she doesn't smile more often. I jot down a few talking points, which I will need for later next week, before turning my attention to James. He and I have had differences of opinion over the years. He is sometimes a bit overzealous enforcing some of the rules associated with his job. "So, James, are things still running smoothly concerning pill and water administration?"

"As a matter of fact, they are. Every once in a while, citizens try to supplement their diet, which as you know is against regulations. Just last night a few of our soldiers stumbled upon two violators who had roasted a rabbit. There were also a number of backpacks scattered around, so the Security Unit is investigating whether this was part of an escape attempt."

I was expecting James to gloat about this incident during the staff meeting this morning. I have already received a summary of last night's incident, but I'm curious to know how much James has learned. There was further evidence, included in the report, to indicate an escape attempt, so I decide to probe him further.

"Is it possible this was just a few kids out on a harmless camping trip?" Jim stops what he's saying and gives me a disgusted look before responding to my question.

"First of all, they had clothes for more than a few days. Secondly, one of the criminals tossed evidence into the fire before the soldiers could stop him. The paper appears to contain some sort of coordinates, but it was mostly destroyed in the fire. They captured a third individual early this morning, and a fourth person is under surveillance as we speak."

Jim awaits my response with a satisfied look on his face. I'm alarmed to discover the amount of information he is privy to already. I maintain eye contact and attempt to hide my concern as I address his comments.

"Since they haven't been formally charged with a crime, I'd be careful throwing the word criminals around. If it turns out they weren't escaping, then we are left with the deaths of two young kids, due to the excessive enforcement of a Food Ordinance."

As expected, James begins to show irritation as his neck and face begin to redden. He regards the regulations as black and white, while I firmly believe common sense and discretion should be applied in certain circumstances. The problem is James has the support of people in high places. They regard discretion as a form of weakness. James rolls his eyes, crosses his arms, and leans back. I don't need to be a psychiatrist to recognize a textbook defensive posture. "You mentioned there is possibly another person involved."

"The two deceased and the third individual who was captured were part of an Environmental Unit. Their Group Leader is Dennis Jones, and they all live in the same house. Naturally, the Security Unit believes he was involved and intend to question him today. Even if they can't immediately prove his involvement, there's a good chance our sensors will detect something when he makes his scheduled appearance at the Food Dispensary this week. Our monitors are sensitive enough to pick up the elevated protein and B-12 levels 3 to 4 weeks after ingestion of animal meat. If he doesn't show up for his allotted time this Wednesday, we will take him into custody and perform a scan. By the way, Michele, can't your group come up with any original surnames for your Lab Rats? Our database is full of kids named Johnson, Smith, and Brown."

Michele immediately whips around to address James. "Could you please not use that nickname here? That is an extremely inflammatory name we highly discourage our youth from using. I wouldn't expect it to be uttered in a professional environment. To answer your question, since a newborn's true identity is provided by their number, we cycle through about a dozen surnames when naming each Mandatory Reproduction Age (MRA) baby. Perhaps we should reconsider this process."

As usual, James has found a way to cause animosity during a meeting. I probably should save him for last next time. I need to make one more attempt to get something productive from him this morning. "Did you have anything further to report other than the tragic incident which occurred last night?" His cocky smile signifies he thinks he has won this round.

"Things have been running smoothly, even before the events of last night. Once word circulates, concerning the fate of the violators, the remaining citizens will most certainly appear at the Food Dispensary at their allotted times. People respond to strength and consistency. Any sign of weakness will eventually lead to rebellion. Do we want a repeat of what happened ten years ago? How many citizens did we lose then? The good news for us is those rebels probably didn't get far. Some neighboring bears had a nice feast, and it ended up working as a deterrent to anyone else with ideas of leaving."

I can see we are getting nowhere fast, so I decide to change topics. "Thanks for the update James." I shift my gaze to the other side of the table to Stuart.

You can feel the tension in the room begin to ease. "Stuart, any good news on the population front?"

"We continue to monitor a few issues concerning our population. First of all, our population growth has leveled off over the past seven years. This dates back to when the controversial Maximum Expiration Age was instituted. Many of us believe this was the final straw that caused the rebellion which James just referenced." Stuart gives a slight nod toward James. "Word was leaked leadership was considering a maximum age limit of eighty years old and some people decided to make a run for it."

I immediately cast a disapproving glare at James while addressing Stuart's last remark. "It appears those of us who were against MEAs are being proven correct." My remark produces the desired reaction as James bolts upright in his seat and turns to respond.

"You can't blame the leveling off of the population on the MEAs. There are a number of reasons for the population to experience a leveling off. People had to go through a period of adjustment to our new society. They are finally getting used to everyday life and entering into a routine. There will soon be an increase in couples starting families, and the population growth will pick back up."

I just shake my head as I listen to the same tired excuses and unfounded optimism. Stuart pulls out a paper that contains a bar graph.

"My group has been tracking births since 2058, which is the first full year we lived underground. We instituted the Mandatory Reproduction Age, during that first year, because we were unsure how we would adapt to life underground. I don't need to remind you that the MRA law, which called for the mandatory, confidential donation of sperm and egg, by the age of thirty, served two purposes. It provided a means to test our Artificial Wombs, and it delivered a needed influx to the population."

As Stuart continues, my thoughts are drawn back to those early days. There was grave concern, back then, that we would experience significant fatalities adjusting to life underground. We did not know how people would adapt to a diet based solely on the Apis Pill and water. Abby, and her group had run exhaustive tests and trials, but they had no long-term data. We were also afraid of disease and the risk of transmission in an enclosed environment.

My attention is drawn back to the meeting, and I realize Stuart is still expounding. He's a reserved person by nature, but when he starts discussing his area of expertise, he could ramble on for hours. I sense him starting to ramp up and need to get the meeting back on track.

"Stuart, we all know the reasons why the MRAs were established. Could you get back to summarizing why our population growth is leveling off?"

"Sorry Mitch, to put it bluntly, many of us feel there is a general feeling of apathy and resentment festering in large segments of our community. Frankly, families are hesitant to bring children into this world, and our compiled data supports this theory. We have separated our data into age groups, each spanning ten years. Families in the 31-40 and 41-50 age groups are having fewer and fewer babies over the past ten years. The majority of our births are occurring in the 21-30 age group. If you zoom in on this data, you will see the bulk of these births are resulting from MRA individuals. A significant percentage of the population is kids with unknown birth parents. They are raised in our child care facilities which are just glorified orphanages. When they grow up, they get placed in apartments. Their life, to this point, is essentially segregated from kids brought up by families. It has caused a divide in our social structure and is becoming a serious problem."

James just shakes his head in disgust, but I can see concern and resignation amongst the rest of the group. This is not a new concern. It's a topic some of us have been discussing more and more lately. The consensus is, even if we could devise a solution, there's little hope the leaders of the territory would give it much credence. I pull myself out of my reverie and turn my attention back to Stuart. "You mentioned earlier there were two issues your group has been tracking."

"They are actually related to one another. Since births, to citizens aged 31-50 years old, have been steadily decreasing our population is becoming more and more top heavy." James, who had been exhibiting false disinterest, takes this opportunity to pounce.

"This is exactly why the concept of Maximum Expiration Age was put into effect. We can't support a bunch of old people who have nothing to offer our community. We have limited resources and need to direct them toward citizens who are working and performing a useful role."

He proceeds to lean back in his chair and refolds his arms. He now wears a smug look signifying who he believes has just won round two. As soon as James finishes, Stuart continues without missing a beat.

"Regardless of regulations and laws, we are still faced with the dilemma of how to fix our population percentages. This problem is going to continue to get worse. We have discussed this before and have determined we must somehow improve living conditions in order to stimulate population growth. The problem is any suggestions we come up with fall on deaf ears. Mitch, perhaps you will have better success at the territory meeting later next week."

I smile at Stuart, but it does not exude the same optimism he possesses. My skepticism stems from years of disappointment and dismissal by the leaders of our territories. In order to be perceived as being more humane, our leaders adopted the moniker of the National Organization for Animals and Humanity (N.O.A.H.). While this acronym is quite accurate in describing the process by which humans and wildlife were saved from extinction, it misses the mark of portraying the actual agenda of our leaders. Prior to the apocalyptic event, the United States had devolved into a more militaristic form of government. Apparently, when our previous form of government became perpetually gridlocked, the government was overthrown, and a more militaristic approach was instituted. Thus, my chances of swaying the opinions of a group of stubborn, power-driven individuals are remote. With these dark thoughts in mind, I search for a life raft in the form of Michele. "It looks like your previous colleagues set the bar pretty low when it comes to imparting good news. Do you have any laboratory highlights I can present?" Michele gives me her dazzling, white smile that always seems to disarm me a little.

"First of all, the construction of the additional Artificial Wombs has been completed. They have passed all functionality testing and are available for service. We are thinking of utilizing these units as we take other Artificial Womb units off-line for routine maintenance. As Stuart just explained, the number of births has declined. This also includes the number of MRA births. His data shows we currently have approximately 225 citizens in the 21-30 age group. Close to 30 of them will be hitting Mandatory Reproduction Age. Our facility has sufficient Artificial Wombs to handle the anticipated volume. So, the lack of need affords the opportunity to integrate new systems into service."

"Thank you, Michele, for the good news. I will make sure to pass along the great progress your group has made. Do you have anything else to report?"

"I have information concerning a couple of items you wanted me to check into regarding newborn identity tracking and numbering. The placement of trackers is indeed random for all MRA births. Apparently, years ago, the tracker location was coincident with a group of births. It could span a day or two depending on the number of births being handled over that period of time. This made implantation easier for the doctors. During one of the equipment upgrades in 2075, the tracker insertion became automated. All patient information is cataloged and stored using their unique identity number. We still utilize the 17-digit numbering system to catalog each birth. The first eight digits are the newborn's birth date depicted as mmddyyyy. The next five digits are the location of the birth. Evidently, years ago, it was decided to adopt the old zip code system. Since our community currently resides in what was previously Bellows Falls, Vermont the zip code is 05101. Finally, the last four digits are the newborn's unique birth order. Since our current population is just over 1400 citizens, the four digits should last us for quite some time. The identity number continues to be placed on the palm of the newborn's right hand just below the pinky finger. Our sensing stations are designed to scan a citizen's right hand, palm down, so it's important to keep this location consistent." Michele gives a slight nod of her head, which is her way of signaling she's done speaking.

I reply with an appreciative nod of my own and look around at my staff. "Thank you all for the updates. I will summarize the information and pass it along. I appreciate your time and will give everyone a synopsis of the upcoming territory meeting. Hopefully, there will not be any surprises that will affect our day to day activities. Have a good week everyone." With that, the meeting adjourns with some scattered pleasantries and the expected scowl.

4

MARCUS

AT LEAST IT is sunny and warm today. There was talk, back at the depot earlier this morning, about the temperature reaching 75 degrees this afternoon. It's hard to believe, that years ago temperatures commonly reached 90 to 100 degrees during the month of August. Working hard outside, in those temperatures, must have been brutal.

Our crew is continuing to slowly advance up the wide street formerly known as Atkinson. We have been working on this street for a few years, performing demolition and clean-up. Initially, we conduct preliminary building inspections to see if the structures are salvageable and then our findings are turned over to a construction group for verification and eventual refurbishment. If the building can't be saved, then we knock it down with either machines or explosives. Everyone looks forward to blowing things up. It's the clean-up that's the longest and most tedious part of the job.

I have been told this area used to be called Bellows Falls and was located in the former state of Vermont. This region was known for its lush green forests, but when we surfaced from the Grounding, back in 2072, everything was brown and covered with dirt and snow. Most of the buildings were flattened, or well on their way, and the streets were littered with fallen trees, debris, and a variety of abandoned vehicles. My friends and I were only 13 years old, at that time, and we were tasked with clearing the streets of all obstructions. We would salvage usable wood and materials and move the rest to a separate site in the southern part of the community. The vehicles were also gathered and moved to the storage area. Since all vehicles used today are electric powered, these gas-powered antiques were useless. After the lengthy, initial clean-up task was completed, we were able to concentrate on the buildings themselves. Some of the stone structures were salvageable, but the majority of the wooden buildings were ruined.

Our job today is to continue with the clean-up of an apartment house we knocked down last week. I look over at Cowan stepping down from his bulldozer which is equipped with a universal blade, or 'U blade'. The tall wings, on the side of the blade, are used to move large quantities of dirt and debris.

Cowan and I have been best friends for as long as I can remember. Even though I am comfortably over six feet and pretty solid, he's one of the few guys I wouldn't mess with. We make quite a pair, with his pale skin in direct contrast to my black skin color. When the sun strikes his long, red hair, it appears to be on fire. The way the temperature is steadily rising today, he will have it pulled back in a ponytail by mid-afternoon. At the moment, he's struggling to move a fallen tree from the front of his dozer. He seems to be a little sluggish today, so I decide to lend a hand and poke a little fun in the process.

"Hey man, do you need a hand lifting that little branch?" He glances over and glares at me, but I know he's not serious. He's used to me busting him up, and he does not hesitate to give it right back. "You know, you've been dragging all morning. Are you feeling okay?" Cowan slowly stands up, puts his hands on his hips, and stretches before replying.

"Bree and I were up late watching the meteor shower out behind the school."

"How did you convince her to go near the Dead Stones?" I remember when Bree found out the purpose of the Dead Stones, her skin went whiter than Cowan's and her eyes bugged out. She wouldn't sleep alone for an entire week.

"I made sure we stayed far away from the stones and found a new place further north."

"What you're innocently trying to tell me is you found a safer place which just happened to be more secluded. It's always the quiet ones you need to be careful of." I wink at him as I give him a good-natured punch in the arm.

"Real funny, now help me pick up this tree." Cowan turns to begin moving the tree, but I'm not going to let him get off that easy.

"Seriously Bud, what's up with you two? If you haven't noticed, Bree is an attractive woman, so how come you're not going after that?"

"We're just really close friends, and for some reason, I don't see her that way."

"You do like girls, right? It's cool if you don't. You're a good-looking guy and all, but I definitely like girls. On top of that, I don't go for redheads."

"Don't worry, I like girls, and you wouldn't be my type anyway. I prefer to be with a person who has brains so I can have an intelligent conversation."

We just look at each other and start laughing. The tree just continues to lay there not enjoying our banter as much as we do.

A few moments later my attention is drawn to an object flying in our direction over the trees. At first, I assume it's a hawk, but then I notice its wings aren't moving.

"What the heck is that?" Cowan turns around and looks up to see what has peaked my interest.

"I believe it's called a drone. Drew and Kenji were talking about them a few weeks ago. Drew said they are used to monitor the wildlife population."

I was not expecting an answer from Cowan. After the object passes overhead, I look down at my friend hoping to get more information.

"How do you monitor animals with a flying object?"

"Drew said the bottom of the vehicle is equipped with sensors aimed at the ground. These sensors are used to detect signals, which are transmitted from devices attached to the animals. This information can be used to monitor animal population and to track their movements."

"Wow, that's amazing! I didn't know we had such technology. I thought everything was destroyed during the Grounding."

"I think for the most part you're right, Marcus. Kenji and I were talking about this very topic. He's convinced that if our society hadn't experienced a catastrophic event, technology would have advanced far beyond our imagination. Not only would airplanes be flying overhead, but cars as well. The incident not only destroyed buildings but the people and information associated with the various technologies. Our community is left with only a small sample of the technology which existed years ago."

It's depressing to think of everything that was lost. I contemplate this as I stare up into the sky. I look for the drone, but it's nowhere to be seen. It is pretty cool to think an object, that high in the sky, can monitor a tiny animal. Suddenly, I'm struck with the thought that if they can monitor animals, what would stop someone from using drones to monitor people. The idea of being watched from above gives me the creeps and instantly changes my opinion towards drones.

It's getting late in the afternoon, and the sun is nearing the tops of the trees off to our west. This would be the nearest thing we have to a forest. The Forest Ordinance prohibits civilians from entering the wooded region unless they are employed by either the Wildlife or Environmental Units. My friend Dennis has been working for the Environmental Unit for the past five years. He said it's tough getting around with all the fallen trees. Some of the new trees are up to 10-15 feet in height. He has seen mostly small animals, but occasionally he sees a bear or a deer. They have to carry stun guns in case they are attacked because the Hunting Ordinance prohibits killing or hunting of any kind.

I turn back to the housing lot we've been clearing all day. It will take a number of weeks to finish this job. I glance to my left at the next few houses on this side of the street. They are primarily three-story apartment houses with their roofs collapsed into the two upper floors. Some of them may be perfect candidates for explosives. Cowan walks up as I'm planning our next projects.

"Hey, are you going to help me pack up our equipment or what?"

"You seemed to be doing a great job without me. I was just trying to figure out what we're up against over the coming months. We may get to play with some explosive charges." Cowan's face brightens at the prospect of imploding more structures. I walk over and help him gather up the remaining tools.

"You know Marcus, you're like a little kid with those explosives. By the way, don't let me forget to charge the dozer and the dump truck when we get back to the depot. They're running low on juice."

"No problem, I know how forgetful you can be sometimes. As a matter of fact, let's test that little brain of yours with some college sports trivia. How about an easy one to start? Duke?"

"Aw c'mon Marcus, not that game again! I suck at it! Aren't they some kind of devil? Just give me a second. Blue Devils!

"Good job! How about Arizona?"

"I remember you asking me this one a few weeks ago. Bulldogs?"

"That's not a bad guess since it's one of the more popular nicknames, but it's incorrect. I'll give you a hint. They have the same mascot as Kentucky."

"Wildcats!"

Cowan breaks out into a grin as he climbs into the dozer to drive it up onto the trailer. I guess my boy has been studying the sports magazines I gave him. Once the bulldozer is pulled up to the front of the trailer, I secure it with the appropriate chains and then hop down onto the ground. We both climb up into the truck and start heading back to the depot. "How about I give you a mascot, and you have to come up with the school? How about Longhorns?"

"Longhorns are found in the former state of Texas. I guess sleeping with those magazines under my pillow really does work."

5

MITCH

I T HAS BEEN a long day to start a long week, so it feels good to finally sit down and relax with a drink. It is one of the perks of being in the territories upper management. I lean my head back in my favorite chair and watch the last vestiges of light slant through the living room window. I hold up my glass of bourbon and gaze at the light through the caramel colored liquid as I review the day's events.

The monthly staff meeting was contentious as usual with James, once again, being at the center of everything. While differences of opinion can be beneficial to a group, his constant abrasive behavior creates too much animosity. A few members have already complained to me privately, but the fact remains that his appointment to our staff came directly from territory Management. They love the uncompromising attitude he brings to our company. Rumor has it that he's being groomed to take over my position. He is probably supplying them with his own, biased version of today's meeting. I can count on a lukewarm reception at the territory meeting later next week.

It only seems a short time ago that I was the Golden Boy representing Apis Corporation at the initial planning meetings. However, these were held years before the volcanic eruption took place. I can remember the complete shock, exhibited from everyone around the table when General Taggert presented the outrageous plan our nation's military leaders had concocted along with a group of hand-picked researchers. He warned that the content of the meeting was classified and anyone caught discussing the subject matter, outside the room, would be charged with treason and immediately imprisoned. The intensity of his glare left no doubt to anyone sitting around the conference table. The general turned over the meeting to his researchers, and everyone's disbelief was slowly dispelled.

The researchers had been tracking a Supervolcano located in Yellowstone National Park in Wyoming. Seismic activity had dramatically increased over the previous few years. The caldera, which capped the underground reservoir of magma, had risen to unprecedented levels. Their data, derived from multiple sources, predicted it was only a matter of time until the volcano was going to erupt.

They listed a number of sobering facts concerning the imminent eruption. Volcanic ash, measuring over ten feet deep, could potentially cover a radius of over 1000 miles. This ash would spread eastward to cover almost the entire United States. It would essentially render this country uninhabitable. The ash cloud would cause the temperatures of the earth to plummet and thus trigger a 'Mini Ice Age'. The duration of the Ice Age could last for decades. The entire population of this country, and large segments of Canada and South America, would perish. The severity and length of the Ice Age would dictate the impact to the rest of the planet. At a minimum, famine and disease would devastate the remaining population. It was impossible to predict what population would remain once the temperatures began to rise and the snow and ice receded.

Their plan was to build six underground facilities at various locations in the United States. The facilities would be spread out across the country. Each facility would be located near a hydroelectric power plant for its major source of power. Wind farms would also be constructed to supply power. Emergency power would be provided by nuclear reactors from decommissioned submarines. They estimated approximately 1000 citizens could be supported underground at each site. These citizens would include our top military leaders and a representative cross-section of the population. Selected specimens of plants and wildlife would also be brought underground and housed in separate, secure areas to repopulate the land upon returning to the surface.

I can remember the room being deathly quiet while the scientists continued to outline their extraordinary plan. Everything was meticulously planned except how to feed the underground population. Finally, I raised my hand and asked the obvious question concerning food. The assembled group of leaders and scientists smiled and turned to my mentor Dr. Howard Langfeld who was seated to my left. I can still remember the proud look on his face as he stood up, patted me on the shoulder, and then walked up to the front of the meeting room. Dr. Langfeld was a brilliant man in his early seventies. He was the founder and president of Apis Corporation. He was a tall, lean man with thinning white hair. His wire-framed glasses magnified the green eyes that blazed with excitement.

He proceeded to summarize the Apis Pill which his company had developed. What I had considered to be only a dietary supplement was presented as the complete solution to our food needs. The main constituent in the pill is honey, which contains vital enzymes, vitamins, and minerals. The honey is combined with additional vitamins and proteins to create a pill capable of sustaining life. As my old friend and mentor finished his presentation, a satisfied look came over his face. At that moment, I understood that his lifelong dream had just been realized.

The sound of footsteps, coming up the front stairs, distracts me from my reflection. The front door opens, and Stuart walks into the living room. Suddenly, the room is bathed in bright light, causing me to partially spill my drink as I quickly turn away from the glare.

"Mitch, what the heck are you doing sitting here in the dark?"

I look at my watch and realize how much time has passed. "Hey Stuart, I was just planning my week. It looks like that boss of yours had you working late again." Stuart chuckles as he pours himself a bourbon and plops himself down on the couch near the front window.

"You got that right! He has this big territory meeting, later next week, so he has his staff working overtime to make him look good."

I smile at him as we sip our drinks in silence. My friend looks like he has had a long day. A white dress shirt is half untucked from his beige khakis. Two bloodshot eyes are the result of hours in front of a computer monitor crunching data.

We met shortly after going below ground and quickly hit it off. He was assigned to the Population Monitoring group and immediately displayed an aptitude for numbers. His tireless work ethic made him an easy choice for my staff. Since neither of us has any family, we decided to share this house when it was time to resurface. Our house was one of the first to get refurbished. It's a large, two-story stone building, located on Westminster Street, just west of the Apis Corporation building. It is one of the few homes with both electricity and running water.

"You look exhausted Stuart. You need to delegate some of your work. Do you have enough help?"

"It's not the number of people, but their capability that's the problem. I have to be careful not to overwhelm them with certain jobs. Keep in mind, some of my staff are the product of MRA births. The education they received falls short of high school equivalency with regard to math and science. I still don't understand why we still segregate these kids from the general population in school. Some of these kids have potential. Kenji is a prime example."

"You have mentioned his name on a few occasions. It is interesting how people are born with certain gifts."

"Kenji is obviously naturally intelligent, but he utilizes our vast database of information to further enhance his knowledge. Recently, I've been monitoring some of the areas he has been visiting, and they raise some red flags."

"What do you mean by red flags?"

"Our security software enables me to track where he goes in the database. He leaves virtual footprints I can easily follow. Lately, he has been researching apocalyptic events. His main area of concentration appears to be Supervolcanoes."

"Well, it looks like your little genius has solved the big mystery. I would not concern yourself too much with his studies. Even though our great leaders would frown upon such activity, I believe, at this point, people deserve to know what happened. It made some sense, at first, to shield the general public from some of the horrors associated with such a tragic event. I try not to dwell on the fact we were only able to save one thousand citizens in our facility. Everyone lost close family and friends when we had to retreat underground. I shudder to think what gruesome sights the initial 'clean-up' crews faced when they resurfaced. The snow and ice had just receded, leaving the remnants of the last survivors. Not much was left of the remaining bodies, but there were signs of mass slaughter and cannibalism. By the time the rest of us resurfaced the bodies had been incinerated, and we just had to deal with the widespread destruction of buildings and the environment."

"I agree with you that it is senseless to continue with the veil of secrecy surrounding the eruption. People are over the initial shock, and most seem pretty ambivalent about what occurred."

"I have attended the territory meetings for years and have come to the disturbing conclusion that the real reason our leaders regulate knowledge is to maintain control over the population."

"Mitch that's crazy!"

"Come on Stuart think about it. What other reasons are there for the regulation of information and education? I think you were dead on with some of the observations you presented at the meeting this morning. Over the years, we have gradually created a society that has promoted segregation. As you have rightfully concluded, this has caused a general feeling of apathy. I'm beginning to think this was the goal of our leadership all along. A society, comprised of citizens who don't care, is easier to govern and control."

"Obviously, I agree with you about the mindset of a significant percentage of our citizens. However, I do not share your cynicism about this being some master plan concocted by our leadership."

We spend the rest of the evening, either lost in our own thoughts or discussing simple topics. Stuart, by nature, possesses a more optimistic personality. Just give him a little more time, living with me, and I will taint his positive attitude.

6

KENJI

AS I SIT in my bedroom reading an American History book, I'm amazed at the senseless loss of life that has occurred over the years. One of the main reasons for studying history is, so people don't repeat past mistakes. After reviewing some of the events, I'm gravely concerned the majority of us are ignorant of our past. It turns out the sum total of our historical knowledge has been obtained through rumor and hearsay. Somewhere near the end of the chapter on World War III, my concentration is interrupted by the sound of Drew's voice.

"Hey Kenji, where are you? We need to get going."

It's not like there are many places to hide in our small, single-story house. It only has five rooms, which include a living room and dining room on either side of the front door. The back of the house consists of a small kitchen sandwiched between two bedrooms. Drew and I share one, while Carmen gets the other. Like the other houses on the northern side of the community, there is no electricity or running water. We obtain our water, along with our Apis Pills, during our weekly visits to the Food Dispensary. Some of the apartments and homes, further south, have a small hand pump in the kitchen to obtain water from underground wells. There are a few homes, where the community leaders and some of the families live, that have both running water and electricity. We utilize battery operated lamps for our lighting purposes. Marcus and Cowan recharge our batteries at work. Our restroom consists of a rustic shack in the back yard, which ensures visits are painfully quick in the middle of the winter.

I hear Drew walking down the hallway, so I close the book, tuck it under my arm, and walk out into the kitchen. He just turns around and shakes his head as he walks back to the front door where Carmen is waiting with her arms folded.

"Oh, I see you found him. Let me guess, he had his face buried in a book, and he lost track of time?"

I open my mouth to apologize, but realize there is no point. We've been down this road many times before, so it's best to just follow them outside for the short walk next door. It's almost 7:00 p.m., which means the sun won't be setting for another hour. As I look south on Green Street, it appears empty all the way down to where it meets School Street.

Immediately upon entering the house, I see the rest of our gang in the living room off to the right. Cowan and Marcus are in their customary chairs across from Bree and Grace, who share a couch along the front wall. As everyone says hello, Drew and Carmen walk across the room and sit down in the loveseat while I grab the chair near the door. It doesn't take long for everyone to start chattering about their day.

This group has literally been together since birth. Our birthdays are all within a day of each other as a result of the Mandatory Reproduction Age Law. The tattoos, on each of our right hands, are a constant reminder of our kinship. Even though we all have different personalities, we have always been a close-knit group. Glancing around the room, and watching the animated conversations, causes me to realize how fortunate I am to have grown up with such close friends. With the discussions as a backdrop, I open my book to get a little reading done. As soon as the book opens Cowan starts calling my name.

"Hey Kenji, what are you reading this time?"

"This is the American History book you found a few months ago. It's hard to believe some of the events that occurred in this country over the years." Conversations begin to break off, and everyone gradually turns to listen. Bree is the first to join the discussion.

"What events, in particular, are you talking about?"

I look down at the book and select a bookmark about one-third of the way into the book.

"This chapter describes the Civil War which occurred between the years 1861-1865. Apparently, this country had a war with itself, and the sides consisted of mainly northern states versus southern."

"What could possibly cause people, in the same country, to fight each other?"

It never takes Carmen long to join the conversation. She's the most outspoken person in our group. It's best not to get on her bad side because she has a short fuse. Even through her olive complexion, her face can get pretty red. She is beautiful with her long dark hair and large brown eyes. Personally, I find her temper, and her flirtatious personality, to be a turn-off.

"The main cause of the war was slavery. Slaves were predominantly people of African descent who worked for landowners in the south. They essentially had no freedom and lived in harsh conditions. The people in these pictures have the same color skin as you Marcus." I turn the book around so everyone can see the pictures. "The northern states wanted to eliminate slavery, and this triggered a war. The northern states eventually won, but over 600,000 people died."

"So, my relatives were probably from Africa? It's amazing how little I know about my history."

"We are all pretty ignorant about the history of this country and our nationalities. Apparently, my ancestors did some deplorable things over the course of history." I look down at the book and select the appropriate tab about halfway through the book.

"How did you find out about your ancestors?"

I look over to my left to answer Cowan's question. "Well I'm not 100% sure of my nationality, but if I were to guess it would be Japanese. This chapter describes the bombing of Pearl Harbor. Pearl Harbor was an American military base located in the Pacific Ocean. Evidently, Japan conducted a surprise air attack on Pearl Harbor, killing almost 2500 Americans. The United States eventually retaliated by dropping nuclear bombs on the cities of Hiroshima and Nagasaki in 1945. By the end of the year close to 150,000 people were either killed or injured." The room becomes quiet while they digest the information. I just sit there feeling somewhat embarrassed, even though I have no reason to be. It's Cowan who finally breaks the silence.

"Kenji, even though your nationality may have been Japanese, it doesn't mean you should feel responsible."

Leave it to Cowan to pick up on my distress. He has always been the unofficial leader of our little gang for as long as I can remember.

"It just concerns me that throughout history different races and nationalities have clashed. Not too long ago, in 2021, the United States built a wall across its southern border to keep Hispanic immigrants from entering the country. The wall took almost four years to build and was almost two thousand miles long." I hand the book to Cowan so he can pass it along to everyone. When it finally makes it over to Carmen, I hear her gasp.

"These people look kind of like me. They have dark skin and dark hair like mine."

The room remains quiet as everyone either looks through the book or becomes lost in their own thoughts. This time it's Drew, of all people, who speaks up.

"Guys, just because these events happened before, doesn't mean anything like them will happen again. We all look different, but we get along just fine."

"Drew is right. I don't sense the same prejudice my supposed ancestors from Africa experienced. We're all pretty much equal in our community."

"What the hell are you talking about! Do you really feel equal to the families in the southern part of this community? Do we have running water or electricity like they do? What about all the insults we have to put up with? I'm sick of being called a 'Lab Rat' or a 'Tubie' by those creepy guys! It's not our fault how we were born."

"Sorry Carmen, I didn't think about that. At least we are better off than the victims in that book!"

We spend the next few minutes complaining about our living conditions. I decide it's time to ask Cowan why he called this meeting in the first place.

"So, Cowan, why did you get us all together tonight?"

"While I was watching the meteor shower the other night with Bree, I started thinking again about the Grounding. We really should know what happened. How do we know it won't happen again in the near future? That history book showed the destruction from a couple of bombs. Is it possible the United States went to war with another country?"

"I researched the possibility, and I doubt it because the bombs would have made the soil uninhabitable. The soil in our community is very rich. The trees and plants have been flourishing now that the weather has been getting steadily warmer over the past few years. There would also have been more devastation to the buildings, not just collapsed roofs."

"I heard some people talking about global warming. What exactly is that Kenji?"

"I initially thought that was a possibility Bree. It's also known as climate change. There should have been a gradual change in temperature leading up to the event. From the data I've seen, the temperature drastically changed just after people fled underground. Researchers claim an 'ice age' would result, that could last hundreds of years. From all reports, most of our community was underground for only ten years."

"So, do you have any idea what happened?"

I look back toward Cowan and nod. "I was able to access different databases at work, over the past few weeks, and discovered some very interesting pieces of information. I believe a Supervolcano was the cause." The room is filled with sudden outbursts and looks of disbelief. When everyone finally settles down, I continue with my explanation.

"When a Supervolcano erupts, incredible amounts of volcanic ash are spewed into the sky blocking out the sun. A 'mini ice age' would result. Depending on the severity of the eruption the ice age could last between 10-20 years. This would fit within the timeframe we spent underground. The land would be covered with a deep layer of snow causing buildings to collapse. This could explain the destruction we witnessed when we resurfaced. The fertile soil would be a direct result of the volcanic ash. The sky would gradually clear, which would cause the temperatures to gradually increase. This would account for the increasing number of stars in the sky and the reason you have only been able to enjoy the meteor showers over the last few years. There are a number of active volcanoes in the Western part of the former United States. This makes sense since the devastation would be the most severe closest to the eruption."

The looks on the faces of my friends are priceless. Only Carmen is able to respond when I finally finish my explanation.

"I will never make fun of you again for having your face buried in a book."

I smile at Carmen knowing this is the closest she will ever come to an apology.

"Well Kenji, I called this meeting without much hope of coming to a resolution, but after hearing your explanation, it makes a lot of sense. You mentioned the devastation would be worse closest to the volcano. Does that mean the people out there didn't make it?"

"From what I have read it would be harder to survive the closer you are to the eruption. We need to come to grips with the fact we may be the only survivors remaining in this country.

7

BREE/MARCUS

DARK CLOUDS ARE slowly rolling in as I wait in line with Carmen and Grace for our food. It's kind of funny what we call food nowadays. I can remember looking through some books with Kenji and being amazed at the different meals people used to eat. He explained that people would spend significant time preparing and cooking food. Now things are much simpler since we only need to take an Apis Pill once a day. It can be a hassle having to wait in line for our weekly supply of pills and water. This is especially true in the winter or on a day like today when it threatens to rain. Let's just hope we can get back home before the rain starts. This is highly unlikely since it's a long walk from the Food Dispensary, which is located along the river at the back of the Apis Corporation building. For the time being, we just stand in the middle of a parking lot in a long line. The Headquarters building looms over us and gives me the creeps with its tinted windows. I always have an eerie feeling of being watched.

I look toward the back of the line, where the boys are standing, and give them a wave. The four of them are an odd-looking group. Cowan and Marcus stand out from the rest of the people in line because of their size and Cowan's long, fiery-red hair. Marcus is muscular, like Cowan, but is a few inches taller. Kenji looks tiny standing next to the two of them. The top of his head barely reaches Marcus' chest. His round glasses and thin body fit his brilliant mind. I'd bet Kenji and Drew, together, don't weigh as much as Marcus. While Drew may be six inches taller than Kenji, he might even weigh less. His curly, blond hair contrasts with Kenji's spiked, black hair.

"Oh crap, here comes those two idiots!" I look at Carmen who is trying to ignore the two guys who are approaching us. I don't know if it's the fact that Carmen is attractive or that she can be loud, but these guys always seem to find her.

"Hey Cole, look what we have here? It looks like the Lab Rats are standing in line waiting for their cheese."

The two guys start laughing as they walk up to us. We all try to ignore them, but it's obvious they are more interested in Carmen.

"Danny, I think the one with the dark hair has been having extra cheese. Check out the tail on her!"

More laughter follows this latest comment. People in line start turning toward us and listening, but nobody seems interested in helping out. Even the guards, standing near the window of the Dispensary, are watching but making no attempt to intervene.

"By the way Tubie, I was fondling your mom the other day while working in the laboratory. Her curvy, glass bottom looked just like yours!"

This time a few of the other people join the laughter. Suddenly, I feel a presence to my left. I glance over to see Marcus and Cowan glaring at our uninvited guests.

"Carmen, do we need to remove these pieces of trash for you?"

Immediately, color drains from the faces of our guests. Danny nudges Cole in the side, and they both turn and begin walking away from the line. Marcus puts his arm on Carmen's shoulder and turns her body to face him. I can see Carmen's eyes are watery and she is visibly shaken.

"Are you okay?"

"Yes, thanks for showing up guys. It's not the first time those two have bothered me. I never did anything to them. I don't understand why they single me out."

"Some guys are just morons. They probably think you're pretty and this is their screwy way of showing it. We will be right back there if you need us again."

With that, he and Cowan turn and start walking back to their spot in line.

"I'm telling you, Cowan, I was ready to give them a good ass-kicking."

"It's not worth it. You'll either have to spend time in the Detention Facility or end up losing your job. You handled it fine. Hopefully, we put a scare into them, and they won't bother the girls again."

I know Cowan is right, but it doesn't change the fact they pissed me off. My mood now matches the skies overhead. It looks like another late afternoon storm, which is common during July and August.

We slowly start moving up in line. I can see the girls have already received their food and water and are heading back home. I wish they would wait for us before heading back. I'm suddenly distracted by a commotion at the front of the line. Three guards seem to be struggling with someone near the window. The line begins to fan out to make room for the three figures clad in green. The guy has his back to us as the guards try to pin him against the wall. Suddenly, he flashes out his left elbow and knocks the helmet off one of the guards. The people in line start cheering. The young man shakes loose and turns left to get away. I finally get a look at his profile and realize it's my friend Dennis. My stomach rolls as I see the guards reach for their weapon belts. The helmetless guard pulls out a black stick, while another is now holding what looks like a gun with no barrel. A blue spark suddenly appears at the end. The third guard is holding onto the back of Dennis' shirt, trying to keep him from getting away. The black bat comes whizzing down and connects with his upper right arm. An audible crack can be heard all the way from where we are standing. The other guard places the black device in the middle of Dennis' back. Immediately, Dennis begins shaking and drops straight to the ground where he begins to convulse. At the same time, the bat comes arcing down and lands on the back of his head. A sickening sound follows, and Dennis' body goes limp. The guard raises his bat for another strike but is halted in mid-air when one of the guards grabs his arm. He stands up and kicks Dennis in the ribs with his black boot. The other two guards get on either side of Dennis and reach under his arms to pick him up. They slowly drag him through a doorway in the front of the building. The door closes, and all that remains is a small pool of blood. An eerie silence hangs over the crowd. A low rumble is heard overhead and is immediately followed by rain. The steady downpour causes the blood to move off in red rivulets. I quickly turn away and stare up into the sky. The rain disguises the tears that begin flowing down my cheeks.

8

GENERAL TAGGERT

AS I LOOK around the table, at some of the anxious faces, I wonder if any of these people will ever be fit to help run a country. Some of these spineless individuals are having enough trouble keeping a single territory running. Until worthier candidates materialize, this motley crew will have to suffice. At least I can enjoy making a few of them squirm today.

"Let's not have a repeat of last month's staff meeting. Keep your presentations short and concise. The goal is brief updates, people. It wouldn't hurt to mix in some good news either. Elliot, have we been able to contact any other territories?" My communications expert looks up from his notes with a steady gaze. He's one of the few members on my staff with some backbone.

"We are still limited to shortwave radio communications. The only territory we have been able to reach is the Southeast Territory. Their community remains near the Cheoah Dam, which is located on the western border of North Carolina. They have also been unable to contact the other four territories. They are considering sending out a search party to the Southern Territory site located at the Buchanan Dam near Burnet, Texas. Our Communications Unit has also been unsuccessful reaching any survivors on other continents. We remain optimistic, but no shortwave transmissions have been detected."

"Perhaps I should speak with Colonel Travers and organize a joint search effort. We could send our own contingent to the Northern Territory stationed near the Oahe Dam just north of Pierre, South Dakota. Clark, how are our population numbers looking? Can we spare the personnel without hampering our own rebuilding efforts?" Clark, on the other hand, is your prototypical, skinny nerd. He adjusts his tie, which is always four inches north of his belt and takes an unsteady breath.

"Sir, our latest calculations estimate our total population at just over 1400 citizens. Our birth rate continues to gradually decrease, while the annual number of deaths is rising. The increasing deaths are a direct result of the Mandatory Expiration Age."

"Well, at least that process is working. You assured me the birth rate would start turning around. Why isn't this happening?"

"Sir, we haven't found a definitive reason. People just seem reluctant to start families. Our sources feel that people are unhappy with the living conditions and are waiting for things to improve."

"I'm sorry we can't provide five-star hotel accommodations! Have they forgotten we saved their damn asses? I'm sure the victims, who were left on the surface, wouldn't mind changing places!"

I can feel the vein pulsing near my right temple. What a bunch of unappreciative bastards. There are probably a few vermin contaminating the thoughts of the masses. I need to figure out a way to find them and eliminate the cancer once and for all. It's not like I can depend on Clark to solve the problem. He looks like he's about to wet himself. It's best to just finish with him and move to the next topic.

"We need to make progress in this area soon. Our population is already getting top heavy. Get more people to analyze the data and find me some answers. Is the news any better in the Southeastern Territory?"

"Sir, as you know, their total population is lower due to the radiation leak which occurred while they were underground. The reactor, they were forced to temporarily use for emergency power, took out a large segment of their population. The good news is their Child Care Facilities were spared. Thus the majority of the deaths were adults. Their last update listed their current population around nine hundred."

I turn my attention to Claire Townsend, the head of the Environmental and Wildlife Units. It looks like Claire has found a few more gray hairs since our last meeting. Apparently, the stress of her position is taking its toll.

"Claire, how are things looking from an environmental perspective?"

"The higher temperatures and the ash-enriched soil have combined to stimulate plant and tree growth throughout our community. Forests are starting to mature in the surrounding areas, and the increased foliage has improved the habitats for our neighboring wildlife. We have been able to implant trackers in a variety of species, which has provided valuable data relative to their movements and breeding grounds."

"Finally, some good news. Have you had any further instances of unlawful hunting?"

"There have been no violations reported since the incident a few weeks ago. I believe Roddy will be providing an update shortly."

"Thank you, Claire, for the encouraging news. Roddy, we might as well hear your update now. I turn my attention to my chief of Security and Law Enforcement. His immense body is a stark contrast to Claire's tiny frame. Massive shoulders and a thick neck stretch the dark green fabric of his guard uniform.

"We apprehended the fourth hunting violator last Wednesday at the Food Dispensary. Our scanners picked up the excessive levels of protein and B-12 in his blood. He was quickly escorted inside the Dispensary where he was terminated. The entire episode will serve as a deterrent to the rest of the community."

I like Roddy's no-nonsense approach to Law Enforcement. The general public looks for any sign of weakness and wastes no time using it to their advantage. "Any other incidents to report, or signs of dissension?"

"Everything appears to be pretty routine with no visible signs of resistance at the moment."

"Thank you, Roddy. Keep up the good work. A firm hand prevents peace from slipping through its grasp."

A quick glance at the clock suggests I need to start wrapping things up soon.

"We emphasized Construction and Education at last month's meeting. If there are no new issues to discuss, I propose we end the meeting with a quick Apis Corporation update." Trevor and Susan nod in agreement. The head of my Education group exhibits genuine relief on her face. I can't say the same for Mitch Andrews who heads up Apis Corporation. We have been at odds on a number of topics lately. I welcome strong personalities on my staff, but Mitch has been showing signs of being a bit defiant regarding some of our new laws and regulations lately. I train my eyes on my next victim and await his summary.

"Apis Pill production is going well. We are somewhat limited by our bee population. Honey production, in our open-air facilities, continues to be a concern due to insufficient plant growth. Hopefully, Claire's encouraging news will translate into improved above ground honey production. Fabrication of the additional Artificial Wombs is complete. These will be introduced into service while older units undergo routine maintenance. We anticipate no interruption in service."

Mitch lays his notes on the table, folds his hands, and gives me his cocky smile. I look forward to the day I knock that smile off his face and have someone else sitting in his seat. For now, I need to wrap up this meeting and move on to more important matters.

"As you've just heard, we are faced with some significant problems. I'm gravely concerned we are still unable to communicate with four of the territories. Assuming there are survivors out there somewhere, it is only a matter of time before another country pays us a visit. Presently, we are in no condition to defend our soil. You need to recognize the sense of urgency and concentrate your efforts. I want to see more progress next month." I can feel seven sets of eyes boring into my back as I swiftly exit the meeting room. There is nothing like a grand exit to get the blood pumping.

9

COWAN

AS I STEP down from our truck, I can feel the cold wind biting through my jacket. It's the middle of November and winter has set in for good. At least Marcus and I will be working inside for the most part. He walks around the front of the truck and joins me as I regard our next project. It's your typical three-story apartment house with a collapsed roof. Chances are the damage will be too extensive to be worth saving. We won't know the extent until we go inside to investigate. I open the rear door of the truck and grab the roll of building plans and two flashlights, before turning toward Marcus to provide instructions.

"Okay, you know the drill. Be careful of unstable debris. I don't need to be spending the better part of the day digging your ass out." Marcus smiles as we make our way around the house. We both realize the inherent dangers of our job. It appears the entire top two floors are collapsed. Since the house has been exposed to the elements, there will be severe water damage to the first floor. We will need to be extra careful walking around inside. Marcus stops as he rounds the corner of the house leading into the backyard.

"At least there's an outside bulkhead leading to the basement. Maybe we can avoid crashing through some floorboards today."

It appears my friend has been reading my thoughts. "You really scare me sometimes. I was just worrying about the same thing."

"I enjoy being inside your head. It's warm, with tons of space to stretch out and relax."

I just shake my head and follow him into the backyard. It looks like another typical day working with my best friend.

We spent the better part of the morning carefully analyzing the exterior of the house and the first floor. Before heading into the basement, we made use of the ambient light to study the plans. After establishing that the basement layout was similar to previous houses on the street, we headed outside to the bulkhead.

Marcus opens the bulkhead doors, shines his flashlight down, and begins walking down the stairs. The strong smell of mildew emanates from the gloom. Small animals can be heard scurrying in the darkness, causing Marcus to immediately hesitate halfway down the steps.

"I freaking hate little critters. If this light shuts off, while I'm down there, you better not be between me and the bulkhead."

I smile and shake my head. We go through this each time Marcus has to enter a dark place. For a big guy, he can be a real wimp.

"Would you like me to lead the way or hold your hand?"

"Real funny Cowan. Who has to climb up most of the roofs, because somebody cries like a cat caught up in a tree? You don't like heights. I don't like the dark and critters."

The big man does have a point, but I won't give him the satisfaction. We finally make our way into the basement and shine our lights around. Other than a few puddles and scattered dirt, the cellar is in pretty good shape. The rafters look sturdy, so the threat of falling debris is low. As I shine my flashlight around, something doesn't feel right. I seem to remember the space being much larger on the plans. I finally turn to Marcus who is standing off to my right.

"Does this area look right to you?"

Marcus pulls the roll of plans from his back pocket and shines his light on them.

"The plans show a large, open rectangular area, but this room has more of an L-shape."

"That's exactly what I was thinking." As I get closer to one of the walls, I notice a lack of foundation at the bottom. I keep walking along the wall while scanning it with my flashlight. Finally, I walk around the corner of the L-shaped section. Pieces of plywood are stacked against this section of the wall.

"Hey Marcus, come over here and check this out." I can hear Marcus' footsteps round the corner behind me.

"What did you find Cowan?"

"I'm not sure, but keep your light on this wall while I move some of these boards out of the way."

I begin moving the plywood away and stacking them against the outside wall. Once the plywood is removed, a single 2X4 is left against the wall. It appears to be wedged between the ceiling and the floor. I try to move it, but it won't budge.

"Why don't you try using the rusty crowbar that is lying on the floor?"

Sure enough, there is a crowbar lying at the base of the wall near my feet. I jam it behind the board and give it a good yank. The board comes flying off and misses my head by inches. We both look up to see a vertical seam in the wall. About halfway up is a worn notch that appears to have seen some use. I place the end of the crowbar in the notch and apply pressure. A section of the wall comes easily away. After making the opening wider, we both train our flashlights into the void exposing a hidden room.

The beams of our flashlights reveal a makeshift meeting room. The center of the room contains a collapsible table surrounded by folding chairs. Assorted charts and diagrams are scattered on the tabletop. At the far end of the room stands a large chalkboard on wheels. Marcus and I walk over to the table and shine our lights on the various charts. There's a large map of the United States in the center. The map has been broken up into six territories. They are labeled Northeast, Southeast, North, South, Northwest, and Southwest. An area, in southeastern Vermont, is circled to indicate the location of our community. A few smaller maps are scattered on the table. There are topography maps of the states of Vermont and New York. There is also a street map of Massachusetts. I pick up a tattered piece of paper with a short bulleted list.

o Nuclear war unlikely; soil not poisoned
o Global warming?
o Possible volcanic eruption
- Everything covered in fine dust or ash
- Constant overcast skies
- Temperatures colder than usual

"Hey Marcus, check this out? It looks like this resistance group was on the right track." I hand the list to Marcus and continue scanning the room. The chalkboard attracts my attention, so I make my way over to it. I shine my flashlight on the board revealing another bulleted list. Marcus' flashlight beam soon joins mine. He starts reading the items written on the board.

"What the heck do these mean?

o Water tainted
o Trackers embedded at birth
o Bees are the key
o Need to find survivors

They're supplying us tainted water!"

"Marcus, we better copy this stuff down and show it to the rest of our group." I see Marcus turn over the tattered document and begin writing. While he is writing the list down, I continue checking the rest of the room. My brief scan of the room yields nothing of further consequence. My attention is suddenly disturbed by the sound of Marcus' voice.

"We should take whatever information we can and erase or get rid of the rest. We don't want any of this being discovered after we've already been here."

My friend has a valid point, so we gather the maps and other documentation. We use a dirty rag to erase the writing on the chalkboard and perform a final inspection of the room before exiting. Standing near the opening, I turn to my friend.

"I guess we will need a few more explosives to ensure the room isn't discovered by anyone." Marcus nods and returns a big smile. I don't have to twist his arm to make a bigger boom.

10

KENJI

SOMETIMES I FEEL like a mushroom sitting in this computer lab. It's a small rectangular room with no windows. Workstations are placed around the periphery of the room, away from the lone exit door and the door leading to the back room. The only ambient light comes from the overhead lights, which reflect off the computer monitors. This is probably the source of my headache, as I sit by myself in the dark searching our databases for answers.

I certainly hope the gang appreciates what I have to go through to obtain information. Even though I've been conducting research after hours, I could still lose my job, or worse. The way information is protected, it's hard to imagine that accessing some of these databases wouldn't be frowned upon. This is coupled with the fact that my boss has definitely been keeping a closer eye on me lately. It looks like I'll be here late tonight gathering the necessary information to discuss with the group. Crap, was that the door to the lab? I turn around to see my boss entering the lab.

"Hey Kenji, working late again? Have I been overloading you with too much work?"

"No, I almost have the newest population projections done. I just need to double-check a few of the curve fit routines." Mr. Barnes returns a smile, suggesting he knows bullshit when he hears it.

"Kenji, I am willing to bet you had those projections completed hours ago. How about you tell me what you're really researching?"

I feel like a cornered mouse, with no means of escape. Mr. Barnes has always been nice to me, but I fear this is about to end. I just sit there with my mouth open, searching for an appropriate response. As if sensing my dismay, he breaks the awkward silence.

"How about I save you the trouble of explaining it to me? You see, I've been tracking your extra-curricular research for weeks. I must say that I am very impressed with your detective skills. You're very intuitive Kenji."

I continue to sit with my mouth just opening and closing, like a fish looking out of a tank. Finally, words start spilling out.

"I'm sorry Mr. Barnes, but we have just been curious about what caused people to flee underground. Everyone is so tight-lipped about everything." Before I can continue, Mr. Barnes holds up his hand to stop me.

"I'm beginning to understand what you must be going through. My boss, Mitch Andrews, finally convinced me that you have a right to know about certain things. He's eager to speak with you. If you have time, he would like to have a quick meeting. Perhaps we can shed some light on a few things."

With that, Mr. Barnes turns around and heads for the door. I quickly gather up my notes and follow him out of the lab.

We finally approach a door with the name Mitchell Andrews stenciled in black letters. I suddenly realize that I'm about to speak with the president of Apis Corporation. My stomach balls up into a knot, and my pulse begins to quicken. Mr. Barnes knocks on the door, and I hear a muffled reply. He opens the door and steps aside to allow me to enter.

Mr. Andrews is seated behind a plain oak desk with folders stacked neatly on the right side. Curtains are drawn on the windows behind him. Bookcases line the walls on either side of his desk. The room is lit by a floor lamp in the corner and a small desk lamp. Two empty chairs are angled in front of his desk. As I enter the office, he smiles and gets up from his chair.

"Kenji, I'm so glad to finally be able to meet you. Stuart has told me so much about you. Please sit down and make yourself comfortable."

I proceed to take the seat on the right, while Mr. Barnes sits in the other. I'm not sure what to say, so I decide to just remain quiet for the time being. Luckily, Mr. Barnes rescues me by initiating the conversation.

"My associate has been tasked with finding out some answers to a few long-standing questions. I figured we could save him some time by having a brief meeting."

"That's an excellent idea, Stuart. You see Kenji, I have come to the realization that our citizens deserve to know what happened. Our pig-headed leadership firmly believe it's necessary to keep the general public in the dark. They feel this is the only way to control the citizens of our community. It is my opinion that this only creates feelings of animosity toward leadership. How do you and your friends feel?"

I am caught off guard by the beliefs of Mr. Andrews since he has just described the mindset of our group perfectly. My apprehension persists, however, as I'm not convinced his views aren't merely a ploy to acquire information. As if sensing my trepidation Mr. Andrews interrupts my internal conflict.

"Kenji, I understand if you are hesitant to share the feelings of your group of friends. How about if you just ask questions and we will do our best to answer them?"

I look straight into his eyes to see if there is a hint of deception, but they just seem friendly, yet troubled. While his face looks youthful, I get the impression the pressures of his position are taking their toll. His brown hair is showing hints of graying over the ears. While his smile appears genuine, it doesn't quite make it to his eyes. My gut tells me the man sitting before me can be trusted, so I make a critical decision.

"The mindset you just described is exactly how we feel. While we are grateful to still be alive, we feel isolated. It's not only from information that we have a sense of detachment but from segments of the community. The southern part of our town is comprised of the leadership and wealthy families, while the northern section is primarily children who are the product of Mandatory Reproduction Age births. This has caused a distinct void between the youth in both regions." I sense understanding in Mr. Andrew's eyes as I finish my explanation and eagerly await his response.

"We have been trying to convince leadership of this developing issue. It has manifested itself in a number of areas. We have been tracking population data, over the years, and recent trends are alarming."

My feelings of apprehension slowly ebb during the course of our impromptu meeting. I get the impression the meeting is not just therapeutic to myself, but to them as well. Our conversations stretch into the night, and the flow of information continues unabated. It becomes apparent that while we may come from different walks of life, we have a common foe. I sense a bond forming that will forever change the course of our lives.

11

COWAN

FRIDAY IS FINALLY here, and the gang is once again together at our house. Everyone is in their customary spot, recapping their respective week. A small fire is crackling in the fireplace, removing the chill from a damp November evening. The flames and the familiar banter provide a cozy feel to our living room. It's during times like these I really appreciate the close bonds that have formed within our small group. As I gaze at the fire, my thoughts are drawn to the reason for getting everyone together. Marcus and I have been pondering the contents of the secret meeting room all week. We decided it would be a good idea to have Kenji analyze the material before presenting the information to the rest of the group. The duffle bag I gave Kenji is laying on the floor beside his chair. Drew told me earlier that Kenji spent long hours at the lab this week. Kenji seems distressed about something tonight. He keeps fidgeting with his glasses and glancing at a few sheets of paper in his lap. I wonder if it has anything to do with the information he uncovered this week. I guess now is as good a time as any to find out.

"Hey guys, this wasn't just a social visit tonight. Marcus and I have something we want to discuss with all of you. On Tuesday, we made a very interesting discovery at the house we were preparing for demolition. In the basement of the house, we found a secret meeting room." Scattered murmurs and questions are blurted out by the group. Carmen, as usual, is the most vocal.

"Why did you wait until Friday to tell anyone?"

Nods in agreement follow Carmen's question. We had expected this reaction from the group.

"First of all, we wanted to get everyone together to discuss our findings which is easier said than done. We also wanted to give Kenji the opportunity to analyze the items we removed from the room." Everyone turns to look at Kenji, only adding to his distress. It's apparent I need to finish my introduction quickly, so we can all hear what Kenji has to say.

"Marcus and I believe it was a secret meeting room used by a resistance group. There were various maps on a table in the center of the room. One of these was a map of the United States showing the current six territories with our community highlighted. There were also random notes and a large chalkboard containing cryptic clues. These notes and maps were the items we gave Kenji to research. Kenji, would you mind taking it from here." My bespectacled, little friend looks up with concerned eyes and clears his throat. My feelings of apprehension grow as he begins to speak.

"First of all, I was able to gather a wealth of information on the items you provided. What I would like to explain is the manner in which I obtained most of the material." As usual, Kenji has the rapt attention of the entire group.

"I was in my lab searching through the various databases when my supervisor, Mr. Barnes, entered the room. He had been watching me closely over the past few weeks, so I knew it was only a matter of time before I got caught."

Kenji's peculiar behavior now makes sense. We should have realized the danger associated with our data gathering assignments. Marcus must have read my mind.

"Dude, I'm sorry we put you in that position. Are you in trouble? Did you lose your job?"

"That's the funny part of the whole thing. At first, I tried to pretend I was simply staying late finishing an assignment, but Mr. Barnes didn't buy my explanation. He informed me that he'd been monitoring the sites I'd been visiting during my database research. I was then invited to a meeting with his boss Mr. Andrews."

A series of concerned groans and questions are launched at Kenji from the group. Everyone is anxious to hear the result of the meeting. Kenji patiently waits for the chaos to die down before proceeding with his summary.

"Mr. Andrews turns out to be, Mitchell Andrews, the president of Apis Corporation." Once again, an uproar ensues, and Kenji has to patiently wait for everyone to settle down. "The three of us sat in Mr. Andrews' office and talked for a long time, sharing similar beliefs regarding a number of issues facing our community. Eventually, they began answering some of my questions."

"Please tell me you didn't share the existence of the secret meeting room?" My anxiety grows as I await Kenji's response.

"Of course, I didn't. I just said we've been hearing rumors in the community. Although I'm pretty much convinced, we can trust both of them."

"How about if we don't take any chances?" A number of affirmations show that the room is in agreement. Marcus finally beats everyone to the punch.

"So, did they explain what the clues from the secret room mean?"

Kenji nods and looks down at the sheets of paper he has been nervously gripping. A weight seems to have been lifted from his shoulders. He was obviously concerned about notifying the group of his meeting.

"Apparently, our rebel friends correctly identified the apocalyptic event. It indeed was a Supervolcano, which erupted in Yellowstone National Park in Wyoming."

"Congratulations Kenji, you were also correct about the cause."

"Thank you, Bree, but it was pretty obvious once you pieced all the clues together. The most amazing thing they shared is that an underground facility was built in each territory."

The room erupts, once again, with a barrage of questions? The final question coming from Carmen.

"So, there are other survivors?"

"They've only been able to contact the Southeastern Territory using shortwave radio. The remaining four territories are unresponsive."

A bittersweet silence settles over the room while the group digests the magnitude of the last statement. It's great to hear that we are not alone, but realization sets in that the rest of the country, to the west, may have perished. I am distracted from my thoughts by Kenji's voice.

"How about I summarize the information that was obtained from the meeting and then we can have a discussion?" Heads solemnly nod and turn toward Kenji. "The Apis Pills are primarily made from honey, and they contain the required vitamins and nutrients to support life. I have verified this over the last couple of days. You can also relax with the knowledge that the water is not tainted. The scanners, at the Food Dispensary, are used to scan our blood. They can use this data to check our health and to identify if we have any foreign substances in our bloodstream."

"So, that's how they nabbed Dennis? The scanner must have picked up the wild rabbit meat, in his blood, and the bastards killed him."

"I'm sorry to say you're probably right Marcus. The rabbit meat must contain some vitamin or protein not found in the Apis Pill."

"If Dennis would've skipped going to the Dispensary, for a while, I imagine the banned substance would eventually become undetectable."

"I suspect that would be the case Cowan, but I'm fairly certain they would've noticed his absence and arrested him anyway. It took me a while to get them to admit that trackers are, indeed, embedded at birth."

Bedlam breaks out in our living room when the rest of the group hears about the existence of trackers. Marcus and I had assumed the trackers were simply a paranoid concept dreamed up by the resistance group. Heated discussions ensue focusing on a variety of topics including the violation of privacy. Kenji also found out that trackers were not implanted during all births and that certain families were granted special dispensation from tracker implantation. This fuels the groups' sentiment of being further discriminated against. It takes a long time before the discussions slow down, and the anger begins to subside. I decide to use this opportunity to broach a subject that has been on my mind for some time.

"Hey guys, I have been wondering about something for a long time, and the discovery of the secret room only rekindled my curiosity." I sneak a peek around the room and see I have everyone's attention. "I've noticed the living conditions in our community, especially for people like us, have been getting worse and some of Kenji's findings support this opinion. I keep asking myself if this is where I want to spend the rest of my life. Now that it's confirmed there are other survivors to our south, should we be entertaining the thought of leaving this place." As expected the idea of leaving is not well received, by the rest of the group, as a variety of responses are cast in my direction.

"Hey buddy, being unhappy with a few rules and regulations is one thing, but uprooting your life and blindly traveling south is more than a little crazy."

I look over at Marcus and smile, realizing that what I'm proposing must sound ridiculous.

"I know what I'm saying may sound irrational, but I can't stop thinking there may be a better life for us out there somewhere. Perhaps, it's not in the Southeastern Territory, but in another region, that was not hit as hard by the volcano. Who knows, maybe the group who used the secret room made it out safely and settled down somewhere else."

"It's a common belief they were eaten by wild animals not that far west of here."

"Bree, that may just be what they want us to think. After hearing what Kenji just said, I'm beginning to trust our leadership less and less. All I'm saying is it wouldn't hurt to find out as much as we can about areas outside of our community in case we need the information in the future."

A series of nods follow my request, but it's evident the rest of the group doesn't share my optimism. Perhaps they will all come around in time.

12

CARMEN

IT LOOKS LIKE it's going to be another boring Saturday night hanging out with the gang. Don't get me wrong I love my friends, but I'm getting sick of playing cards, or charades, or whatever tired game the group decides to play. I just want to do something different and exciting. I'd really like to get Cowan alone. Every time I see him, he's either with Marcus or Bree. What I wouldn't give to be in Bree's shoes. She gets to live in the same house as Cowan. I just don't understand those two. They seem to get along so well, yet there has been no evidence of them ever dating. I certainly would be paying the red-head some late-night visits.

"Hey Carmen, are you going to sit there with a stupid grin on your face, or are you going to pick up a card?"

Marcus' voice causes me to jump. Chuckles are heard around the table as I unsuccessfully attempt to regain my composure. I glance across the table and catch a good-natured smirk from Cowan. This causes heat to slowly creep up my neck. I reach down and pick a card from the deck and quickly discard a random one. Bree immediately snatches it up

"Gin! Read 'em and weep guys."

"What do you have a horseshoe up your ass? It's probably because you're following Carmen. She keeps feeding you whatever cards you need."

I just glare at Marcus as I get up from the table. He's a nice guy, but he can really get on my nerves sometimes.

"How about if we take a break from cards? I look directly at Cowan. "Would anyone like to go for a walk?" Heads turn toward Cowan to see if he caught my not so subtle hint.

"I think I'll pass. Even though it's mild tonight, I'd rather stay in and see if my luck changes."

He starts sweeping up the cards with his hands. The rest of the crew seem content to keep on playing. Frustrated, I stomp out of the dining room and grab my jacket off the hook by the door. After one final glance over my shoulder, I open the door and give it a little slam before making my way down the steps to the sidewalk.

It's a beautiful, clear night and I reluctantly put on my jacket. The moon, which is almost full, will have to serve as my flashlight. With no destination in mind, I decide to head north on Green Street. The street ahead looks abandoned with the occasional light spilling from a window. For no apparent reason, I take a quick right on Cherry Street and head east. This road will lead past the Dead Stones which is Bree's least favorite spot. It would have been a perfect night for a romantic walk. That big dope doesn't know what he's missing. Perhaps a stroll along the Connecticut River will raise my spirits. I could just keep walking until the memory of Cowan's snub is forgotten.

The road begins to bend to the right, and I can just make out the field with the Dead Stones on my left. Small groups of trees are scattered throughout the field. Many of the stones are toppled over with high grass covering the rest. The field reminds me of Bree, and this causes my anger to return. Without thinking, I turn left and start walking into the field. I'll show Bree that her fear is ridiculous. It'll be fun teasing her about it tomorrow. The beginnings of a smile appears as I imagine the scene in the morning. Even though my eyes have become accustomed to the darkness, my progress is slow due to the ground being riddled with branches and twigs. The neat rows of markers have turned into an obstacle course. By concentrating on the ground, I'm able to avoid falling or twisting an ankle. I know, from my previous visits, that a small road will eventually cross my path up ahead.

The sounds of voices stop me dead in my tracks. They seem to be coming from somewhere off to the north. Suddenly, the idea of walking through this field doesn't seem like such a good one. Standing motionless, I try to remain completely silent, but my growing anxiety begins to affect my breathing. Just when I begin to think the voices were a figment of my imagination, I hear someone nearby. The footsteps seem to be heading toward the spot where I entered the field.

"Hey Cole, are you sure you heard something? Maybe it was just a wild animal."

Crap, don't tell me it's the two guys who harass me all the time. My circumstances are just going from bad to worse.

"If it was an animal, it sounded awfully big. Let me get a light."

Panic begins to grab hold of me as I search frantically for a place to hide. The stones are too small to conceal a body. A small copse of trees stands about forty feet away. My best chance is to get there and hide out until they get tired of looking and head home. A flashlight beam suddenly appears to my left, about a hundred feet away. A short distance behind, I hear the sound of water splashing against rock.

"Hey Danny, any luck yet?" This voice comes from the direction of the flashlight.

"I'm a little busy cleaning off one of these gravestones." A juvenile laugh is followed by the sound of a zipper being closed.

"I'm sure you can go to hell for that."

There's something odd about the way the two of them are acting. Their speech seems slow and somewhat difficult to understand. My anxiety increases as I slowly creep toward the trees. All of a sudden, my right foot sinks into a hole left by a fallen stone. My momentum carries me face first into the ground. Breath is forced from my lungs as my body impacts the stone marker. The sound of footsteps can be heard from the area I just left. I try to scramble to my feet in a last-ditch effort to get away. Just as I begin to run away, a body tackles me from behind. My body crashes to the earth a second time. A sharp pain flashes from the side of my body that previously landed on the stone.

"Well, it looks like this little critter has two legs. Hey, Cole, I found our intruder."

Struggling, with all my might, I almost free myself as the sound of running footsteps nears. As I get up on all fours, a beam of light shines directly into my face.

"It looks like you caught yourself a rat. I guess this night isn't going to be boring after all."

I start to scream, but a hand is quickly clamped over my mouth. My legs are then lifted off the ground, and the two boys start carrying me away. Repeated attempts to kick and squirm out of their grasp are futile due to their strength. We eventually reach a blanket laid out on the ground. My body is thrown roughly onto the blanket. There are a number of empty bottles strewn on the ground. One of the boys jumps on top of me and straddles my waist as the other walks around the blanket. Once again, a hand is clamped over my mouth as I start to scream. The force of the hand makes it impossible to bite his fingers. He leans down, and I can see that it's Cole. I start punching his arm when I hear a click, and a knife materializes in front of my eye.

"If you move or scream then you will become a one-eyed Lab Rat. Hey Danny, how about if we teach our friend the correct way to make babies?"

The smile on his face, and the dark look in his eyes convince me that he means business. His hands are quickly undoing my pants and pulling them down my legs. Any attempt to squirm results in the knife being held just below my right eye. Ultimately, I surrender to the inevitable and let the vermin have their way. I start counting stars hoping my thoughts will get lost in the dark expanse. Eventually, this becomes difficult due to the tears blurring my vision.

13

BREE/GRACE

"HEY GRACE, I am going to head to work. It doesn't sound like the boys are up, so I'll pound on their door on my way out."

"Okay Bree, have a good day at school. Hopefully Drew and I will get to work in the greenhouse all day."

I'm fortunate to have an inside job, especially during the winter. I'll take a bunch of screaming preschool kids any day, versus manual labor outside in the cold. Although, catch me on a hot day in the classroom and I may sing a different tune. They wouldn't let me work in the Environmental Group anyway since I don't have a green thumb.

As I make my way across the kitchen, the boys' side of the house remains completely silent. Monday mornings are the worst with those two. I feel like their mother, having to make sure they get out of the house on time. Standing at their door, I raise both fists above my head and smile. Let me see how far I can make them jump this morning.

"Hey boys, it's time to wake up!" The sound of someone banging a body part against the wall brings a smile to my face. Thrashing and moaning can be heard through the door as I exit the kitchen and head up the hallway. Hopefully, Carmen is ready so we can make our trek to school together.

As I step outside, the chill of winter makes me yearn for the warmth of our home. The sun is painting the eastern sky with a beautiful array of red and orange colors. The wispy clouds seem to soak up the sunshine and magnify the radiance of the sun. It is amazing how pictures and paintings fall short of the real thing. Reluctantly, I turn away from the spectacle and jog across the front yard to Carmen's house. As I raise my hand to knock, she opens the door.

"Hi, Carm, ready for another week?" She just stares straight ahead and gives a slight nod. Distinct dark circles can be seen under her eyes even through her olive complexion. She looks like she hasn't slept in days.

"You look exhausted. Are you feeling okay?" Her vacant stare doesn't seem to change. A slight turn of her head is the only indication that she heard my question. Without answering, she begins shambling down the sidewalk and then turns south down the street. Why would she head that way? We always walk down Cherry Street to get to school. At first, it bothered me because it goes right by the field with the Dead Stones. Carmen used to tease me about it, but she finally stopped.

"Hey, Carmen, why are you going that way? We always walk down Cherry." Carmen just continues walking, as if she didn't hear a word I said. I hurry down the steps and start walking beside her. Her jacket is wide open, and the wind is turning it into a cape, but it doesn't seem to faze her.

"Carmen, why don't you zip up your jacket? You must be freezing." Again, she ignores me and just keeps on walking. It's as if she's pissed at me about something. This would not be the first time since she does have a temper. I try to think what she could be upset about. The last time I saw her was when she stormed out of the house Saturday night, while we were all playing cards. She had tried to get Cowan to go for a walk, but he refused. Could she be jealous of Cowan? Everyone knows Cowan, and I are just friends. We get along great, but something just doesn't feel right. He must feel the same way because he has never, once, tried to kiss me. I continue to rack my brain, about what could be bugging her, as we turn onto School Street. Finally, it reaches a point where I can't take the silence.

"What's your problem today? Did I do something to piss you off?" She just stares straight ahead and ignores my question. Fine, if she wants to be that way, we can walk the rest of the way in silence. Eventually, we reach the front entrance of the school. After climbing the steps, she opens the door and walks through without holding it open. I have to reach out quickly in order to prevent it from smacking my shoulder. I look up to say something, but she's already heading for the stairs which lead to the basement. Carmen works for the Janitorial Services Group at school. The kids love when she visits my classroom because she likes to act silly. It's unfortunate she was placed in the Janitorial Group because she'd have made a great preschool teaching assistant. My sympathy is short lived as I remember her mood this morning. My irritation returns and the thought of Carmen possibly having to clean up kid puke brings a fiendish smile to my face. My mood brightens as I head down the corridor to my classroom.

"I was looking forward to working in the greenhouse today, but I'm roasting in this beekeeper suit."

"Really, Grace. You were hoping to work inside today and yet you still complain. Would you rather get stung by a swarm of bees?"

Drew does have a point. Our job, for the foreseeable future, is to take care of the plants and honey bees in the greenhouse. During the winter months, the plants are critical to the survival of the bee population. The bees are kept in the greenhouse to pollinate the plants and collect nectar which is used to produce the precious honey for the Apis Pills. The greenhouse can be turned into an open-air facility, during the warm weather months, to enable the honey bees to pollinate the surrounding plants in the community. The large greenhouse is located on the northern side of the Apis Corporation building.

"That's okay. I'll rough it in this sweaty suit. I was stung this past spring, and my hand was swollen for a week. It's not easy working with these gloves on. So, did you guys do anything interesting yesterday?"

"It was pretty boring. Kenji had his face buried in books, as usual. I read for a while, but I ended up falling asleep. Carmen stayed in her room for the entire day."

"Do you think she's sick?" The Apis Pills are supposed to help our immune system in addition to providing nourishment.

"I have no idea. We tried to find out what was wrong, but she'd just roll over and pull the blanket over her head. She did get in late Saturday night, so perhaps she was just tired and needed to catch up on some sleep. It's probably nothing serious because she did go to work today."

"I'll talk to Bree, when she gets home from work, and see what Carmen told her today."

The rest of the day was spent quietly tending to the lifeblood of our community. Our dependency on these little critters is a little unnerving at times. I shudder to think what we would do for food if anything tragic happened to our tireless workers. Our group often talks about the short-sightedness of our leaders to rely on them solely for our food. They must have their reasons to continue using the Apis Pills as our only food source. Kenji thinks that it's another way of ensuring our dependence on the community and to discourage any thoughts of escape. Given the subsequent discussions from our meeting last month, I am beginning to understand some of his theories and concerns. For the time being, however, Drew and I need to take care of our most important natural resource.

14

MITCH

AS I WALK down the hallway, leading to Michele's office, my anxiety grows. The trick is to play it cool or else she'll never provide the information I need. She'll hide behind the very same patient confidentiality policies I helped write. Just a few pieces of information should be enough to narrow down the possibilities. Reaching her open doorway, I see her sitting at her desk concentrating on some documents. She has her long, black hair pulled back in a ponytail. My nervousness shifts from the anticipated topic to just being in her presence. Even though we've worked together for years, her beauty still transforms me into a young schoolboy. Before my nerves win the battle, I rap lightly on her doorframe. Her head lifts and the captivating smile begins to turn my legs to jelly.

"To what do I owe this unexpected visit?"

"Good afternoon Michele, do you have a few minutes?"

"Come on in and have a seat."

The chair, in front of her desk, seems miles away. I attempt to cross the distance, while exuding an air of confidence.

"Well, as you know, there is another territory meeting coming up, and I was hoping to get a little background information." A little white lie never hurt anyone.

"So, what information, in particular, are you looking for?"

"How often do you conduct MRA births in a given year?" I already know the answer to this question, but I need to get her comfortable.

"We conduct these twice per year. Since the percentage of our population in the 21-30 age group is decreasing, we may return to once per year."

"How long ago did you abandon the once per year methodology?" The answer to this question is important since it will reduce the number of possibilities in half.

"Let me think. I believe it was only during the first four to five years that we limited the MRA births to once per year. Being forced to handle 6 to 10 births became cumbersome on our staff, which is why we switched to twice per year."

"How long do you retain a person's sample before it is either used or discarded?" My pulse begins to quicken as I await her answer. Michele stares at me with a quizzical look.

"Are you talking about someone's sperm sample?"

Michele's eyes bore into mine, and the faint smirk signifies she is on to me. I can only supply a timid nod and hope the beads of sweat stay safely hidden beneath my hairline.

"We retain samples for a maximum of one year, and then they are discarded."

At least I have things narrowed down to a single group of candidates. Michele holds my gaze until I'm forced to look down at my lap.

"Mitch, what are you up to? Why do I have the feeling these questions have nothing to do with your next territory meeting?"

I look up but avoid making eye contact, knowing full well my eyes will betray me. I need to come up with a believable excuse and then somehow make a graceful exit.

"I just like to stay informed in case questions are asked." I follow this with my winning smile, hoping she'll be convinced.

"Do you know what I think? I think you're trying to find the name of your MRA offspring. That's what I think. Even though you know, it's against regulations."

She clasps her hands on the desk and patiently awaits my response. I feel like a child caught stealing candy at the corner store. A nervous chuckle escapes as I slowly rise from my seat.

"Don't be silly. I was just trying to refresh my knowledge on a few things." I slowly move toward the door which seems further away than a few minutes ago.

"You keep on babbling Mitchell Andrews, but I'm on to you. If you think, for a second, that I'm going to tell you her name, then you are sadly mistaken."

I momentarily freeze, and my jaw drops. A knowing smile crosses her face, and I realize my plan has been exposed. All that's left is to give a sheepish nod and slowly exit her office.

As soon as I get back to my office, I boot up my computer and pull up the company's database. Using my special access code, I'm able to open the confidential patient files. Since I now know the time period my sample was used, I pull up the MRA births that occurred in 2059. This was only a year after the MRA regulation was put into effect. If Michele's recollection is accurate, there should be only a single group of MRA births during that year. The data confirms only one group of MRA births were recorded between September 8th and 9th of that year. A total of seven births occurred over the course of the two days. After tapping a few keys, a listing of the seven names is displayed. The list includes four males and three females. The records provide a variety of information including the blood types of the father, mother, and baby. I hold my breath as I scan the column containing the fathers' blood types. Only three fathers are listed with type O. I look to the left under the column containing the sex of the newborns. Two babies are male, and only one baby is female. My heart begins to race as I stare at the name of my daughter, Grace Johnson. I slide the cursor over her name and hesitate.

For years, I have wondered about the identity of my child. This desire has increased over the past few years. As my distaste of our leadership intensified, my concern over the welfare of my offspring has increased. Is my child still alive? What is my child's living conditions? How has life been without a parent? As a result, my hatred of the MRA regulation has grown. Its sole purpose is to maintain the population numbers. The long-term effects, on a large segment of our population, are ignored. I am not the only person to share these beliefs, but they have fallen on deaf ears. Now that the moment has arrived, when many of my questions will be answered, my hand is paralyzed over the mouse. Finally, I am able to click the button. A file opens, and a photo of my daughter fills the left side of the screen. My green eyes are staring directly back at me. The reality that I have missed out on the first twenty-five years of my daughter's life comes crashing down. I bury my face in my hands as I am suddenly overcome with emotion.

15

GENERAL TAGGERT

STANDING AT EASE in my office, looking out my interior window, I feel the weight of the community on my shoulders. The window overlooks the nerve center of our community, which contains the numerous computers and large displays that continuously monitor the various aspects of our town. Even though it's late on a Monday afternoon, the large room is bustling with activity. Each station is manned by personnel from the various units.

The Wildlife Unit has a number of trackers displayed on their large screen. Judging by the number of dots moving on the screen, I can tell the unit has been busy implanting new trackers. Two members of the Law Enforcement Unit are cycling through the various cameras mounted around town. During our last meeting, I tore into Roddy because of the lack of coverage in our community. There are too many blind spots around town. He assured me that more cameras would be mounted to provide additional surveillance. We also need to install some early warning systems and sensors along the outskirts of our community. It's only a matter of time before we are attacked by another country. Just because we've been unable to contact another country doesn't mean there are no survivors. The early warning systems may afford us sufficient time to retreat to the underground facility. We may need to add additional patrols in the surrounding woodland areas to supplement the guards posted on the major highways. There are so many things to worry about when you're in a position of authority. It must be nice to be an average citizen without a care in the world. People just assume someone else will provide protection. The clock on the far wall reads 4:50 p.m. I turn away and head back to my desk to prepare for my meeting with Jim.

As I prepare the materials for the meeting, I realize it's already December 18th. Another year is almost over, and it doesn't seem like we have made much progress. It feels like our rebuilding process will never end. One thing a traumatic event will do is realign your priorities. Years ago, people would be rushing around with only seven shopping days left until Christmas. Now holidays are a distant memory. The only two days we acknowledge are Remembrance Day, on July 28th, and Resurface Day on May 24th. Remembrance Day honors the citizens of the United States who were left behind when we were forced underground. Flags are flown at half-mast, and most citizens get a day off to reflect on the Americans who perished. It wasn't until ten years later that the first group resurfaced on May 24th. Some of the sights we encountered, as the initial clean-up crews, still haunt my dreams. The depths humans will sink to when their food supply disappears proves we are no better than the animals that prowl the outskirts of our community. The frigid temperatures preserved evidence of mass murders and cannibalism. We stayed in groups, worrying creatures lurked in every abandoned building. Finally, after weeks of searching, we came to the realization that any survivors were long gone.

In some respects, we still have two-legged animals living within our community. They prey on the fragile psyche of our citizens and spread lies. For a number of years, their misguided messages brainwashed a few weak-minded individuals into leaving. This undoubtedly resulted in some tasty meals for some of our neighboring wildlife. The time has come to find the source of this cancer that is growing in the bowels of our community. I have stood by long enough, allowing these vermin to exist. The only way to exterminate them is to find their lair. My thoughts are interrupted by Jim Moeller knocking at the door.

"Good afternoon Jim, come in and take a seat. You are probably wondering why I asked you to come here today?" Jim walks in and takes the seat in front of my desk. He's one of the few people at Apis Corporation I trust, which makes him a perfect choice for the job I have planned.

"I must admit, General, I'm a bit curious."

"I have a very sensitive assignment, which requires someone I can trust implicitly."

"General, I believe that I have proven my loyalty in the past."

"Which is why I have requested your attendance today. I'm becoming more and more convinced we have a growing rebel network in our community. We need to infiltrate these rebels. The best way to accomplish this task is to plant spies in their midst. These files contain a few individuals I've selected. I'd like you to head up this spy network. I want you to meet regularly with these individuals and to keep me appraised of any developments. Any questions?"

"Have you approached these people already?"

"No, I'll leave that up to you. The candidates I've selected appear to be extremely close to their family. Utilize coercion to convince them to cooperate. Threaten their family's safety and their job security in order to get them to perform. You have full authority to obtain rebel information by whatever means necessary." I reach across my desk and hand Jim the folder. He immediately starts looking through the material. As he flips one of the last pages, his eyes widen.

"Apparently one of the candidates has peeked your interest. Is there something you'd like to share?" Jim looks up from the open folder with a sinister look in his eye. At times like these, I'm glad he's on my side.

"General, I believe I'm going to enjoy this new assignment."

16

GRACE/MICHELE

WHAT I'D GIVE to be the boys right now. They're just about done getting their pills. Soon they'll be enjoying the warmth back home, while we continue to freeze standing in line. The cold is bad enough, but the wind makes it unbearable. The gray skies appear ready to dump a load of snow any moment. If only Bree and I didn't have to wait for Carmen to get ready, we would be heading back with the boys. She has been acting very strange for over a week. Right now, she's just standing there with her jacket open, oblivious to the cold.

"Hey, Carmen, why don't you zip up your jacket before you catch a cold?" She just turns and gives me a vacant stare before returning her attention to the front of the line. I can see the boys walking away from the window. They all wave in unison with stupid grins on their faces. Bree and I half-heartedly wave, before tucking our hands back in our pockets. The first snowflakes begin to fall on the remainder of people in line. I turn to huddle a little closer to Bree when I notice the two boys, who like to harass Carmen, standing off to the right. As soon as she sees them the color seems to drain from her face. She quickly turns away and stares at the ground. Bree notices her reaction and puts her arm around her.

"Carmen are you okay? You look like you just saw a ghost."

Carmen just shrugs off Bree's arm and shuffles forward as the line finally moves. As I edge forward, I glance off to my right and see the boys walking away. At least we don't have to worry about dealing with them without Cowan and Marcus around. I guess the earlier threats served their purpose.

As we near the front of the line I see the same woman sitting behind the window. A guard, dressed in the customary green uniform, stands to the left of the window. He looks to be the same guard who used the electric gun on Dennis. Standing in the room, behind the woman, is a man that I have been noticing lately. He is a handsome, middle-aged man who appears to be in charge. He looks up and smiles when we reach the front of the line. Carmen approaches the window and places her right hand on the sensor. Usually, it takes about five seconds for the light on the top to turn green. The appropriate time passes, but the light remains off. Suddenly, the light turns red causing the woman behind the counter to look up. She turns to look at her monitor and begins to type on the keyboard. A concerned look appears on her face, and she turns to address Carmen.

"I'm sorry, but you'll have to come inside for a quick examination."

Carmen just keeps her hand on the sensor and continues to stare at the woman. The guard begins to move toward Carmen. I try to react, but my body remains frozen in place. Bree moves to get between the guard and Carmen.

"Miss, please stop right there. I am just going to escort your friend inside for her examination. There's nothing to worry about."

I notice the man and woman inside the booth are having a serious conversation. He turns and heads for the door leading outside. Once outside, he immediately heads toward the guard who is now standing next to Carmen.

"Paul, let me escort the young lady inside. I'll take her to see Dr. Timms."

He then turns toward the two of us and smiles.

"My name is Mitchell Andrews, but please call me Mitch. Don't worry. I'll make sure nothing happens to your friend."

He extends his hand in my direction. I reach out and shake his hand.

"My name is Grace, and this is my friend Bree." He reaches over and shakes Bree's hand.

"I'm sure there is a simple explanation for the sensor behavior. Your friend just had some readings that were slightly off. It's probably a malfunction, but it's best if we verify that nothing is wrong. Why don't the two of you follow me and I will lead you to a waiting room where you can get out of the cold?"

His green eyes have a calming effect. I look over at Bree, and she just shrugs her shoulders. Carmen is just standing there, seemingly unaware of what's going on. The three of us begin to follow Mitch inside the Food Dispensary. We head down a short hallway that's lined with large, framed photographs of bees in different settings. Apparently, Kenji wasn't exaggerating when he explained how important the bee has been to our survival. The hallway eventually ends at a nurses' station with separate hallways heading off in both directions. Behind the desk are two nurses. The nurse on the right looks up and smiles at us as we approach.

"Good afternoon Mr. Andrews, is there something I can do for you?"

"Hello Carol, do you have any idea where I can find Dr. Timms."

"I believe she's in her office. Would you like me to page her?"

"That won't be necessary. I'll just swing by her office. Could you take this young lady to an examination room and keep her company until we can have her seen by Dr. Timms?"

"I will take her to Examination Room #2 and check her vital signs. She looks like she hasn't slept in days."

Mitch nods and then leads us into a waiting room located diagonally across from the nurses' station.

"Why don't you make yourselves comfortable while I go find Dr. Timms?

He has a soothing voice to go along with his eyes. My heart has slowed, and my anxiety has lessened from the initial shock. I turn and grab a seat next to Bree. The remaining seats in the waiting room are empty. Mitch turns and starts walking down the hallway. I look at Bree and see the same concern in her eyes.

"Do you have any idea what is wrong with Carmen?" The tremor in my voice reveals my stress level. Bree just shakes her head while she reaches out to hold my hand. There's nothing we can do but helplessly sit and wait.

★ ★ ★

My lower back has been tight all afternoon. It's amazing how stiff I get sitting at my desk for an extended period of time. First, my eyesight started going in my mid-forties. Since I hit fifty, a few years ago, a simple yoga session induces soreness lasting for a couple of days. I remove my readers to give my eyes a break and arch my back to ease some of the stiffness. All I have left to do is enter the remaining Artificial Womb results and then I can call it a day. I could have one of the lab assistants enter the data, but I somehow feel closer to the babies by personally monitoring their development. Nothing can match the emotions I experienced monitoring my own daughter's development. She was the product of an Artificial Womb birth. After she was born, I legally adopted her, but nobody knows she is my biological daughter. When she was old enough, I secretly revealed I was her biological mother, but I made her promise to keep it a secret. Not only did I violate the company's Patient Confidentiality policies, but I altered the parent data so the birth couldn't be traced to myself. I feel a little hypocritical giving Mitch a hard time the other day when he was obviously trying to find out information about his daughter. The sound of approaching footsteps interrupts my train of thought and who else but Mitch appears in my doorway.

"If you keep this up, people are going to start talking." He just leans against the doorframe and smiles. Mitch is a very handsome man and the fact that he doesn't realize it makes it more so. There seems to be an unspoken chemistry between the two of us, but the fact he is my immediate supervisor squashes any hope of an office romance.

"It would be an improvement over some of the stories that I've been associated with in the past."

His smile turns into a mischievous grin that is accompanied by a subtle glint in his eyes. My face starts to flush, and I can feel my pulse quicken a bit. I'm forced to smile and break eye contact. Mitch has always handled our personal dealings professionally in the past. This is the first time he has exhibited the slightest hint of playfulness. I realize, by my reaction, that I like this side of him. Misreading my reaction, he quickly changes the subject.

"The reason I'm here is to ask you a favor. Would you mind examining a young lady in the Dispensary?"

"This wouldn't happen to be a certain young lady that you were trying to locate?" My eyebrow raises to emphasize my point.

Mitch produces a mock, confused look and holds out his hands innocently.

"I have no idea who you're talking about. There's a young lady that triggered our sensor outside. I was at the window and observed what triggered the sensor. Apparently, she exhibited high hCG levels. Her behavior is somewhat alarming, so I thought it would be a good idea for you to examine her."

My interest is suddenly peeked because High Human Chorionic Gonadotropin levels indicate pregnancy. The hormone is produced during pregnancy and is made by cells formed in the placenta. Typically, the hCG levels will double every 72 hours and peak in the first 8 to 11 weeks of pregnancy. Our sensors can usually detect a change in hCG levels about 10-12 days after conception. Since our sensors did not pick up her elevated hCG levels last week, her conception most likely occurred within ten days of last week's visit. A quick estimate would bound the date of conception somewhere between December 4th and 10th.

"What was so alarming about her behavior?"

"She almost looked like she was in shock. She had dark circles under her eyes and looked like she hadn't slept in days. I guess it was just a gut feeling that something was amiss."

Mitch has excellent instincts, and I trust his judgment. If this girl's behavior raised a few red flags, then it warrants further attention. I immediately get up from my seat and start walking around my desk.

"Lead the way, Sherlock. Let's see if we can get to the bottom of this mystery." He turns and starts heading out the doorway. He chuckles and looks over his shoulder with a wry grin.

"I guess that makes you Dr. Watson."

He thrusts out his stomach and proceeds to waddle down the hallway. I give him a playful punch on his left shoulder. I think I'm going to like the new Mitch.

As we pass by the nurses' station, I see two young ladies sitting in the waiting room. They both look up as we approach and it strikes me that the girl on the left looks familiar. She has dark brown hair, but it is her eyes that draw my attention. As we get closer, the overhead lights enhance the greenish tint in her eyes. She produces a nervous smile, and suddenly I realize where I've seen her face before. I turn toward Mitch, and his face confirms my assumption.

"Hello again ladies, this is Dr. Timms. She will be examining your friend. Dr. Timms, this is Grace and Bree."

I nod at both of them and smile in an attempt to ease their apprehension.

"I am going to take care of your friend, so there's nothing to worry about. Mitch will stay here and keep you company. The examination should not take long."

"Dr. Timms, I believe Carol brought the patient to Examination Room #2."

I nod and head in the direction of the examination rooms. Upon reaching the appropriate room, I knock on the door and enter. Carol looks up from the chair next to the examination table. A young, Hispanic female is sitting down on the edge of the examination table. She is an extremely attractive young woman, but she looks exhausted. What is immediately troubling is her vacant stare. Mitch's instincts, about there being more going on than a simple pregnancy, appear to be correct. Hopefully, she'll provide some answers during the examination.

"Good afternoon Carmen, my name is Dr. Timms. Hi Carol, would you mind helping out during the examination?" The young woman barely acknowledges my presence. I asked Carol to stick around because a second set of eyes is always helpful.

"Of course, Dr. Timms. I'd be more than happy to assist."

"Apparently, the scanner has picked up some abnormal readings. Do you mind if I perform a quick examination?" The young patient shakes her head while continuing to avoid eye contact. "You look exhausted have you been sleeping well?"

"I've been sleeping fine."

"Have you been experiencing any nausea?"

"I've been a little nauseous in the mornings"

"Carol, how were her vital signs?"

"Her blood pressure was slightly elevated, and her pulse rate was a little high. These readings could have been attributed to nervousness. I drew some blood and sent it to the lab. The results should be available within the hour."

"Thank you, Carol." I turn back toward Carmen and complete my examination. Usually what I am about to say is received as good news, but my instincts tell me this is not going to be the case. I remain hopeful and optimistic my instincts are wrong.

"Well I don't want to get your hopes up until the results of your bloodwork are back, but I'm pretty sure you are pregnant." The young girl's eyes pop wide open, and she suddenly breaks out into hysterical sobs. Carol and I dive forward to console her as she bawls in our arms. Eventually, the sobbing subsides, and she just leans against me while I stroke her hair. I stand there, looking over at Carol, trying to figure out what to do next. She's obviously in no condition to discuss her situation. My best option is to talk with her two friends, and hopefully, they can shed some light on things. I slowly get up from the table and lay her back.

"Carmen, I just need to go out for a minute. Just relax here, and Carol will stay with you."

I look over at Carol, and she returns a nervous nod. I open the door and head in the direction of the waiting room. Mitch is still sitting there chatting with the two girls. They immediately stand as I approach.

"Please, sit down and relax. Your friend is fine. I just need to ask you a few questions if you don't mind. We need to monitor Carmen over the next few weeks, but I'm pretty sure she's pregnant." The two girls have identical stunned expressions. Bree is the first one to speak.

"That's impossible. There must be some mistake."

"Why do you say that?" Now it's Grace's turn to find her voice.

"Because Carmen doesn't have a boyfriend!"

17

CARMEN/DREW

HOW COULD THIS be happening? What did I do to deserve this? I don't even know whose baby it is. The doctor said it's early enough to abort the pregnancy. How can I keep a baby that's the result of a rape? How could I possibly get rid of the baby? I feel like my head is going to explode under all this pressure. Now my friends know there's something wrong and I just can't face all the questions.

We're almost home from the Dispensary. The man who kept Bree and Grace company nicely offered to give us a ride home in a company car. Bree is sitting in the back seat holding my hand. My friends are extremely worried, but I can't bring myself to talk about what happened. I just want to go to my room and sleep for a few days. Hopefully, when I wake up, this will all have been a nightmare. The car takes a right onto our street and pulls up to the curb in front of our house. The front door immediately opens, and Cowan rushes out the front door followed by Marcus, Kenji, and Drew. Bree and Grace get out of the car and hurry around to my side. They open the door and help me out onto the curb. Cowan is the first to reach us and puts an arm around my shoulder.

"Carmen are you okay? We've been worried sick. We were getting ready to start walking back to the Dispensary? What the hell is going on?"

"Let's just get Carmen inside, and we'll explain what happened. Guys, this is Mr. Andrews. He works at Apis Corporation and was nice enough to give us a ride home." Bree looks from the boys to Mr. Andrews who is standing next to the driver's door. Mr. Andrews walks up to the boys and extends his hand to Cowan.

"It's nice to meet you. I wish it were under better circumstances, but Carmen is a strong girl, and she obviously has great friends."

Cowan keeps his left arm around my shoulder while he shakes hands with Mr. Andrews.

"Thank you for taking care of Carmen. Would you like to come inside?"

"Carmen should get some rest, and I have to be getting back. Please keep me posted on her condition. Kenji, I'll try to drop by and see you tomorrow."

After saying goodbye to Bree and Grace, Mr. Andrews gets into the car and pulls away. The gang leads me into our house and to the couch near the front window. Bree and Grace sit on either side with the rest of my friends grabbing seats around the living room. I just want to go to my room, but I know it would be impossible until the boys receive a summary of the day's events. It's Cowan who breaks the ice.

"Could someone please tell us what the heck is going on?"

Bree provides a quick summary of what happened after I tripped the sensor at the Dispensary. She explains how Mr. Andrews escorted us inside and how he stayed with them while I was in the examination room with Dr. Timms. Grace goes on to describe how nice Mr. Andrews had been while he patiently sat down and kept them company. They both stop short of announcing my condition. I know it's only a matter of time before that bomb will have to be dropped. The boys sit there, after the girls finish talking, with expectant looks on their faces. It's obvious they are reluctant to be the one to announce my pregnancy. Eventually, Marcus grows impatient when it becomes apparent the girls are not being totally forthcoming.

"Carmen, what was the result of the examination?"

I look up at Marcus, but can't maintain eye contact, so I turn to look at Cowan. As soon as I look into his eyes, I start crying. Bree and Grace immediately put their arms around me.

"Carmen, we're your friends, and we're just concerned. Bree, if you know what's going on could you please share it with us? Not knowing is driving us crazy?"

I can feel Bree's body stiffen. I can feel her lean over and whisper in my ear.

"Is it okay if I tell them?"

All I can do is nod in response.

"They're not totally sure about Carmen's condition. They need to monitor her over the next few weeks, but the doctor at the Dispensary is pretty sure she's pregnant."

I can sense the air suddenly leave the room. There is an awkward silence for a while until Cowan finally speaks.

"That's impossible. There must be something wrong with their test results. I'm sure they will discover their mistake the next time Carmen goes in for a visit."

I can hear the other boys murmur in agreement, and then I feel Grace straighten up and turn in the direction of the boys.

"What if the test results are correct? Why are you so sure the results are wrong? Why are you being so defensive? Is there something that you are hiding?"

"What the hell are you talking about Grace? Are you implying that I had something to do with her pregnancy?"

Suddenly all hell breaks loose, and everyone is talking at the same time. Everyone is trying to shout over each other. It gets to the point that I can't stand it anymore. I finally jerk my head up and scream out at everyone.

"I was raped! I was raped in the fields behind the high school. It wasn't Cowan or anyone else in this room."

It was almost a relief to finally utter those words. The entire room falls silent. Everyone looks like they are frozen in time. Finally, the shock wears off, and everyone starts moving and blurting out questions. Eventually, I find myself surrounded by concerned faces. They all want to know who is responsible. Before I can respond, Cowan bends down in front of me and lifts up my chin. His eyes are so intense.

"Was it the two guys who were harassing you in line a few months ago at the Dispensary?" His eyes bore into mine. I try to respond, but I'm overwhelmed with the caring in those eyes. We communicate without words. I eventually drop my gaze. He immediately stands up and walks toward the door. Bree jumps up and tries to stop him from leaving. He grabs his coat and stands glaring down at her.

"Bree, get out of my way. I'm going to make those guys pay."

The white-hot intensity in his eyes forces Bree to step aside. He wastes no time rushing out the door. Marcus, Drew and Kenji quickly grab their jackets and hurry out the door after him. Bree hopelessly yells after them, but they're already down the sidewalk and determined to catch up with Cowan. I close my eyes and pray that somehow they come home safely.

I have never seen Cowan like this before. He has always been the calm one in our group. The fire that appeared in his eyes, when he realized the truth about Carmen's rape, was frightening. Marcus, Kenji, and I are just trying to keep up as he turns left on School Street. A thin layer of virgin snow covers the street from the brief storm that came through this afternoon. The wind has died down, and the skies are beginning to clear. The moon finally appears from behind some clouds. A combination of the moonlight and my eyes adjusting to the dark improves my visibility. I can see the high school looming off on our left up ahead. A few battery-operated lights can be seen through random windows as we make our way along School Street. Cowan eventually takes a right onto Hadley Street. The homes are starting to get bigger as we make our way into the nicer part of town. I finally work up the courage to say something.

"Hey Cowan, do you have any idea where you're going?"

"Just follow me, Drew, I know exactly where those guys live. They share a house on South Street."

"Just two of them share an entire house?"

Cowan looks at me with a knowing leer.

"One of them is Cole Taggert. His daddy makes sure he has the best of everything."

I see Kenji jerk his head toward Cowan and his eyes have a startled look.

"Please tell me that his father is not General Taggert, who is the very same man who runs this territory with an iron fist?"

Cowan stops and turns toward Kenji.

"He is the one and only. We're going to teach Cole and his daddy a lesson tonight."

Cowan then turns and continues walking down Hadley Street. The three of us just walk on in silence zig-zagging our way south. A pit begins to form in my stomach as we turn onto South Street. I don't know what the game plan is, but it can't be good. We eventually bear right and continue down South Street. Cowan begins to slow his approach as he scans the homes coming up on the left.

"It's the second house on the left."

I look up on the left and see a dark, three-story apartment house, similar to some of the others on the street. There doesn't appear to be any lights on inside the house. My heart is beating like a jackhammer as we walk closer. Finally, Marcus breaks his silence.

"Hey Bud, you don't plan on just walking up and banging on their door, do you?"

Cowan turns his head and smiles. The cold look in his eyes provides the answer. He continues up the front steps and walks right up to the door and begins pounding. The three of us have no choice but to follow. Cowan stops pounding, and we all listen for someone inside. My heart continues to pound in my ears, so it's unlikely I'll be able to hear anyone approach. Cowan tries pounding again but eventually stops. It becomes apparent that nobody is home. I quietly breathe a sigh of relief. It looks like fortune may save us from making a terrible mistake. Marcus reaches over and places a hand on Cowan's shoulder.

"Dude, let's take this as a good omen. Why don't we head back and plan an appropriate revenge for these two? I'm just as pissed as you are, but we need to act on this with clear heads. Rushing down here, in a blind rage, was not the best idea in the world."

Cowan's shoulders begin to sag, and his head tilts forward in clear resignation. He finally turns to face us. The fiery look has dissipated to smoldering coals. We all put a hand on his shoulder to show our support.

"Thanks for coming with me tonight guys. All I saw was red when Carmen confessed about what happened. We need to make these guys pay for what they did."

His intensity flickers for a moment before calming down. I give his shoulder one last squeeze before releasing my grip.

"Don't worry we'll think of something. Those guys will rue the day they messed with someone in our gang."

The four of us begin to make our long trek home.

18

MARCUS

I T IS SO peaceful out here early in the morning, especially on a Saturday. Walking on the paved path along the river, before the rest of the town wakes up, has become a weekend ritual whenever the weather cooperates. This morning is clear and cold, but the air is perfectly still. Snow and ice line the banks of the river. I stop to watch the rapids as they flow over the frozen rocks. The morning sunlight is caught in the mist and gives the impression of ice chips floating in the air. The sights and sounds of the rapids have a calming effect, which is much needed after the stress of the past week.

Finding out about Carmen's rape was traumatic for everyone. She has been adamant about not going to the authorities to report the rape. We initially tried convincing her otherwise, but she refused. Over the past few days the realization has set in that reporting the crime is probably futile. Since one of the boys is General Taggert's son, the chances of an arrest happening are zero.

It's possible that Carmen would get in trouble for falsely accusing the two boys. At the very least we would draw attention to our group and eliminate any chance of exacting revenge in the future without getting caught. As a result, Cowan has been skulking around like a caged animal the past few days feeling helpless. He keeps mentioning about paying the two boys another visit, but we all know how that will turn out. Thus, we have focused our energy into finding a method to seek revenge that won't be traced to our group.

The sound of falling stones interrupts my thoughts. I look off to my right to see a young woman carefully stepping down the short embankment leading down to the path. After she steps on the path, she turns and starts walking in my direction. Her white, winter coat and hat are a stark contrast to her dark skin. Her long, black hair is pulled back in a ponytail. As she gets closer, I begin to recognize her from the Dispensary. I remember seeing her leaving the building a few times. It's funny how attractive women find a way to stick in your mind. As she passes by, I politely nod and receive a smile in return. I try to act cool, while I turn to face the river. My thoughts are fixated on the smile and her big, brown eyes. She continues walking and eventually stops a short distance away. She proceeds to leave the path to climb on a big flat rock overlooking the river.

Other than the Dispensary, I don't remember seeing her anywhere else in town. She probably lives somewhere in the southern part of the community. I could either head back home or continue my walk past the rock outcropping where my visitor is standing. I decide to try my luck and resume walking up the path. As I get close, she turns and smiles. I figure that I have nothing to lose, so I might as well strike up a conversation.

"It's a beautiful morning for a walk. Do you come down here often?" I try to look calm, but I feel sweat starting, even in this cold. She smiles and turns to face in my direction.

"I woke up early this morning and couldn't get back to sleep, so I figured I'd take a walk. I guess I've been missing out. My name is Simone."

"Simone is a very pretty name. My name is Marcus. Would you like some company walking up the path for a bit?" The smile returns to her face, which I take for a good sign.

"That sounds like a great idea Marcus."

I like how my name sounds coming off her lips. She steps off the outcropping and joins me on the path. We start slowly walking up the path, each in our own thoughts. We pass the hydroelectric power plant on our right. It's hard to believe that the vast majority of our electricity was produced by the water flowing through the plant. Kenji tried to explain how the process worked one time, but it was way over my head. I try to think of something to say when Simone thankfully breaks the awkward silence.

"So, do you have to walk far to get here?"

"My house is on Green Street, so it's probably less than a mile. I guess far is a relative term when it comes to our community."

"I guess you're right. It doesn't take long to walk across town."

As we pass the first bridge, I glance east and see a guard house stationed on the far end. I can see a few guards sitting inside talking. I turn to Simone as we pass the bridge.

"Sometimes I wonder why they call them 'guards'. Are they guarding us from outside danger or preventing us from leaving?"

Simone's eyes dart toward the guards and then look back in my direction. For a split second, she seemed apprehensive. It's almost as if I struck a nerve, but the moment soon passes, and she returns her attention to the path ahead. The old abandoned buildings on Main Street pass by on our left. Some of the buildings have been renovated for particular community purposes. Up ahead is a factory which produces clothing for the town. Every citizen has an allotment, with each article cataloged in order to keep track of how much is used.

"Do you ever wonder what it's like outside of our community? I hear rumors of possible communities in other parts of the country."

Simone's question catches me a little off guard. My instincts awaken for a second time, and my apprehension returns. It's not often I meet someone who is inquisitive about the world outside of our community. Everyone is pretty tight-lipped when it comes to topics concerned with life outside our town's borders. I don't know if it's out of fear or resignation. I attribute my anxiety to a simple case of nerves and decide there is no harm in having a harmless conversation about the topic.

"My friends and I have wondered about the same thing. Supposedly, there has been some contact with a community south of our site. I haven't heard of any other successful contacts. It's hard to believe our two sites may contain the only survivors."

"It's depressing to think about all those people who died."

Simone turns away and stares straight ahead as we continue to walk along the river. We pass the second bridge as we continue our trek north.

"Have you ever thought about leaving town and trying to see what's out there?"

Simone surprises me again during our short walk. This is the first time anyone outside of my friends has asked me this question. Are there really other people who entertain these thoughts? The idea should not surprise me, yet we haven't found anyone who has shown any interest in our inquiries in the past. My group has felt increasingly isolated over the years. While it's exciting to finally find someone who shares similar thoughts, my instincts warn me to be careful.

"I think it's natural to wonder about what's happening outside of our little world. The only glimpses we have, of life outside, is what we read in books or hear through rumors and gossip. However, I believe such thoughts and actions are frowned upon by people in positions of authority." She returns a nervous smile and looks away. Perhaps she's just as concerned and confused about our situation as I am. It would be nice to have someone else to confide in. I ponder this possibility as we continue walking along the river.

★ ★ ★

The last few weeks seem to have passed by in a blur. I tried to see Simone as much as possible when I wasn't working or hanging out with my friends. I probably should bring her over to the house to meet the gang soon. Some of them know that something is going on, but I have used the excuse of Carmen's situation as the reason for my frequent walks. Cowan has asked a few times during work, but I've just avoided the subject. He apparently thinks I'm dealing with the same demons that have been plaguing him lately. He has definitely become more serious over the last number of weeks. I get the impression he feels responsible for what happened to Carmen. He has been reluctant to talk about anything associated with the incident. Perhaps I should try to get him to talk about it before we get home from work.

It's hard to believe we are already nine days into the year 2085. It's late on a Tuesday night, and we are driving the truck back to the depot to drop it off. Cowan has been silent the entire way back from our latest job. He finally pulls into the long driveway that runs alongside our building complex, which contains the maintenance facilities for the town. The buildings are located just south of the large Headquarters building. I wait for him to park the truck in the back parking lot before attempting to discuss the subject of Carmen.

"Hey Bud, you know that you can talk to me about anything. We are best friends, so if something is bothering you let's talk about it. Two people can carry a load much easier than one." I concentrate on his eyes as he continues to stare straight ahead. I can tell he's wrestling with the prospect of opening up about his problem. Finally, he takes a deep breath and then lets it out. It looks like he has reached a decision.

"I should have gone for a walk with her. If I had gone, then none of this would have happened."

His voice cracks at the end and I can see his eyes getting moist. I reach out and place my left hand on his arm.

"We all look up to you Cowan. You've become our unspoken leader, but you can't feel responsible for the entire group all the time. As far as I know, nothing like this has happened in this town before. So why would any of us worry about her going out for a walk alone? I have been doing that a lot lately, and I feel totally safe."

"The difference is you are a large man, and you can defend yourself if someone tries to attack you."

"Regardless, this wasn't your fault. If those creeps had their mind set to attack Carmen, it was going to happen eventually. They are the people responsible, and they will be the ones to pay."

"I guess you're right, but it just eats at me that they haven't been punished for their actions yet. They are free to live their lives while Carmen has to deal with the aftermath. She needs retribution. We all need it."

"I agree with you Cowan, and I promise you that we will find the right time and place to exact our revenge."

"Thanks, Marcus, I really appreciate it."

Cowan looks at me and smiles before sitting back in his seat and staring out the windshield. We just sit there for a few minutes, each of us lost in our own thoughts until he finally speaks.

"Since you brought it up, how have those solitary walks been going?"

I look over at him and see a mischievous glint in his eyes. It's obvious he suspects that something is going on. I'm tempted to continue the charade, but I feel guilty since he just opened up about his true feelings regarding Carmen.

"Well if you must know, I have not always been alone."

"The way I figure it, there is only one reason a man will wake up early in the morning to go for a walk in the winter. I'm willing to bet that reason is a woman."

19

MITCH

I AM STILL upset with some of the decisions that were made at the territory meeting yesterday. Taggert, and most of his followers have no feel for the mindset of large portions of the population. They are so concerned with our stagnated population growth that it affects their decisions on laws and regulations. Yesterday they voted to increase the number of Mandatory Reproduction Age births going forward and are actually considering decreasing the minimum age to twenty-five. They ended up tabling the vote until next meeting pending the results of Stuart's Population Growth Study. I told Stuart I'd stop by today to discuss his study and to see if there are any positive trends developing. We both agree that MRA births are causing a significant void in our society, between citizens with and without parents. Increasing the number of MRA births will only exacerbate this situation.

Stuart's computer lab is just ahead on the left. As I reach the door, I see Kenji sitting with his back to me working at a terminal on the other side of the room. I knock on the door, so I don't startle him while he is deep in thought.

"Good afternoon Kenji, how are things going?" I walk into the lab and lean against the table on Kenji's left.

"Hi Mr. Andrews, I've been working with Mr. Barnes on his newest population study. I'm trying to figure out the best way to display some generated data."

Kenji has proven to be a valuable asset to the company. He's naturally bright with a tenacity to solve problems. I've enjoyed talking with him over the last few months. His comfort level, with Stuart and I, has increased over time, but he still persistently calls me Mr. Andrews.

"Kenji, will I ever get you to call me Mitch? Have you seen Stuart around lately?"

"Sorry, Mitch. Mr. Barnes, I mean Stuart, was here a little while ago. I think he went to his office to get some research notes."

Stuart's office is just up the hall. If he doesn't return to the lab soon, I'll stop by on my way back to my office. I figure while I'm waiting I can get an update from Kenji on his friend.

"By the way, how's your friend Carmen doing?" His eyes look away, and I notice a subtle change in his demeanor.

"She seems to be doing much better. She works at the school, so I only get to see her briefly at night and on weekends."

Kenji definitely appears fidgety as if the topic is making him uncomfortable. I can remember thinking that something didn't seem right the afternoon I met Carmen in the Dispensary. It has been almost a month, and I can feel the same red flags returning. I realize that I'll need to be cautious if I'm going to obtain any useful information today.

"Carmen was understandably shocked when she was told about her pregnancy. I assume her shock has worn off over the last month."

"It took everyone by surprise, but she seems to be handling it well. We're all keeping an eye on her."

I notice there's no mention of a boy being involved. I remember her friends were emphatic about her not having a boyfriend. My gut tells me something is not right with the situation. I decide to push my luck a little further.

"I assume her boyfriend was excited when she shared the great news." Kenji definitely appears anxious and seems to avoid making eye contact. Before I am able to press him further, Stuart walks into the lab.

"Hey Mitch, I grabbed some notes for our meeting. Has Kenji been keeping you company?"

"He was just explaining some of the algorithms he is using to crunch through the population data. Do you want to go to your office to brief me on your progress?"

I start heading for the door and glance at Kenji to say goodbye. The relief on his face is obvious. Something is going on with his friend and I make a mental note to revisit the topic soon. Perhaps Michele may have some insight into what's going on. If I have time, after my meeting with Stuart, I'll pay her a visit later this afternoon. After all, any excuse to see Michele is a good one.

My meeting with Stuart lasted longer than expected, but I still may be able to catch Michele before she heads home. I hustle down the hallway leading to her lab. At the end of the hallway, a set of double doors serve as the entrance to the Artificial Womb Laboratory. Due to the sensitive nature of the work performed in the lab, access is limited. To the right of the door is a scanner similar to the unit outside the Dispensary. There is also a screen, mounted to the wall above the scanner, used for retinal identification. The security protocols seem a bit extreme, but if they help keep leadership off our backs, then I can put up with a little inconvenience. I place my hand on the scanner and wait for confirmation. A few seconds pass before I see my name appear on the retinal screen in green. I lean forward and place my right eye in front of the screen. A vertical, yellow line slowly moves across the screen from left to right. The word CONFIRMED is eventually displayed, followed by the time and date for logging purposes. After a few moments, there's an audible click indicating the door is unlocked. The door relocks within five seconds, so I quickly grab the handle and make my way into the lab.

The sheer size of the lab always impresses me when I first enter. The front half of the lab comprises the Artificial Womb units, while the back half contains the nursery. There are twenty Artificial Womb units arranged ten per side. The primary section of each unit is a large, black spherical shell which houses the fetus. Inside the shell is a sack comprised of thin, man-made material that mimics the lining of the female uterus. The sack is filled with artificial amniotic fluid which is maintained at a constant temperature and suspends the fetus in the sack. A number of tubes regulate blood flow, oxygen, and critical nutrients and hormones to the fetus. Vital signs are constantly monitored to ensure an optimum environment for the fetus. The process has become so routine that it's easy to take the incredible scientific achievement for granted.

Michele has her back to me while she works at a computer terminal which is interfaced to one of the Artificial Womb units. As I walk over, she stops typing and turns in my direction. I actually receive a smile when she sees her late afternoon visitor.

"Now you are coming to visit me in my lab. We are definitely going to have people talking."

"Hey let them talk. It's about time this town had something interesting to talk about." Even though the lab is kept at a comfortable seventy degrees, I can feel sweat starting to form on my brow. How is it that I can stand up to General Taggert, yet turn into a puddle in the presence of Michele?

"I'm actually glad you came by this afternoon. There's something I've been anxious to show you. Come on over to unit number four."

I make my way to the fourth unit on the right. Michele powers up the monitor which is mounted to the front of the spherical shell. The monitor displays readings from dozens of sensors mounted to the inside of the shell.

The resultant video is a high-resolution sonogram of the fetus. I lean forward and look at the monitor. My eyes fly open in disbelief as I stare at the image or should I say images displayed on the screen. Michele must have seen my reaction because I hear her chuckling off to the side. I turn toward her, but I'm temporarily speechless. Finally, I'm able to formulate my thoughts.

"Is this what I think it is? Do you have two fetuses in one chamber?" She smiles and nods her head.

"You've warned us for some time now that our leadership has been entertaining the possibility of increasing the number of MRA births. Even though we have twenty chambers, we could run out of capacity if they significantly increase the required numbers. We figured that one way to meet their quotas, using our current facilities, would be to double their output."

"Michele this is amazing! Nobody has ever successfully developed twins in an Artificial Womb before."

"Actually, it has been done once before." She promptly smiles and pretends to fiddle with some hoses and connections.

"What are you talking about? You're the one who made human ectogenesis a reality. This is one of the few facilities where it would have been possible." Michele turns and has a mischievous look on her face. I'm rendered speechless once again. I turn to face the two healthy hearts beating in the monitor. Eventually, Michele walks over and stands by my side.

"So, what was it that you wanted to talk about this afternoon?"

20

SIMONE

IT'S A FRIGID Friday night and I can't wait to get inside out of the cold. The wind, blowing out of the north, makes walking outside unbearable. For the time being, the school is blocking the wind as we make our way to Marcus' house. The closer we get to his house, the more apprehensive I feel. Even though it was my idea to meet all of his friends, I can't help but feel awkward about the whole situation.

"Perhaps we should wait a little longer before we do this?"

"Don't be silly Simone, it has been almost a month since our first date, and it's about time you met everyone."

I nod and face the road ahead pondering my current dilemma. When I first met Marcus, I promised myself I would keep my distance and not get involved. I was convinced I could handle the situation and keep my emotions in check. As the weeks went by it became apparent his interest was growing along with my guilt. Over the past week, I began to realize that I have been fooling myself about my own feelings toward him. He's a good-looking guy with a great sense of humor. Under different circumstances, I'd be thrilled about our relationship, but I have resigned myself to the fact that the closer we get the more disastrous, it will end. This mindset has dampened my mood as we turn the corner and approach his house. As we near the walkway leading to his house, I feel his hand on my shoulder. He lifts my head gently, and I can see concern in his eyes.

"Hey, is something bothering you tonight because you haven't said more than a few words since we left your house."

Telling the truth is not an option, so I force myself to smile as I reach down and grab his hand. The ease with which I'm able to transform my personality is disturbing. Marcus appears to relax as we make our way up the stairs and into his house. As we enter, I can see a bunch of people sitting in a living room off to my right. Marcus hangs up my coat and leads me into the living room. I welcome the warmth from the fireplace that services both the living and dining rooms.

"Guys, I'd like you to meet Simone. Simone this is the gang."

One by one his friends get up from their seats and introduce themselves. They all seem extremely friendly, and I immediately feel welcome as Marcus and I sit down on a small couch at the end of the room. I recognize most of the faces from the Dispensary, but Kenji looks very familiar.

"Kenji, you wouldn't happen to work at the Apis Corporation building?"

"As a matter of fact, I work for Stuart Barnes in the Population Monitoring group."

"Stuart is good friends with my mother. He stops by my mother's lab every once in a while."

"What exactly does your mother do for Apis Corporation?"

I turn toward Bree who is sitting on the couch to my left with Drew and Grace.

"My mother heads up the Artificial Womb Laboratory. I work there as a lab assistant." Everyone turns and stares at me with their mouths open. The room is silent for a few moments before I hear Cowan speak off to my right.

"If it weren't for your mother we wouldn't be here today. You're surrounded by a bunch of Lab Rats."

At first, I'm not sure how to respond until the entire room erupts in laughter. I look over at Marcus and see genuine enjoyment in his eyes. A sudden pang of guilt hits me at that very moment.

The rest of the evening is spent just sharing stories and chatting about a variety of topics. I'm tempted to steer the conversation in certain directions, but my conscience prevents me from pursuing my agenda. I realize that I'm squandering a perfect opportunity, but I find that I'm actually enjoying the company of this group of friends. Every once in a while the name Carmen is mentioned, but the conversation is soon redirected to something else. I make a mental note to ask Marcus about this person during our walk home.

At some point, late in the night, the conversation slows, and everyone looks ready to call it a night. Eventually, Marcus and I make our way around the room to say good-bye. Everyone is quick with a hug which makes me feel like part of the gang, at least for one night. Marcus helps me on with my coat, and then we are welcomed by a blast of cold air as soon as the door is opened.

The frigid cold does nothing to dampen his spirits. As we make our way down the street, he will not stop talking about how well the evening went.

"I told you my friends would love you. You were a big hit tonight. I don't know why you were so nervous about meeting everyone."

Even though the night went very smoothly, I have trouble sharing his jubilation knowing it will only be temporary. At the same time, I hate to pour cold water on his great mood.

"I had a really nice time, and your friends made me feel very welcome."

He smiles and kisses the top of my head as we continue our trek to my house. Near the halfway point of our walk, I recall the topic I wanted to talk about.

"I heard the name Carmen mentioned a few times tonight, but everyone seemed to quickly change the subject. Is she one of your ex-girlfriends?" An awkward silence follows before I hear Marcus respond to my question.

"I figured you would ask me about Carmen eventually. First of all, Carmen is a close friend, but she has never been my girlfriend. Carmen had a traumatic experience recently and is still trying to emotionally recover, which is why she wasn't there tonight."

I stop walking and look up at Marcus, who is noticeably shaken. He tries to maintain eye contact but eventually looks off to a point further down the street. I'm stunned to see that his eyes are actually tearing up. I'm tempted to press the issue, but decide to give him time.

"Carmen used to be an energetic, talkative person to the point of being borderline annoying. Whenever the gang was together, you could always count on her to be the center of attention."

He pauses and just stares off into the distance, obviously troubled by something. When it becomes apparent that he's going to need some prodding, I decide to probe a little further.

"Marcus, what happened to your friend?"

My question distracts him from his thoughts, and he looks back down into my eyes.

"Carmen was raped by two boys about six weeks ago. She was catatonic for a few weeks following the incident and has been slowly coming out of her shell."

I'm stunned by this revelation and find my head spinning with a bunch of questions.

"Oh, my god, that's terrible! I don't remember hearing about any arrests recently."

"Carmen was adamant about not reporting the rape. After she told us who one of the boys were, we understood her reasoning."

"Marcus, it doesn't matter who they are. They have to be brought to justice."

"When one of them has the last name of Taggert then justice is not an option.

My jaw drops and I quickly understand how hopeless and frustrating the situation must be for Carmen and her friends. I also realize that my dilemma is getting more and more complicated every day.

21

JAMES

AS MY OFFICE door closes, I lean back in my chair and cover my face with both hands. So far, my little spy network is producing a big fat zero when it comes to useful information. General Taggert entrusted me with this task, so I better start producing some results. He either selected complete incompetents for spies or his paranoia, concerning another resistance group, is being proved false. My last mole will be arriving shortly. I'm almost hoping she demonstrates some resistance, so I have an excuse to exercise my new-found authority. Taggert did stipulate I could use whatever means necessary to obtain information, including utilizing their family members. With respect to my next operative, I know exactly which family member I would like to exploit.

A knock at the door signifies her arrival. She has a similar look of despair, which adorned my previous visitors. I put on a winning smile and motion for her to enter the room.

"Good afternoon Simone, please have a seat."

Simone timidly enters the room and takes the seat in front of my desk. When she glances up, I immediately see the strong resemblance to her mother. She only holds my stare for a few seconds before glancing back down to her lap.

"So, what information have you been able to gather over the last month? I certainly hope it's more useful than our last meeting." She reaches into her jacket pocket and produces some folded sheets of paper, which she hands over. I unfold the sheets and begin scanning the information. The paper lists seven names, along with physical descriptions, addresses, and job titles. A short summary regarding each person is provided under each name. The information is pretty comprehensive, but I can't let on that I'm remotely impressed.

"This is material I already know. I need you to find out how they feel about their living conditions and if they have any grandiose plans to change things in the future. Are they planning on leaving or starting a rebellion? You see Simone, large rebellions start with small plans. We aim to thwart any movements before they get a chance to start. Your information is critical to making this possible."

"My meetings have primarily been with Marcus. I've met the entire group only once, and even then, one of the group members was not present. The group appears to get along very well with each other. I doubt that they associate with people outside of their group because there were very few references to other community members. A few of them expressed feelings of isolation from the rest of the town. This is not only a result of their living conditions but also how they're treated."

I've heard these theories tossed around during our weekly meetings and each time I get irritated. It's apparent Simone is being brainwashed by her mommy.

"They should feel fortunate they're even alive. Without the technology we developed, they would never have had the opportunity to whine about their minor problems."

"Actually, it's the technology my mother and her team developed."

"Don't get smart with me Simone. You know exactly what I mean. Since you mentioned your mother, I assume you would want her to remain unaware of our little arrangement. It would be unfortunate if she were to be negatively impacted due to a lack of cooperation on your part." Simone immediately lowers her eyes and remains quiet.

"Why have you only been meeting with this boy Marcus?" Simone looks up briefly, but the look in her eyes indicates that I struck a nerve.

"Oh, I see, don't tell me you're starting to have feelings for him. Please tell me the feelings are mutual. Perhaps I've underestimated your abilities as a spy." A smile spreads across my face as I ponder the ramifications of this development.

"I do not have feelings for Marcus. He's just a friend, and we simply enjoy hanging out together."

"You better make sure your feelings don't interfere with how you perform this job. If the poor boy has become infatuated with you, then you must nurture those feelings. Gain his trust and use it to gather as much information as you can. Don't worry about hurting him, since there is no future in this relationship. As soon as he finds out that you've been using him as a conduit for information, he'll drop you like a bad habit."

Watching my little mole squirm is extremely gratifying. The only thing that could make this moment more enjoyable would be if her mother were seated in her place. Simone remains silent, hoping the meeting will be over soon. I use the opportunity to examine her information more closely.

"I notice that you have supplied a detailed physical description of everyone except a young lady by the name of Carmen. I assume she's the person who was not present at your little get together."

"That's correct. She was not there because she has not been feeling well lately."

"What is wrong with her?" Simone just sits there fidgeting with the zipper of her jacket.

"I can easily look up her medical records to find out her condition. Why don't you save me the trouble and tell me what you know?" Simone sits and stares at the wall behind me while she appears to gather her thoughts. She eventually reaches a decision and meets my gaze.

"Carmen was apparently raped by two boys a few months ago and is subsequently pregnant. The traumatic event has had a significant impact on her both physically and mentally. Marcus said that she was essentially catatonic for a few weeks following the attack."

"This is the first I've heard about this crime. When did she report the attack? I'm surprised it wasn't mentioned during our weekly Apis meetings or the recent territory meetings." I find myself verbalizing my thoughts and stop to await Simone's response.

"Apparently, Carmen has not reported the attack and feels that doing so will just cause additional trouble for her and her friends."

"An alleged crime of this nature must be reported to the authorities. If indeed this attack occurred, then the animals need to be brought to justice before they attack someone else." Simone looks at me with a cold stare for a few seconds before responding.

"Even if one of the animals has the last name of Taggert?"

The mention of the name forces me to pause for a moment. It's no wonder the alleged victim has remained quiet. General Taggert would respond by protecting his own kin. An unfortunate accident would most likely befall the young lady. If this did not silence her friends, then similar incidents would follow. General Taggert will be most appreciative that I've uncovered this bombshell. Mitch's position is even closer to my grasp.

"I understand her hesitation with approaching the authorities about the attack. Let's keep this information between us until I can figure out how best to handle it. I assume that I'm the only person you've shared this secret with."

Simone stares at me for a few seconds, but the anger that accompanied the latest outburst soon dissipates. Her shoulders sag as she nods and then proceeds to stare at the papers on my desk. I imagine she's realizing just how deep her predicament has become with her recent admission. I had planned to take out some insurance tonight, and recent events make it imperative.

"Your throat must be parched after all of this talking."

I pour water, from the pitcher on the corner of my desk, into two glasses. I make careful note of which glass I hand to my partner in crime. Simone accepts the glass but proceeds to just hold it in her lap showing an admirable amount of caution. I grudgingly admit that if our roles were reversed, I wouldn't trust me either. I proceed to take a generous swig from my glass to set her at ease. This seems to alleviate her apprehension as she proceeds to take a drink from her own glass. It doesn't take long for her eyelids to get heavy from the drug that was laced inside of her glass. Soon my little spy is fast asleep.

Reaching into my lower desk drawer, I remove the Tracker Administration Gun which has been getting a workout today. I swiftly walk around the desk and carefully open the left side of her jacket, exposing the upper part of her left arm. Once the TAG unit is positioned on the meaty part of her shoulder, I depress the trigger. The miniature tracking device will not only provide valuable information but assurance of future cooperation if utilized correctly. A quick swipe of the tiny entrance hole with an antiseptic wipe, which also contains a numbing agent, completes the process. Now all that remains is to wait for my patient to awaken from her afternoon nap.

A rustling, in front of my desk, indicates that Simone is recovering from the effects of the drug. I look up from my reading to see her eyes fluttering open. As she raises her head, a stream of spittle stretches from the left arm of the chair.

"Welcome back Simone. It has been a while since someone has drifted off in the middle of my conversation. If I didn't have thick skin, I would take it personally." Simone rubs her eyes and yawns, as she attempts to wake herself up.

"What happened? Why do I feel so foggy and why is my left arm numb? How long was I out?"

"You have been out for about fifteen minutes. You slept on your left side so that probably explains the numbness. I'm sure it will clear up very shortly. Why don't you head home and get some rest?" Simone gets up and makes her way slowly to the door.

"Oh, and Simone, don't forget about our understanding."

22

ARLEN

I CAN SEE the two boys hard at work from my vantage point, inside an abandoned apartment house, across the street. The collapsed structure affords little protection from the cold weather outside. It's a typical morning, in early March, and at least the weathered walls block the majority of the wind that's buffeting my temporary shelter. It's a good thing the boys have been exerting themselves today because it must be the only thing keeping them warm.

While keeping an eye on Cowan and his friends has been a tedious assignment at times, it has been gratifying watching them grow into adulthood. I knew full well the sacrifice I was making a decade ago when I volunteered to stay behind and oversee the next potential wave of rebels. We had such grandiose ideas, back then, thinking that we were paving the way of freedom for future generations. I can remember the excitement around the table, during those secret resistance meetings, as we carefully discussed our future options. The gradual infringement on our freedoms, by various rules and regulations imposed by the community's leadership, stoked the fires of rebellion. When our operatives leaked word of impending legislation, which would enforce a maximum age limit, our resistance group expedited plans for an exodus from the community. We could not imagine living in a society that thought so little of its elders. It was decided that some of us should remain behind to slowly infiltrate key areas in the community and to keep the fires of rebellion stoked. This strategy worked for a number of years, as a slow trickle of rebels were able to follow in the footsteps of the initial group. Over the last few years, the results have been disappointing, due to the increased security measures imposed on the community. One escape attempt, in particular, ended in the tragic deaths of four citizens. The leadership has also methodically dampened the hopes and dreams of its citizens to the point that everyone is petrified to even utter the words resistance or rebellion. Thus, I find myself monitoring a small group of kids who unknowingly find themselves in the crosshairs of our heartless leaders. This, coupled with the fact my eightieth birthday is mere months away, has created a small window to fulfill my obligation. I check my pocket once again to ensure its contents and get up from my perch to meet my younger recruits.

As soon as I open the battered door, the cold wind tempts me to turn around and reconsider my decision to leave. Making my way slowly across the street I note that the boys have moved inside, which means we can at least talk free from this relentless wind. Voices emanate from the house as I mount the front stairs. The conversation stops as they become aware of a visitor outside. The front door swings open before I am able to raise my arm to knock. Cowan fills the doorway with his impressive frame, his bright red hair spilling out from under a woolen hat. My immediate impression is that I'm staring at a younger version of the man I hugged for the last time ten years ago. This triggers an unexpected emotional response as tears begin to well up in my eyes. In the meantime, Marcus walks up behind Cowan and looks at me over his friend's shoulder.

"Is there something we can help you with?"

Cowan's voice has the same bass undertones as his father's. It takes me a few moments to regain my composure and reply to his question.

"Cowan, I have something I need to discuss with you and Marcus? May I come in?" The boys' faces share identical confused looks before Marcus has the obvious response.

"Hey, wait a second. How do you know our names?"

"I know more about you and your friends than just your names and I will gladly explain if you would just allow me to come inside. It's probably a bad idea for us to be seen talking out in the open."

Cowan finally steps back to allow me to enter the house. A dining room is located off to the left with a weather-beaten table and chairs. I make my way over and sit down to await my hosts, who eventually join me at the table.

"My name is Arlen, and I've been entrusted, by the previous resistance group, to remain behind to watch over, recruit, and shepherd future rebels to their freedom. I've been watching over this territory for the past decade since your father led the original group to safety."

"Are you saying that my father made it out alive and is living somewhere else as we speak?" Cowan stares back at me with a hopeful expression on his face.

"That's my belief, and none of the lies our leaders have spread will ever convince me of the contrary. I have no definite proof, but I've proceeded under that certainty over the years, and I entreat you to do the same. As I've said, my mission was to collect individuals who exhibited the determination to escape their bonds and reunite with people who share their beliefs. While you may not be chained, don't fool yourself into believing that you're not enslaved to the current regime. Your plight will only get worse in the coming months and years."

"How do you know this to be true? You expect us to risk our lives, on a pilgrimage to who knows where under the remote possibility that the previous rebels made it out alive. Why should we put our lives in danger based on the words of an old man?"

I look over at Marcus and smile, not surprised by his reaction. Cowan, however, has a different determination in his eyes. He's the leader of this group and the lone person I need to convince. Reaching into my pocket, I remove the envelope and slide it across the table in his direction. Cowan picks it up, reaches inside, and removes the picture.

"Does that face look familiar. I was amazed by the resemblance when you first opened the door. The same fire blazes in your eyes that he exhibited during our secret rebel meetings. Don't fool yourself, Cowan, your father is still alive and awaits you and your friends." Cowan's eyes glisten with tears as he stares down into his father's face. He eventually flips the picture over and reads the information on the back.

"What do these numbers mean?"

"That's the location of a cabin which you need to locate. It's a way station of sorts. I was told that you will find a contact there who will direct you on the next phase of your journey. For security purposes that's the only information, I was given. The resistance group did not want the leaders of the community to have a way to discover their current location."

"How do you know the cabin is there? How do you know that your contact is still waiting or even alive?"

"Marcus, I cannot answer either of those questions at this time. I just have faith that my friends completed their journey and have maintained a route for others to follow. Hope is a dwindling resource around here. You need to redirect your thinking and follow a path which leads to something much better."

Marcus shakes his head in disbelief, folds his arms, and leans back in his chair.

"Why did you pick today to deliver this message?"

"First of all, I only have a few months remaining. My eightieth birthday is May 15th, so I was faced with the choice of delivering the message myself or entrusting it with one of my few rebel friends. Second, and most important, your lives are in danger. My contacts have recently informed me that your group is being monitored by our paranoid leadership. Recent events have increased their scrutiny and have placed you and your friends in danger."

"I think you are the one being paranoid. What recent events are you talking about?"

Taking a deep breath, I look toward Marcus who is leaning forward with a skeptical look on his face.

"General Taggert is aware of Carmen's rape, and he knows that his son was one of the boys responsible. I am trying to find out how he obtained the information, but the fact of the matter is he will not allow the information to become public knowledge. Arresting and terminating your group, under the pretext of rooting out a resistance group, will serve two purposes. His son's despicable crime will die along with your group. Even if it surfaces later, it will be waved off as the last desperate appeals of traitorous individuals. Your deaths will also serve as a deterrent to anyone contemplating rebellion."

My answer has the desired effect, exhibited by the stunned looks on the other side of the table. Cowan abruptly pushes away from the table and starts pacing back and forth.

"We are so screwed, Marcus. We should've killed those bastards when we had the chance. We should've searched them out and made them pay."

Images of his father stalking around the meeting room flash through my mind as I watch his son rant and rave. Similar to his dad, the trick will be to harness that energy for leadership purposes, while keeping him from doing something drastic.

"Cowan, even if we were able to exact our revenge, it would only have resulted in getting our group arrested and killed." Cowan stops pacing and glares at his friend.

"Your friend is right, there is a correct way to honor your friend, and we will plan it together." Both heads turn in my direction, but this time there is hope and determination in their eyes. "Please sit down and let us discuss our initial plans."

Cowan eventually returns to his seat, and a thoughtful silence descends upon the room.

"I realize this is a lot to digest all at once. The good news is that I don't believe you are in immediate danger. You two need to meet with your friends and convince them of the gravity of the situation. For the time being, continue with your daily activities as if nothing is wrong. I realize this will be difficult, but you need to convince whoever is watching that you are unaware of anything going on. I'll talk to my own moles and attempt to uncover how General Taggert found out about your friend's attack and if he has any near-term plans. Does that sound like a good initial plan of attack?" Both heads nod in response to my question. Marcus, surprisingly, is the first to reply.

"How can we get in touch with you if something comes up?"

"Don't worry about that right now. I have been monitoring you closely and will be back in touch soon. I live in the gray house at the western end of Henry Street. You can reach me there if an emergency comes up before then, but it's probably best if we avoid too much contact."

"So, what was my father like? If you knew about me, then did he also know. If he did, then why did he leave without me?"

I can see the anguish growing in Cowan's eyes with each question.

"Cowan, there will be time to discuss things further. Let me just assure you that your father never knew who you were. I only put the pieces together over the last few years, as I watched you grow up. Your features are a little out of the ordinary you must admit." This produces the first smiles since I entered the house and eases the tension in the room. I slowly get up from my seat and head toward the door followed by the newest members of the resistance.

23

MICHELE

IT HAS BEEN a long week, and I'm about ready to head home. I should be done reviewing this week's Artificial Womb results by the time Simone finishes up in the lab. My vision is starting to blur from hours of staring at this computer screen. The data and the photos captured from the chambers are fascinating, so it's tough to pull myself away. I keep returning to the information pertaining to the twins.

The twins are about four months along and are each about the size of an avocado. This corresponds to about three to five ounces. The babies' circulatory systems are up and running and pumping over six gallons of blood per day. I marvel that such tiny hearts are capable of moving so much blood around. Their ears and eyes have finally arrived in their final positions. I may be biased, but they are cute little things all snuggled up together and suspended in the synthetic amniotic fluid. All signs, thus far, are pointing to two healthy babies.

As I examine some projected size and weight graphs, I get the impression I'm being watched. I look up to see my daughter standing in the doorway.

"Simone, how long have you been standing there?"

"Only for a few minutes, I didn't want to disturb your concentration."

"Don't be silly, come on in and sit down. I'm almost done here, and then we can head home and relax."

Simone makes her way into the room and sits down in the lone chair in front of my desk. She seems unnaturally quiet lately, which is unlike her. Her buoyant, talkative personality has been missing for a few months now. At first, I thought she was just preoccupied with the new boyfriend, but she seems withdrawn and depressed lately.

"I'm just finishing up reviewing some of this week's data. Do you want to see some recent photos of the twins?" I turn the monitor around so that it faces Simone.

"They're very nice."

Simone looks away and stares off into space. Something is going on with this girl, and I'm determined to get to the bottom of it.

"Very nice? We're not talking about a new dress or a pair of earrings, Simone. We're talking about a set of twins who are developing in an Artificial Womb. This is ground-breaking stuff, and all you have to say is very nice. What's going on with you lately?"

Simone looks up, and I can see that something is troubling her, but she refuses to reply.

"Simone, we have always been able to discuss things in the past. Does it have anything to do with Marcus? Did you guys break up?" She continues to maintain eye contact, but she can't seem to find the appropriate response. I can see her eyes welling up with tears, yet she seems incapable of expressing what's bothering her.

"Honey, whatever it is we can get through it together. Just let me know what's troubling you so I can help you." I can sense Simone's emotional turmoil, but I'm forced to sit here until she decides to reveal the source of her problem. Finally, after sitting there staring at each other, she bursts into tears and starts talking and sobbing at the same time.

"He forced me...I had to spy or...he said he would take it out on you...I was worried about your job...I didn't want to hurt anyone...I love him."

She eventually buries her face in her hands and bawls uncontrollably. I get up and rush around my desk to console her. As I wrap my arms around her, she collapses in my grasp. It's almost as if she has no energy left to support herself. We remain that way until she begins to regain her composure. I continue to hold her head against my chest and stroke her hair like I used to do when she was little. She needs to come around on her own or else she'll shut down again. When her emotional outburst appears to have ebbed, I attempt to revisit the conversation.

"Sweetie, what did you mean by he forced me? What's this stuff about spying and my job?" I continue to stroke the back of her head awaiting a response. After what seems like an eternity, she begins to answer my questions.

"He threatened that if I didn't spy for him, he would take it out on you. He also warned that if I told anyone about our agreement, then he would be forced to take action."

"Who are you talking about?"

I can't believe my daughter waited this long to come to me about this situation.

"His name is James Moeller."

My stomach rolls and my breath catches when I hear the name. I begin to imagine the torment that piece of trash must have put my daughter through and the bile begins to rise.

"Who did you spy on Simone?" My daughter looks away, and the truth immediately hits me as the puzzle pieces fall into place.

"Oh, my god, so that's why you have been so miserable lately. We need to talk to someone about this situation, and I know the perfect person."

★ ★ ★

Simone finally finishes recounting the events surrounding her spying, including her meetings with James. The three of us sit quietly in Mitch's office as he digests the information. After a few moments, he looks over at my daughter and smiles.

"First of all, Simone, you have nothing to be ashamed of since that bastard left you no choice. James Moeller works directly for General Taggert. Since Taggert's son is directly involved, I'm afraid to say that your friends are in danger. It's imperative we meet with your friends soon to come up with a game plan."

A slight bob of the head indicates Simone's understanding as she continues to look down at the floor. It's obvious the process of bearing her soul has been both liberating and exhausting. She needs to just get home to regroup before discussing this topic any further.

"Honey, why don't you go to the lab and gather your things so we can head home. I just need to talk to Mitch for a few minutes, and then I'll meet you down there."

Simone stands up, nods to Mitch, and then makes her way out of the office. I wait for her footsteps to fade away before attempting to talk, but Mitch beats me to it.

"Poor kid, she's way too young to be forced to carry something this big around."

Mitch smiles, but the look in his eyes shows grave concern. I can tell the information Simone provided has him worried and I feel bad for dropping it into his lap.

"Mitch, I really appreciate you taking the time out to meet with us. I didn't know where else to turn."

"I wouldn't be a true friend if you couldn't rely on me during a crisis. I hate to admit it Michele, but this situation is serious given the people involved. We need to meet with those kids as soon as possible because their lives are in danger."

The look in Mitch's eyes chills me to the bone. He referred to them as a group, but I know that he's mainly concerned for the welfare of his daughter. My guilt increases when I consider the danger Grace and her friends are in due to my daughter's actions. Apparently, he senses my apprehension and gets up from his seat and walks around his desk. On instinct I stand up and face him, my pulse rate starting to quicken. He puts an arm on each shoulder and smiles. I look into his eyes and find it easy to get lost.

"Don't worry about anything right now. Let me talk to a few trusted friends and figure a few things out. See if Simone can set up a meeting over the weekend with her new friends?"

"Who are you going to talk to and how do you know they can be trusted?"

"Michele, in the spy game there are always two sides."

Mitch gives a subtle wink and smiles. Before I realize what's happening, he leans in and presses his lips gently to my mouth. Reflexively my lips respond, and we stand there passionately kissing for a few moments. Eventually, he pulls away, and a large grin is spread across his face. I am momentarily speechless, so I'm relieved when Mitch fills the silence.

"Well, I guess I can cross that off my bucket list!"

24

MITCH

AS WE DRIVE to Grace's house, I feel a variety of emotions coursing through my body. I'm excited to meet with my daughter again, even if the circumstances are far from ideal. This excitement is dampened by the grave concern I feel for her and her friends. Looking over at Michele my pulse quickens when I think about the passionate kiss from yesterday. Hopefully, later tonight, we will have a chance to talk about what happened in my office. For the time being, I need to focus on how to keep my daughter and her friends safe. As I review the framework of the plan we will be presenting to the kids, my stomach tightens. You can add apprehension and fear to the potpourri of emotions fighting for control inside my body. Looking in the rearview mirror, I can see that Simone is experiencing some of the same emotions in the back seat. She must be dreading the moment Marcus and his friends find out about her spying activities. My heart goes out to her as I glance at her troubled face in the mirror.

Pulling up in front of Grace's house, I can feel my nerves tingling. Her home radiates a cozy feeling as the flickering light from the fireplace dances in one of the rooms. It looks like the gang is all settled in the living room awaiting the start of the meeting. One of the shades is pulled aside indicating that they are aware of our arrival. I turn toward Michele and attempt to exude confidence as I reach over and take hold of her hand.

"Well, are you guys ready to get this show on the road?" Michele smiles and nods, but concern is etched on her face. We climb out of the car and make our way slowly to the house. As we near the top step the door opens and Marcus appears in the doorway. Michele steps forward and introduces me before I have a chance to open my mouth.

"Hi Marcus, this is Mr. Andrews from the Apis Corporation. We thought it would be a good idea to meet with everyone tonight."

I extend my hand to Marcus, and he politely receives it, but a forced smile remains on his face. He looks over at Simone, but she avoids making eye contact causing him to shrug his shoulders and move aside. He escorts us into the living room where he introduces Michele and I to the rest of the gang. Once we are all situated, everyone sits in awkward silence for a few moments until Michele finally nudges me in the side. Apparently, this is my cue to get the meeting started, although I'd rather wait until one last person arrives. Perhaps I can stall for a bit to allow for more time.

"Before I start, let me introduce ourselves for those of you we haven't met already. This is Dr. Michele Timms, and I am Mitchel Andrews. Please call me Mitch." I glance over to my right and wink at Kenji. "I guess you're all wondering why we're here tonight. I asked Simone to set up this meeting because we are all concerned for your safety." Puzzled looks ensue from the kids seated around the room. As if on cue, a knock is heard coming from the front door. Kenji starts to get up to answer it, but I place my hand on his knee and rise instead. I make my way over to the door to welcome my guest. As my friend ambles into the room and takes an empty chair, I observe recognition on two of the faces.

"For those of you who haven't had the pleasure of meeting my close friend, this is Arlen. Arlen has been a guardian angel to your group over the years. He was associated with the previous resistance group and volunteered to stay behind to assist any future recruits. In an earlier encounter, Arlen indicated that he had rebel friends who provided him key information. Well, I am one of those friends." I glance over at Michele and see a surprised look on her face.

"As Kenji, may have indicated, we share common beliefs and frustrations regarding the current conditions in our community. While the conditions themselves may not warrant drastic action, recent events have placed your safety in question. Arlen, informed you previously, that General Taggert is aware of the atrocity committed by his son Cole." I look over at Carmen, who is sitting next to Grace, and see her wince. My anger begins to rise as I imagine the emotional damage that fateful night has caused. I take a breath to prepare myself for the repercussions my next statements will create.

"General Taggert stumbled upon this information while trying to root out potential rebel groups. He hatched a plan to forcefully employ spies to infiltrate different parts of the community." A chorus of grumblings and questions ripple throughout the room. Simone covers her face with her hands and begins to weep. Marcus instinctively turns to console her when realization strikes him suddenly.

"Simone, no not you?"

His worst nightmare is confirmed when Simone starts sobbing hysterically. Marcus recoils and jumps out of his chair. His face becomes contorted as he screams at his girlfriend.

"How could you do this to us? I love you! I thought you loved me!"

Group members gradually join the fray as they recover from the initial shock. The meeting is quickly dissolving into mayhem when Arlen stands up and demands silence. Everyone is stunned by the strength and intensity displayed by this frail old man.

"Marcus sit down right now. This is no time to finger point."

The room immediately becomes quiet, as everyone's attention is turned toward Arlen.

"Simone had no choice but to cooperate with General Taggert's wishes. Her safety and the safety of her mother were threatened. Anyone in this room would have acted in the same way."

A few heads nod in agreement, but the rest of the room doesn't appear convinced. The leader of the suspicious group is Marcus, who continues to stand in the middle of the room glaring at Simone. Arlen appears to sense the lingering dissension and continues his entreaty.

"My moles have been closely monitoring Taggert and have indicated that you've been in his sights for quite some time. He has been gearing up to make an example of your group regardless of Simone's information."

I know that Arlen is exaggerating his intel a bit in order to create a better case for Simone. The key result, however, is that a few more group members appear to be joining the pro-Simone camp. It's important to get the support of the group if we have any hope of selling them on our plan. Marcus finally sits down but remains visibly unconvinced as he periodically glances at Simone, who is now sitting quietly staring down at her lap.

"Mitch and I have been discussing your predicament for quite some time and have formulated a strategy. We cannot emphasize enough the gravity of your situation, and I implore you to listen to the outline of our plan."

With that, Arlen turns to me and sits back down in his chair. The room is completely silent as all eyes turn in my direction. Being thrust into the spotlight, once again, I initially panic as I search for where to begin. I can feel the expectant eyes boring down on me and find some temporary comfort in Arlen's calm demeanor.

"As Arlen just explained, we've been discussing your dilemma and carefully evaluating potential options and their possible outcomes. The only practical solution, that has the best chance to ensure your safety, is to carefully plan an escape." Even though the group members have been introduced to this possibility by Cowan and Marcus, a chorus of gasps and frantic questions follow. Arlen takes the initiative to quell the unrest before it derails the meeting.

"Everyone, I know you're anxious and that you have a million questions, but you need to listen to Mitch first."

I wait for the clamor to die down before continuing with my explanation.

"Arlen has provided you with the location of a cabin that was used by the previous resistance group during their escape. We've devised an escape strategy which bypasses the various security measures our paranoid leaders have instituted and will provide us the best chance of success."

Michele's head jerks to the right with a stunned expression on her face.

"What do mean by us?"

"Shortly after the kids escape, Taggert and his henchmen will assume we warned them. It won't take long for them to discover we were involved, so it will not be safe for us to remain behind." I reach over to hold her hand as I prepare to summarize our escape.

"First of all, it's imperative that we remove the trackers from each of you. Michele has the required equipment and instrumentation in her lab to safely extract the tracking devices. While Michele is verifying the location of each tracker and prepping you guys, Arlen, Stuart, and I will pay Cole Taggert and his friend Danny a visit."

"Why are you going to their house?"

I turn toward Marcus and pause for effect, knowing that the next step in our plan will elicit a favorable reaction.

"We intend to kidnap them, bring them to Michele's lab, and have the group's trackers implanted into their bodies."

A confused look persists on Marcus' face.

"Why would you implant them with trackers?"

Before I am able to respond, Kenji provides the answer that was right on the tip of my tongue.

"They are going to use Cole and Danny as a diversion, while the rest of us escape from the community."

I smile and pat Kenji on the shoulder before continuing with my explanation.

"Kenji is right, General Taggert will be able to sense the trackers have suddenly stopped working, so we need to quickly implant the devices to quell any suspicions." Marcus smiles in response to our explanation, while the rest of the room listens attentively.

"In order to facilitate our escape, we have arranged for a rebel friend to program the security cameras to turn off every fifteen minutes for a short period of time. This will enable us to make our way west. At the same time, Arlen will escort our new prisoners back to one of your homes for the night. This will hopefully buy us some time to escape, while Taggert and company assume you are all tucked into your beds." Before continuing, I take a quick glance around the room and observe grins and nods in agreement.

"Sometime during the night, Arlen will start heading south with his captives. He will be equipped with both a tranquilizer gun and a handgun. The objective is for Arlen to buy us as much time as possible. As a secondary diversion, I will provide Kenji and Drew with the coordinates for a location up north. Hopefully, after Arlen is discovered in the south, Taggert will confiscate all of our computers in an attempt to find our true location. We will 'destroy' each of the computers, but the damage to Kenji and Drew's computers will only be cosmetic. We will ensure the phony coordinates are accessible with the hopes of delaying our friends a little longer."

"What is going to happen to Arlen?"

"Cowan, I have lived a long life. Enabling you guys to escape would be a perfect way to cap off my life and complete my mission for the resistance."

Everyone solemnly nods in response to Arlen's selfless outlook. Carmen suddenly looks up and addresses Arlen.

"So, what's going to happen to Cole and Danny?"

"Don't worry. They will never see a trial. The tranquilizer gun will be used if they try to escape, while the handgun will be used when we have bought you enough time or if we're discovered."

A contented smile spreads across Carmen's face. It must have been contagious because it slowly makes its way around the room. I look over at Arlen, and he returns a smile of his own. It appears that we have achieved unanimous approval of our plan.

25

SIMONE/JAMES

AS I WALK along the bike path, behind the Apis building, memories of my first meeting with Marcus play through my mind. It was just a little further up from this spot that I interrupted one of his weekend walks. I'd seen him occasionally walking along the path on previous weekends, but was too shy to introduce myself. It's sad that I used spying as the reason to muster the courage to bump into him. Perhaps, under different circumstances, our relationship would have blossomed into something lasting. Considering his reaction to my covert activities, it's safe to say our relationship is over.

The Headquarters building appears on the right, and the mere sight of it causes my stomach to turn. Hopefully, this will be the last meeting with Mr. Moeller. At least this time I will be helping the gang out by supplying false information. Approaching a rear entrance to the facility, I review the information I'm supposed to pass along to my handler. Arlen and Mitch repeatedly stressed the importance of being convincing during this meeting. Utilizing me as a double agent could provide the window of opportunity necessary for everyone to escape.

Fueled with a newfound determination, I open the back door and take the stairs up to the second floor. As I reach for the door to exit the stairwell, it opens suddenly, and I find myself face to face with another young woman. Her initial surprise is soon replaced with a resigned look as she quickly diverts her eyes. Her expression is one that I've seen many times staring back at me in the mirror. The shame and contempt revealed in her eyes, leave no doubt that she is a fellow spy. A slight nod of my head inspires a faint glimmer of gratitude as we acknowledge a secret kinship of sorts. The moment quickly passes as she hurries down the stairs and back to her dual life.

The brief encounter fills me with anger and raises a number of questions as I make my way toward Moeller's office. How many spies is he controlling? How many lives is he ruining and how does this scheme benefit our community? I struggle to mask my resolve and anger as his doorway comes into view on the left. It's important to appear submissive and fully under his control, in order pull off the ruse. He's seated at his desk, poring over some documents, when I meekly knock on the door. He looks up with a glare that quickly transforms into a calculated smile. The dark look in his eyes quickly begins to melt away my confidence.

"Simone, good afternoon! Come on in and have a seat."

I slowly enter his office and take the seat in front of his desk, while consciously diverting my eyes from his evil glare.

"So, what have you uncovered for me over the past month? Are our mutual friends plotting to take over the territory?"

A sinister laugh follows the last question which makes my skin crawl. The sooner this meeting is over with, the better.

"They are not planning anything against our community. They just want to be left alone to live their lives in peace, without constantly worrying about looking over their shoulder."

"Little do they know that you're the one looking over their shoulder." A wink and a satisfied grin confirms how much he's enjoying himself.

"I just want to complete this assignment and try to get my life back to normal. I'm not cut out for this." He sits back, crosses his arms, and stares at me, while he appears to consider my last statement.

"Well, if you could only provide me some useful information there may be a way to relieve you of your duties. I can't guarantee anything, but I promise to put in a good word for you with General Taggert."

This is as good a time as any to see if he will go for the bait. While it's obvious that he can't be trusted, I need to convince him the following information is being provided as a means of obtaining my release from his control and the protection of my friends.

"Before divulging my information, I need some reassurances that this will be our last meeting and that you will do what you can to ensure the safety of the group. They're not the rebel group you're seeking, and they just want to live their lives in peace."

He leans forward, and his demeanor quickly changes.

"First of all, Simone, you're in no position to negotiate. If I have even an inkling that you're withholding something, things will not only get uncomfortable for you but for your mommy as well. That being said, if your intel is deemed valuable enough, I will see what I can do to get you released from future spying activities."

I'm not naive enough to believe that there's an ounce of sincerity in his words, but I need to give the appearance that I'm willing to believe him. I hesitate for the appropriate amount of time to give the impression that I'm struggling with my decision. Finally, I take a deep breath, lift my head, and force myself to look into his deceitful eyes.

"Marcus told me the gang is planning to escape from the territory in late May when the snow is gone and the temperatures aren't freezing at night. Apparently, they don't feel safe here after the Carmen attack. They believe it's only a matter of time before General Taggert finds out what his son did and attempts to cover it up."

I force myself to appear sincere as his eyes bore into mine.

"How sure are you about their intent to escape in May?"

"Marcus asked me to escape with him. I told him that I couldn't leave my mom. He was practically in tears trying to convince me to go." My acting performance is highlighted by a single tear rolling down my cheek. I quickly wipe it off and look down at my lap, attempting to exude as much misery as I can muster.

"Perhaps I've underestimated you, Simone. You have utilized your feminine assets to disarm our poor boy Marcus. What I need you to do is to find out the exact date of this little expedition, where are they headed, and who will be involved. Perhaps we can prevent this mini-exodus from occurring before anyone gets hurt."

I cover my face with my hands and begin whimpering. The final act of my performance needs to be convincing to ensure the hook is sufficiently set.

"Please, I can't take this anymore. Marcus said something about heading south. The gang is going to try and make it all the way to the Southern Territory. They hope to meet some survivors along the way." I punctuate my performance by sobbing and muttering random thoughts as I rock back and forth in the chair. Evidently, I'm convincing because Mr. Moeller attempts to console me with some false words of kindness.

"Let me talk to my superiors and see what I can do. You've done a terrific job uncovering this information. I'm sure that your efforts will be rewarded. Why don't you go home and enjoy the weekend?"

With that, I nod my head and slowly walk out of his office. It takes all of my willpower to suppress a smile until I'm safely down the hallway.

After Simone leaves, I remain seated at my desk pondering the ramifications of the information she's just divulged. Finally, one of my moles has come through with the type of information General Taggert has been looking to acquire. I look down at my watch and see that it's already 5:30 p.m. on a Friday night. General Taggert works long hours so I can probably still catch him in his office or in the main computer lab. I reach down and pick up the folder containing the groups' information and walk out of my office.

Heading down the long hallway leading to the computer lab, I contemplate the prospect of taking over for Mitch Andrews as the head of Apis Corporation. It's not out of the realm of possibility that Taggert will reward me for my efforts. My first order of business will be to fire each of the department heads. The looks on their faces will be priceless when I hand out their pink slips at the first staff meeting. I can feel an extra hop in my step as I reach the double doors heading into the computer lab. The door on the right has a numeric keypad and a thumbprint reader for added security. After entering my six-digit code, I hold my right thumb on the reader and wait for the bright green line to travel across the pad. A few seconds pass before an audible click emanates from the door. Upon opening the door, I'm surprised to see a flurry of activity at this hour on a Friday night. General Taggert runs a tight ship and expects his subordinates to exhibit the same dedication and attention to detail that he portrays on a daily basis. Scanning the room, I see him hunched over one of the central terminals on the far side of the room. He straightens up and begins scanning the three large monitors mounted up on the wall above his head. About halfway across the room, I can pick out his deep voice above the cacophony of noise in the lab.

"Excellent job Sean, getting these additional cameras on line will significantly improve our town's security and provide full coverage of the area. Now I don't have to worry about any of those damn blind spots."

General Taggert turns as I approach and produces a broad smile. My luck keeps on getting better and better. His mood will be off the charts once he hears my news.

"Good evening General, you seem to be in fine spirits."

"That's because my boy Sean is a computer genius. James, I would like you to meet Sean Ramsey, one of the young computer wizards we have supporting the Environmental and Law Enforcement Units."

I reach down and shake the young man's hand who is seated in front of a terminal with three large monitors on the table in front of him. His wavy, black hair almost touches the neck of his olive drab t-shirt. This kid must be a computer wizard to warrant not adorning the preferred high and tight haircut.

"Nice to meet you Sean, my name is James Moeller."

"James works for the Apis Corporation, but he also performs various jobs for me at Headquarters."

I nod toward General Taggert and turn to address the young man who is already obediently typing away at his keyboard. General Taggert turns and begins to walk over to a small conference table located in the middle of the lab. He takes a seat at the end of the table and begins our impromptu meeting before I'm seated.

"So, James, what brings you here on a Friday evening?"

"I've uncovered some interesting news regarding our rebel friends, and their plans in the not too distant future." It's obvious that I have the general's undivided attention at this point. He nods to indicate for me to continue.

"One of my operatives just informed me that the group she's been monitoring has plans to escape in late May."

"How reliable is this information?"

"Very reliable, General. She was invited by her boyfriend to join them on a trek south." A smile spreads across the general's face as he quietly contemplates the ramifications of my intel.

"Excellent job James. I knew you were the perfect man for this job. Do you have the identities of all the members of this group?"

I nod and hand him the folder containing the profiles of each group member. He picks up the folder and quickly thumbs through the pages. He then snaps the folder shut, stands up, and makes his way back to the terminal where Sean is sitting. I hurry over to see what the general has in mind.

"Sean, could you enable the trackers for the seven individuals contained in this folder?"

Sean accepts the folder and opens the cover to display the first profile. He then turns his attention to his monitors and begins typing commands into the keyboard. After about five minutes, he enters a few last commands and then looks up at the central monitor on the wall. The screen displays an overhead two-dimensional image of the town. Outlines of each street and building are shown in white on a black background. Seven flashing green dots are displayed on the map. Three of the dots appear in a house located on Green Street. There are four dots shown along the Connecticut River.

"It looks like four of our targets are working a little late today. Marcus and Cowan appear to be parking their rig in the Maintenance parking lot. Kenji and Drew appear to be working late in the Apis Corporation building."

I marvel at General Taggert's ability to recall information that he only glanced at moments before. I had always heard about individuals possessing an eidetic memory, but to witness it first-hand is amazing.

"General, your ability to process and recall details is truly incredible." My superior glances in my direction and provides a knowing smirk.

"James, a person in my position needs every advantage possible. Just stick with me, and you'll go far."

Little does he realize that I'm way ahead of him in that department. Perhaps tomorrow I'll start scoping out that corner office over at the Apis Corporation.

26

MICHELE/JAMES

I LOOK AROUND my lab and can't believe this will be the last time I ever see this place. It's very depressing to think of all the hard work that I've poured into this job, only to be forced to abandon everything. As much as it hurts to leave, I have to agree with Mitch that there's no way we could remain in this territory after the kids escape, especially considering Simone's status as a spy. At least I can look forward to the prospect of starting a new life with Mitch.

Nervous banter fills the lab, while I prepare the instruments for the tracker location and removal process. The kids are anxious to get things going, but it's important to coordinate the tracker removal with the implantation into their new hosts. It's heartening to see Simone conversing with some of the kids. Marcus' demeanor is still understandably cool toward Simone, but hopefully, he will come around soon.

Glancing up at the clock, I note that the time is almost 7:00 p.m. Mitch's group will be heading out in a little over an hour to begin their part of the mission. Arlen was informed, by his mole at headquarters, that the kids' trackers were enabled a little over a month ago. The group has been going about their daily activities trying to act like nothing out of the ordinary is going on. The fact that everyone is assembled together in this lab will certainly appear suspicious. The next few hours will be nerve-racking since we'll be proceeding in constant fear of soldiers barging into the lab at any moment. However, it's pointless to worry now that the plan is already set in motion. My immediate concern is to locate each of the trackers and prepare each kid for the removal procedure before Mitch's group arrives.

"Abby, can you send the first of our victims in." Abby Chen turns to retrieve one of the kids. I imagine she would prefer being in her lab tackling issues associated with Apis Pill research and production. Being a fellow staff member, Abby Chen has found herself in the same boat as Mitch, Stuart, and myself when it comes to her days being numbered as a citizen in this community. Both Abby and her husband Neil will be accompanying us during our getaway this evening. I hear footsteps and turn to see Abby leading Drew toward our makeshift trauma unit, which essentially consists of the scanning equipment, a hospital bed, and a privacy curtain. There's also room for the two, additional gurney's that Mitch's crew will be wheeling in later.

"Drew we are all set-up to commence the tracker scanning procedure. Let's take care of you first, so you can assist Stuart with preparing the equipment for our departure." As Drew sits up on the hospital bed, I can see the concern etched on his face.

"The scanning procedure is completely painless, so there's no reason to worry. The machine will quickly scan your body and record the position of the tracking device. Since the tracker has been previously activated, the machine will utilize the pings to home in on its location, which will significantly reduce the scanning time."

"The scanning procedure is not the part that worries me."

Drew glances over to the arm on the machine which controls the long needle used for the tracker removal. Beads of sweat are evident on his forehead. I can't help but smile, as I look at the concern displayed in his big, brown eyes.

"Even though the removal head looks imposing it's virtually painless. Once the machine locates the tracker, the needle is lowered into the area. A numbing agent is injected into the incision, while the tracking device is removed. The tiny incision will feel a little sore for a few days, but that's the extent of the discomfort."

I can tell by the pale look on his face that my explanation has done little to sway his fears. It's apparent that I need to just get the procedure over with as quickly as possible. Drew proceeds to lay on his stomach while I activate the instrument and input the unique 17-digit code which is tattooed on his right palm. After the initial calibration sequence, the locating arm begins to sweep over Drew's body. The machine amplifies the ping being produced by the tracker. The tone is reminiscent of the sonar ping that emanated from submarines during those classic naval movies. Eventually, the movement of the arm stops and the head begins to lower directly over Drew's right buttock. This is not surprising since it used to be the most common tracker location for obvious reasons. Given the date that each member of the group was born, I'm quite certain the remaining trackers will be in the same location. After a few moments, the head raises, and the arm moves back to its initial position. I reach up and tap the save button to download Drew's tracker information, which will be used by the removal head later this evening. Drew hops off the bed and heads over to the adjacent room containing the equipment Mitch stored away for our escape. The room has suddenly become quiet, which causes me to look out at six sets of anxious eyes. Something tells me this is going to be a long night.

As expected, the next four trackers were implanted in the same location as Drew's device. While we are just finishing up with Grace, I can hear Drew discussing the operation of the handheld monitor with Kenji.

"Kenji, I'm pretty sure the range settings are adjusted correctly on the tracking channel."

"I agree, but why does the monitor show eight trackers within the confines of this lab. It just doesn't make sense."

"Hold on a second, the TRACKER IDENTIFICATON tab, located in the top pull-down menu can be set to display the ID of each tracker on the screen."

I walk around the privacy curtain and see Kenji look down at his right palm and then at the monitor screen.

"Hey that's cool, I can see my tracker ID on the screen right next to your number. Hey Cowan, get up and come over here, so we can see your tracker move."

Cowan gets up from his chair, on the other side of the lab, and begins walking over to his friends. The way their faces light up, I can tell that their experiment worked.

"This thing works great! Wait a minute, that's strange. Hey, guys, check this out."

Both Kenji and Cowan lean over the monitor to see what Drew has discovered.

"All eight tracking IDs have similar 17-digit codes, but the eighth has the number 02162085051010004 which is a different date than the rest. This number appears to correspond to February 16, 2085."

Simone's head suddenly pivots in the direction of the three boys.

"Did you just say February 16, 2085? That was the Friday I met with James Moeller!"

All heads turn toward Simone, as she quickly gets up to head toward the monitor.

"Oh crap, the ID is moving toward the three of us! Simone, you are the eighth tracking device.

My heart sinks when I hear Kenji's last statement. That bastard must have implanted a tracker during one of their meetings and has probably been tracking her movements ever since. It looks like we are going to have an eighth tracking device to remove this evening.

* * *

Before I head home for the weekend, I can't resist checking in with Sean one last time on the status of our rebel friends. He is seated in his customary spot in front of the three monitors. Various images flash across the overhead monitors on the far wall. It appears that he's cycling through the various security cameras in town to check their functionality for the weekend. The speed that he's able to manipulate the numerous controls on the workstation is amazing. I can see why General Tagger is so impressed with his work.

"What are our rebel friends doing this evening?"

Sean hits a few more keys, and the images begin cycling across the screen automatically.

"I checked on them late this afternoon, and most of them were still at work. I have the tracking program running in the background, so it will only take me a few seconds to bring it up. Hmmm, that's strange."

I look over his shoulder and see a two-dimensional map of the southern section of town. The seven tracking signals are all gathered in the same building.

"It looks like they are all together next door at the Apis Corporation building. What the hell would they be doing there on a Friday night?"

"I was wondering the same thing, Mr. Moeller. I better notify General Taggert about this. Crap, where did I leave my walkie-talkie? Don't tell me that I left it back in my office."

Sean quickly gets up from his seat and heads for the double doors. I turn back to his terminal and examine the program running on the middle monitor. My curiosity gets the best of me, so I sit down and start clicking on some of the menu tabs. One of the tabs contains the subheading entitled TRACKER ID. After clicking on this heading, a small input window pops up containing the label TRACKER ID INPUT to the left of an empty box. I reach into my front shirt pocket and remove the small piece of paper I used to record the Tracker IDs for my four spies. The fourth number of the list is the number associated with Simone. I input the number 02162085051010004 and hit return. A green box appears on the screen containing the words LOCATING TRACKER ID 02162085051010004. After a few seconds, the box disappears, but an eighth tracking symbol appears on the map in the same room at the Apis Corporation building. It looks like my little spy is up to something with her little friends. My blood begins to boil as I watch her signal pulsing on the screen.

Looking up at the menu, I notice a few more unexplored tabs. One of the tabs entitled TRACKER OPERATIONS catches my eye, so I click on it with the cursor. Only three subheadings appear: TRACKER DISABLE, TRACKER RE-ENABLE, RELEASE POISON. I stare at the screen in disbelief. There have been rumors that the tracking devices contained a lethal poison, but they were quickly dismissed. What better way to dispose of my spy then to utilize this function? My finger clicks the mouse before I have second thoughts. A window pops up containing the words INPUT TIME IN MINUTES TO RELEASE (HIT RETURN FOR IMMEDIATE

RELEASE). An empty box sits to the right of the instructions with a cursor ominously flashing. While it's tempting to simply hit return, I decide to delay the release with the hope that I may be able to watch her as the tracker discharges its death sentence. The clock in the bottom right corner of the screen reads 8:14 p.m., so I quickly type 120 into the box and then reach over to the watch on my left arm to set a countdown timer for the same duration. After hitting return, I immediately start the timer. The door to the lab opens behind me, so I hastily shut the most recent window and try to appear casual. Rapid footsteps, accompanied by labored breathing, approach from behind.

"General Taggert is on his way. He also feels that it's extremely suspicious for the entire group to be next door. His orders were to stand down and just monitor the trackers until he gets here to analyze the situation."

I nod and get up from the chair to allow Sean to resume his duties. A smile tries to break through my dour expression, as I consider how the wheels of justice have already been set in motion.

27

MITCH/GENERAL TAGGERT

THE CAR IS COMPLETELY silent as we slowly drive east on Arlen's street toward our destination. The abduction plans were carefully reviewed while we awaited darkness to fall and now we are both deep in thought. Glancing over at Arlen in the passenger seat elicits a mixture of emotions. His calm behavior, in the face of his imminent death, brings forth a sense of pride and sorrow. Even though our contact has been kept to a minimum over the years, a strong bond has developed which I will dearly miss.

"Keep your eyes on the road, Mitch. I certainly don't want to die in a car accident this evening."

The old codger is apparently going to display his sense of humor right until the end. I shake my head and look out the windshield in time to take the right onto Atkinson Street. The walkie-talkie in Arlen's hand squawks and Neil's voice comes through loud and clear.

"The two birds are still safe in their nest. How long until you get here?"

"We will arrive in a few minutes."

Neil's anxiety is apparent by the tremor in his voice. The fact that the outside temperature is just above freezing doesn't help. Neil and his wife Abby were late additions to our group. It was obvious, during today's final planning meeting, that he was still trying to wrap his head around the fact that this will be his last night in this community. Once again, I question if we brought enough manpower this evening. My decision to leave Stuart back at the Apis building to complete our inventory and to finish packing is one of many concerns. Arlen and I finally decided that Stuart's talents would best be served back at the lab.

As we make a left on South Street, my pulse quickens, and a bead of sweat makes its way down the middle of my back. Luckily the street looks deserted with only a few houses lit on the street. The overcast sky, coupled with the new moon, will provide the darkness needed to facilitate our task. Cole and Danny's house is the second to last house on the right. Turning the headlights off, I ease the car to the curb a few houses away, where there are vacant homes on both sides of the street. Double-checking that the interior lights are off I turn to face Arlen.

"Let Neil know that we have arrived. I'll make my way to the predetermined spot, on this side of the street, and await his signal. Are you sure you know how to drive this thing?"

"I can certainly drive better than you, Grandma. At the rate you were driving, the sun will be rising soon."

I give Arlen a warm pat on the shoulder and open the driver's door. The cold air somehow finds the dampness in the middle of my back and causes gooseflesh to immediately break out on my body. As I head down the sidewalk, I reach into my right jacket pocket to verify the location of the taser. Fortunately, the home next door is also vacant, so I'm able to cross the front yard partially shielded by a few trees. Crouching down along the side wall, I pull out the walkie-talkie and press the talk button twice signaling that I'm in position. Neil responds with the same signal as he waits for our prey to be safely away from any windows.

The minutes tick by, and the cold air begins to tighten my muscles, as I attempt to coax the all-clear signal from my walkie-talkie. My position, along the side of the house, feels increasingly vulnerable even with the lack of activity on the street. Finally, I hear the two clicks and begin to slowly make my way to the stairs leading to the front wrap-around porch. I can see Neil making his way awkwardly across the street. Under different circumstances I would burst out laughing, watching him try to force his tall, thin frame into a crouch. It's not long before he's kneeling next to me breathing a little too heavy considering the short distance. We wait a few seconds, to allow Neil to catch his breath, and then quietly mount the porch and head to the nearest door. This is where the plan will get a little sketchy. The trick will be to get both boys together in order to fire the tasers at the same time. Taking a few moments to gather myself, I knock on the door and try to patiently wait. A short time later footsteps can be heard heading toward the door. The door opens, and Cole Taggert appears in the doorway with a questioning look.

"Good evening, Cole, my name is Mitchell Andrews, and I was sent by James Moeller to request the assistance of yourself and Danny for a sensitive mission."

"I don't know a James Moeller or a Mitchell Andrews and how do you know my name?"

"Your father commanded James Moeller to quickly assemble a team of trustworthy citizens to apprehend a group of young rebels who are planning to escape this evening. Do the names Cowan and Marcus mean anything to you?" By the way his eyes suddenly brighten I can see that I've struck a nerve.

"Yes, they live in the northern part of the territory with a few of their friends."

"Apparently, their group is planning to escape tonight, and your father wants to stop them and make an example of them for the rest of the territory. He can't formally apprehend them since they haven't broken any laws, but a group of citizens could pay them a visit and plant some compromising evidence at their homes."

I force a devilish smile, which seems to have the desired effect. Cole's smile widens further as he contemplates my story. I blow on my hands and stamp my feet to exaggerate the cold.

"Would you mind if we came in to discuss our plans further? We didn't have enough time to dress for the weather after our surprise visit by Mr. Moeller."

Cole momentarily considers this request before reaching out to open the storm door. He stands off to the side as we enter his home.

"Cole this is Neil Chen."

Neil reaches out and shakes Cole's hand. Satisfied, Cole leads us into the living room which is off to the left. Danny is sitting comfortably by the fire enjoying an adult beverage as the three of us enter the room. The cozy living space is furnished with dark paneling, plush recliners on either side of the hearth, and an impressive area rug covering the hard wood floor. Obviously, Cole's dad has taken care of his spoiled offspring.

"Danny this is Mitchell and Neil. My dad wants us to help them round up some Lab Rats who are planning to escape tonight."

Danny immediately springs from his chair and walks toward us. The four of us exchange handshakes and then I take the opportunity to quickly scan the room.

"This is a real nice place you guys have here. Do you have the entire place to yourselves?"

"Yes, my dad set us up here years ago. Being the general's son has its perks."

"By the looks of things, I guess it does. Oh, before I forget, Mr. Moeller wanted us to show you guys some pictures so you could hopefully identify some of the group members."

As rehearsed, Neil and I reach into our pockets to pull out the photos but extract the tasers instead. The tips of both guns simultaneously turn blue as two pairs of electrodes streak toward their victims. The two boys instantly drop to the floor and start convulsing. After a few seconds, I release the trigger and quickly grab some heavy-duty tie wraps out of my pocket. In no time both youths have their arms and legs disabled by the tie wraps. I immediately retrieve my walkie-talkie to alert Arlen.

"The packages are ready for pick-up."

Neil and I bend down on either end of Cole to begin hauling him out to the driveway. Luckily Cole's daddy converted the duplex into a single home for his son. A connecting doorway was installed which enables access to the adjacent unit. This will allow us to reach the doorway closest to the driveway from inside the house. By the time we lug Cole out the front door, Arlen already has the car backed up the driveway with the trunk open. We quickly load our package in the trunk and head back inside for Danny.

A few minutes later we are pulling out of the driveway and heading to the Apis Corporation building with our prized possessions in the trunk. The digital clock reads 8:45 p.m. as I breathe a sigh of relief that our plan went off without a hitch. Let's hope that the rest of the evening goes as smoothly.

"So, let me get this straight, it wasn't until after 8:00 p.m. that you noticed our rebels gathered at the same location? If it wasn't for Jim, we may still be unaware of their whereabouts."

My star computer analyst can only bow his head in response. What good is all this technology if we don't utilize its full capability?

"It would be nice to know how long they've been there."

Sean's face pops up, and he turns to the computer and begins to rapidly hit keys.

"I wrote a program that records their tracking information into a database. This information can be easily accessed and reviewed at any time. I will display their positional information from the time I last checked which was about 4:45 p.m."

A window opens on the left monitor, and a similar two-dimensional map of the territory is displayed with the seven tracker signals shown. Two signals are located at the school, and three signals are scattered at various locations in the Apis building. The last two signals appear to be working at a home out on Atkinson Street. A clock located in the bottom right corner displays the time of day. Sean types a few commands and the time appears to speed up as he rolls the trackball on his mouse. The trackers slowly converge in a room located in the Apis building over the next ninety minutes.

"So, it looks like they've been there together for almost three hours."

"Are you going to assemble an assault team and capture them before they have a chance to escape? If so, I volunteer to be part of that team. I know the building extremely well, and I'm pretty sure that room is Dr. Timms laboratory?"

"While I appreciate your enthusiasm James, I want to capture them in the act of escaping. By utilizing the trackers, we have the perfect opportunity to capture the entire group and also arrest anyone who is aiding their escape. Sean, I need you to carefully monitor those trackers and report any movement to me immediately."

Sean immediately turns back to his terminal and gets back to work. It's obvious that he is eager to get back into my good graces. It's always good to keep a subordinate off balance and uncomfortable. Looking back at the center monitor, I try to figure out what the kids could be up to. The eight signals continue to pulse with very little movement happening. That's odd. I thought there were only seven files in that folder.

"Hey James, weren't there just seven kids in the rebel group? How come I see eight trackers on the screen?" James exhibits a surprised expression as he looks up at the center monitor.

"Sir, I meant to tell you that I implanted trackers in my spies so I could monitor their movements. The eighth signal belongs to Simone Timms, who was the spy that supplied the information regarding the planned escape."

While I appreciate Jim's dedication to the territory, he has a tendency to take matters into his own hands on occasion. The trick is to trim feathers, but still provide your underlings with opportunities to fly.

"James, you need to clear sensitive mission-related material with me in the future."

James exhibits the appropriate amount of remorse, but still maintains a backbone which is why I keep him around.

"Your spy's presence in the lab is a source of concern. Is there a possibility that she could have supplied you with false information?"

"I doubt it, sir. She would have to be an extraordinary actress to pull the wool over my eyes. I instructed her to keep close tabs on the group. She's probably just cozying up to Marcus in order to obtain further information regarding their escape attempt."

"For your sake, let's hope that you are correct, Jim.

28

MICHELE/GENERAL TAGGERT

I T'S JUST BEFORE 9:00 p.m. when I hear the security mechanism click for the double doors. I rush out from behind the privacy curtain to see Mitch and Neil wheeling two gurneys into the lab. The two boys are strapped down to the gurneys, but they're trying their best to get free. Mitch looks up, and a huge smile spreads across his face. I can't help but smile when I look at him. It doesn't matter what's happening around him. He always seems to be upbeat and positive.

"We have a couple of live ones here Doc. I think we might need a strong sedative. Do you have that big needle back there?"

"I reserved some room behind the privacy curtain. Just leave them back there, and I'll prepare something."

While Arlen and I follow the two gurneys, I take the opportunity to get his advice concerning our newest development.

"We discovered a possible problem while you boys were busy collecting our hosts. Apparently, our friend Jim Moeller implanted a tracker into Simone a few months back."

Arlen immediately stops and turns toward me with a concerned look on his face. His eyes stare off into the distance while he considers the ramifications of my last statement.

"We obviously have to remove Simone's tracker. We can't just destroy it because they're most likely monitoring it and will know that it has been discovered. If we remove the tracker and implant it in one of the hosts, we will be advertising that she's escaping with us. Taggert will now mistrust any information that Simone supplied. Our ruse about heading south may be scrutinized more closely."

"What alternatives do we have?"

I become aware that we're no longer alone. Kenji and Drew have joined our impromptu meeting. Arlen acknowledges them while he considers his response.

"I'm afraid that our only choice is to implant the tracker into one of the hosts. I have been giving the removal and implantation procedure some thought. You mentioned last week that the trackers not only supply location, but biological feedback information such as heart rate and body temperature. We'll need to perform the removal and implantation procedures extremely fast so that irregularities aren't detected in the data. I wish there were a way to control the temperature to limit the temperature drop before implantation."

"Couldn't you build a tent over the two beds and use a heater to keep the temperature close to our body temperatures?"

We all turn to Drew who sheepishly smiles and looks down at the floor. Kenji enthusiastically slaps Drew on the shoulder.

"Drew that's an excellent idea! We could use some clear plastic and drape it over the equipment and beds to form a tent that Dr. Timms can use to work inside. If the temperature is kept near our body temperature, there shouldn't be any detectable variation in the tracker reading."

Arlen nods his head and smiles at the two boys.

"I believe we have a solution to our problem. C'mon boys let's rummage up some plastic and a heater while Dr. Timms preps her first patient."

Fifteen minutes later I'm already sweating as I get ready to remove Drew's tracker. Drew is also sweating, but it probably has more to do with the upcoming removal procedure and the fact that his bare right buttock is exposed. Arlen is laying on his stomach, in an adjacent bed, with the same area exposed. Even with all the tension and anxiety surrounding this night, it's tough not to find a little humor in these circumstances.

"Drew, as I said earlier there's nothing to worry about. The procedure only takes a few minutes."

Once Drew's file is loaded, I hit the green START button to activate the machine. This time the removal arm, equipped with the extraction needle, begins to move until it's situated over the area of the tracker. The needle hovers over the area for a few seconds before it lowers and punctures the skin. Drew displays a momentary wince, but soon relaxes. About five seconds later the needle begins to rise until it breaks the surface. I quickly grab the joystick which is used to manually move the removal arm. The arm swiftly moves over the appropriate spot on Arlen's body. I reach over and depress the blue IMPLANT button, which causes the needle to immediately lower and pierce the skin. After a few seconds, the needle begins to rise and returns to its starting position. One implant down with seven more to go and the time is already 9:25 p.m. I still have to implant the trackers from Kenji and Carmen before I have to deal with our semi-sedated guests.

Walking over to Sean's area I can see that the kids are still at the lab. What could they possibly be doing there at 9:45 p.m. on a Friday night? Are they having a friggin slumber party?

"Sean, do you have anything new to report?"

"Everything looks fairly normal sir, but there are some anomalies. The pulse rate readings are acting a little funny. If you look over at the left monitor, I'll show you graphs of pulse rate data taken this evening for all eight trackers. As you can see the pulse rates were pretty steady the whole night except for a few increases prior to 9:00 p.m., where the data starts to get a little puzzling. Five of the trackers exhibit gradual increases in pulse rate, and then sudden dropouts occur which last about 25 seconds. The strange thing is that the dropouts didn't occur at the same time, but were spaced minutes apart. A glitch in the program would normally affect all trackers at the same time. The remaining three trackers appear to be functioning normally. The good news is the body temperature readings appear to be well within the allotted error bars."

"See if you can figure out what's going on with the pulse rate readings. I need assurance that these trackers are functioning correctly or we'll be forced to apprehend our rebels. I'm not going to take any chances which could result in them slipping through our net."

"I'll get right on it sir. Damn, another one is starting to increase. I'll bet it drops out in a few seconds. There it goes just like the others. The repeatability of the behavior is bizarre. Now the pulse rate reading is back after a similar amount of time. The readings are somewhat elevated, but the device appears to be working correctly."

"I don't like it. What do you think Jim? Jim, are you paying attention? You keep looking down at your watch. Do you have a date tonight?"

"I'm sorry sir. I was just timing the dropout. It wouldn't hurt to start organizing an assault squad. I'd be more than happy to head up that effort."

"It's always better to be prepared. Go to the barracks and assemble some men. Be sure to grab a radio so that we can stay in contact."

29

MITCH/GENERAL TAGGERT

"CAN I HAVE everyone's attention, while I go over our escape plan one more time?"

The group members look up from the equipment and supplies each of them has received in order to listen.

"In a few minutes, I will take the van with Neil to drop off Arlen and our newfound friends at your house." I glance over at Cowan and Marcus to emphasize my point.

"We will secure Cole in your room since he'll be carrying your trackers along with Simone's. Danny will be kept in Bree and Grace's bedroom for the same reason. Arlen, you will stay in the living room. Hopefully, it will seem like a big sleepover to anyone monitoring your trackers. Stuart, you'll lead the rest of the crew on foot north with help from Drew and one of the handheld monitors. A program has been installed on each of our monitors, which displays a countdown clock for the camera blackouts. Safe zones are mapped out which will keep you hidden from the cameras when they come back on line. After Neil and I finish our delivery, we will join you at one of the safe zones. From there we will cram everyone into the van for our trek north. We will eventually abandon the van at a predetermined location before commencing our final trek west. Our hope is that the van location, coupled with the false information we left on Drew and Kenji's computers, will confuse our friends at Headquarters into thinking that our actual escape route is north. The intent is to buy enough time to escape the sensors placed within this territory. Any questions before we get things underway?"

I look around at all the young, innocent faces and the weight of responsibility presses down even further. Kenji appears to be concentrating on something as he scans the group.

"Kenji, if there's something that concerns you, now is the time to share it with the group?"

"Well, it just dawned on me that there are now eight kids and five adults in our escape party. It's a common belief, throughout history, that the number thirteen is an unlucky number."

This superstition is apparently shared by a large percentage of the group until Bree fortunately responds.

"Kenji, don't forget that Carmen is pregnant. So, our actual number is fourteen. I guess we can consider her baby as our lucky charm!"

The tension is immediately lifted by Bree's observation as smiles, and excited chatter circulate the room. My respite is short-lived when I notice that the clock on the wall reads 10:13 p.m. I need to check on Michele's progress and see if there's anything that can be done to expedite things.

"So, how are you making out back here Doc?"

"Simone's tracker has been located in her left arm, and I just initiated the extraction/implantation process."

"That's good because we need to get moving soon since the camera blackouts are programmed to start at 10:30 p.m."

The removal arm begins to glide over Simone's body. The tension is evident on her face as she lays on her right side awaiting the needle. The removal arm moves to the approximate location where it hovers momentarily sensing the pings from the hidden tracker. The arm finally stops jogging back and forth and begins to lower. Simone suddenly begins to convulse as the needle nears the skin on her upper arm. Michele quickly hits the emergency stop button and rushes over to her daughter. Simone is now lying, with her back arched, writhing on the bed. Her eyes have rolled back into her head, and foam has started leaking out of her mouth. Michele starts frantically moving the instruments and any other equipment out of the way which could cause further harm. At this point, Arlen has joined us as we try to assist as best we can without getting in the way. Suddenly, the convulsions stop and Simone's body goes limp with her head lying off to one side. Michele rushes over and places two fingers on her neck to check for a pulse. She quickly turns toward Abby and screams.

"Abby, get me a crash cart while I start CPR!"

Michele immediately starts compressions as she repeatedly pleads with her daughter to wake up. Arlen and I can only stand and helplessly watch. With all the commotion, I can barely hear the next words out of Arlen's mouth.

"Oh, my God, the rumors were true about the poison. Our time has just run out."

★ ★ ★

"General, you might want to come over here and check this out. The eighth tracker dropped out a few minutes ago and is not coming back. Wait a second, it's back again!"

I get up from the meeting table, where I had been studying the group's files, and walk over to Sean.

"Do you see the bottom graph? The pulse rate had dropped to zero, but now it's back. It's not as steady as before and the pulse rate is faster. The dropout was also shorter than the previous seven trackers. Damn, it just dropped out again."

"What the hell is going on with the trackers, Sean? Now, it's back again."

"The software appears to be working fine. The temperature data and positional information checks out for all eight trackers, but the pulse rate data is still experiencing some dropouts. Now it looks like three of the trackers are experiencing a steady increase in pulse rate."

"This is not good news at all Sean. I better contact Jim and have him get his squad ready to move out at a moment's notice."

This is shaping up to be a very long night. A few eyes glance nervously in my direction as I bring the radio up to my mouth.

"James, do you read me?"

"I read you loud and clear, General."

"I need you to have your squad prepared to leave at a moment's notice. We are experiencing additional problems with the trackers, which may require your men to be closer to the Apis building in case our rebel friends try to make a break for it."

"We'll be ready to move out immediately after your command, sir."

"Hang tight. I'll be in touch."

As Sean analyzes the data, his face takes on a puzzled look, and he starts talking to himself.

"It's almost as if the data is following a strange pattern. There's a pulse rate for about twenty seconds followed by a dropout lasting about six seconds."

As I begin to question Sean, a commotion breaks out on my right involving two members of the Law Enforcement Unit. They're standing up and looking up and down between their computer monitors and the large monitor mounted on the far wall. The large monitor has been cycling through the various security camera feeds throughout the territory.

"Gentlemen, what appears to be the problem?"

"We're not 100% sure yet, General, but it appears that our camera feeds may be frozen."

I immediately begin walking over to their workstations.

"What makes you say that?"

"It's tough to tell at this time of night because there's very little activity. However, some of the cameras routinely pick up tree movements or various items blowing around. For a few minutes, it seemed like all the cameras were frozen, but they seem to all be working now. Perhaps it was just our imagination."

"Find a way to verify that they are all working properly. We cannot afford to lose our security coverage for any length of time."

Michele and Abby are sweating profusely as they take turns administering CPR and using the defibrillator. Arlen and I can tell the situation is hopeless, but neither of us has the heart to intervene. Finally, I walk over and put my arms around Michele. She struggles for a few seconds but eventually collapses in my arms.

"Honey, you did everything you could. I'm so sorry."

She begins to sob uncontrollably into my chest. The entire lab is shocked at the sudden turn of events. Somehow, I need to get everyone out of here before it's too late.

"Michele, I can't even begin to imagine how you feel, but we really need to leave."

"I can't just leave her here. I need to stay here with my baby."

She turns around and reaches down to hold her daughter's hand. My heart breaks as I watch the anguish on her face. Perhaps, if I give her a moment and get everyone else moving, I'll be able to persuade her to leave.

"Arlen there has been a slight change of plans. Tell Stuart to go with you and Neil to transport the boys to the house. Have the kids grab all the equipment and supplies and meet Michele and myself out in the back-parking lot. When Neil and Stuart are done dropping you off, have them meet the group at one of the safe zones. Arlen reaches up and places his hands on my shoulders and looks me in the eyes. I can see that he's trying desperately to keep his composure.

"Goodbye Mitch, thank you for everything you've done for the cause. Please take care of the children."

"It's you we should be thanking old friend. Without you, the kids would have no chance of escaping."

After a brief embrace, Arlen turns and heads out into the main lab. I can hear him reiterating my instructions as I turn my attention back to Michele.

"Michele, let's take Simone downstairs and give her a proper send-off before she's found by Taggert's men."

Michele solemnly nods and then bends over to kiss her daughter's forehead. She then reaches down and pulls the sheet over Simone's body. Abby walks over and hugs her friend before disappearing around the curtain.

We ride the service elevator in silence on our way down to the basement. I try to think of something comforting to say as we push the hospital bed down the long hallway leading to the incinerator room. Everything that comes to mind pales in comparison to the grief she must be experiencing. Eventually, we find ourselves standing in front of an incinerator with the drawer pulled out and Simone laying on the tray. It is truly amazing how the body's defense mechanism takes over and enables a person to function in the harshest of environments. Michele's shock is evident as she prepares her daughter for the incineration process. Finally, she leans over and once again kisses her daughter on the forehead.

"I love you, baby. It's not good-bye, but see you later."

"The trackers are finally on the move. They appear to be heading for the back entrance of the Apis building."

The critical decision is whether I have Jim's team intercept the rebels now or follow them from a distance. The program appears to be tracking their location perfectly, so it should be safe to monitor them once they leave the building.

"It looks like we have seven signals leaving the back entrance. An eighth signal was moving down a back hallway on a lower floor, but now it's stationary."

"Sean, can you find out exactly what room that is and on which floor? Do we have cameras out in the back parking lot of the Apis Corporation building?"

One of the men from the Law Enforcement Unit turns to face in my direction.

"Yes, we do General. Right now, the two cameras show zero activity in the back parking lot."

Sean's head bolts up with an exasperated look.

"That's impossible! My monitor shows seven tracking signals slowly moving around, right in the middle of the parking lot. Whoa, they are now moving rapidly through the parking lot and toward the access road."

"Are you gentlemen catching this on your cameras?"

"That's a negative, General. The cameras appear to be frozen again."

"What the heck is happening to the eighth tracker? The temperature is starting to go through the roof. Damn, the tracker just completely disappeared!" Sean helplessly looks at the seven remaining trackers on his monitor.

"Gentlemen, what's going on with our systems tonight? My patience is wearing awfully thin with this crap. It's time we put a stop to all of this nonsense."

I snatch up the radio and start barking out orders before it's near my mouth.

"Jim, I need your team to jump in the nearest vehicle now. Our rebels are presently in a vehicle heading up Mill Street. I need you to make visual contact and follow from a distance."

"We're on our way, General."

I toss the radio handset down on the computer table and glare around the room. The room is completely quiet with all eyes glued to their respective monitors.

30

ARLEN/JAMES

I STILL CAN'T believe that madman released the poison in Simone's tracker. Witnessing Simone's death, earlier this evening, only confirmed the rumors regarding his manic behavior. It also proved that the kids are in imminent danger as long as they remain in the territory. I just pray we are not too late with this evening's escape attempt. It's this concern and not my looming death, that plagues my thoughts as I sit in the kids' living room. At any moment Taggert could pull the trigger and release the poison slated to kill the kids. My only solace is that he'll terminate his son's life in the process. This thought brightens my mood as I envision Taggert's reaction.

A sudden bang, from one of the back bedrooms, disturbs my thinking. Apparently, one of the boys is trying to escape from his bonds. This is a futile effort given the care we used to fasten their restraints. In a few hours, we will begin our trek south, unless the general decides to take matters into his own hands again.

There's a popular opinion that people experience a sense of calm just prior to death. This always struck me as odd considering the anticipation and anxiety which I assumed accompanied such a significant event. I must admit, as I sit here alone, my expectations are being proved false. I have no feelings of fear or trepidation regarding death. The realization that my life's journey has brought me to this moment produces a satisfied, peaceful sense of accomplishment. My passing will hopefully result in saving the lives of the kids and some dear friends. Their escape will hopefully further the cause of the resistance movement, and my thoughts drift off to those clandestine meetings which we held years ago.

It's difficult to just sit here and wait, after receiving the orders to move out and follow the van. The van was already heading back to the Apis building after dropping the kids off at home, by the time we reached our current position. General Taggert commanded us to stand down and await further orders. He's currently monitoring the kids in one of the houses. Hopefully, something will happen soon, but for the time being, we are parked on Cherry Street in front of an old elementary school. I sent Hodges out to recon the house forty-five minutes ago, and he reported that everything was dark and quiet. The handheld scanner supports his observation by showing three separate groups in the house, presumably asleep. So here we are, patiently sitting in the army truck awaiting our next move. I decide to check in with headquarters to get an update.

"Sean, all is quiet out here. Any changes on your end?"

"There has been no change over the past few hours. The kids in the front of the house appear to be asleep based on their heart rates. The trackers, in the two rooms located in the rear of the house, yield a different story. They seem to be extremely anxious with their heart rates periodically spiking. I find it hard to believe they are all experiencing bad dreams at the same time. My best guess is that they are awake discussing their planned escape. General Taggert believes they may attempt an escape sometime during the night.

"Wouldn't it be a good idea to have my team surround the house to facilitate their capture?

"General Taggert wants to capture them after it's obvious they are trying to escape. He plans to have your team follow the kids, unobserved, from a safe distance. We will have other teams set up on the perimeter road that encircles the community. At the appropriate time, he'll give the go-ahead to apprehend the kids from both directions."

As usual, the general appears to have thought of everything. Capturing the kids, as soon as they leave their house, doesn't provide concrete evidence of an escape attempt. However, capturing them on the fringes of the community, during the middle of the night, would be irrefutable evidence. The general would be able to use this as a deterrent to the rest of the citizens.

His calculated approach to problem resolution is in direct contrast to my own. I have a tendency to let my emotions take over which frequently gets me into trouble. The general was not very pleased when he was briefed about the release of the poison in Simone's tracker. To say that my wings were significantly clipped would be an understatement. The fact that he needed to keep the number of people to a minimum, who were privy to mission sensitive information, was the only thing which saved my position as troop leader. I was ordered to only act on his direct orders and to not deviate one iota.

Hopefully, this evening will provide an opportunity to redeem myself. By the sounds of it, my team would be directly involved in the kids' capture. Since the kids spent most of the night at the Apis Corporation building, it's likely that Mitchell Andrews was involved. At least his company was involved, which makes him responsible. This weekend could see a drastic change in the management structure of Apis Corporation and those people close to General Taggert stand the best chance of benefitting.

My alarm jolts me awake, and my presence at an animated resistance meeting slowly dissolves away. The dream was so vivid, depicting about a dozen of us scattered around the table in the hidden meeting room. Images of my son amongst the members recede back into the deepest recesses of my mind. It's amazing how detailed dreams can be compared to our memories when we are awake. I wish I could see him one last time, but it's more important that I complete my last task this evening.

Glancing down at my watch I see that it's 3:00 a.m. The noises from the back bedrooms have ceased. Perhaps my prisoners wore themselves out and surrendered to exhaustion. It will be a pleasure to awaken them from their slumber. I grab the taser and attach it to the clip on my belt. The handgun goes in the holster on my right hip. I feel like an outlaw in those old western movies. All I need is a black cowboy hat and a long leather coat to complete the outfit.

Grabbing a flashlight, I head down the short hallway leading to the back of the house and walk into the boys' bedroom where Cole is trussed up. As soon as the beam of light shines on his face a cold set of eyes open and he begins to struggle against the heavy-duty tie-wraps. He's on the floor, against one of the beds, with his arms bound behind his back to one of the bed posts. His ankles are also tightly fastened together, so it's amazing he was able to get any sleep. I lean over and place the tip of my knife against his cheek and smile.

"Good morning Sunshine, I hope you slept well. Now we can either do this the easy way or the hard way. We are all going to take a short walk together. As you know, the two of you have been implanted with trackers, so the plan is for the three of us to take a walk south while my friends escape in another direction. If you guys behave, then eventually one of your daddy's underlings will interrupt our little trek, and you'll be safe at home. Nod if you accept the terms of our agreement, so I can cut your bonds, and we can proceed."

Cole gives a nod, but the cold hatred remains in his eyes. I carefully reach behind him with the knife, while keeping as much distance between his head and mine. Getting knocked out by a well-timed headbutt would certainly impact our well-orchestrated escape plan. As soon as he's freed from the bedpost, I step back and remove the gun from its holster. The gun serves as additional insurance that he will continue to comply with our agreement. I keep my distance as I slowly reach down and cut the restraints around his ankles. I keep the gun trained on him as I assist him to his feet. He initially has difficulty supporting his weight, but soon I'm able to guide him out of the room. The two of us walk into the girls' room with the aid of my flashlight. Danny is already stirring at the foot of one of the beds. The process of releasing him will be a bit interesting now that Cole's legs are free. I push Cole onto the other bed and flash the gun in his direction. While keeping him in my field of vision, I'm able to repeat the process with Danny.

Before long the three of us file out the back door of the house to begin our trek. Mitch gave me a headlamp which provides ample lighting up ahead. It also frees up my hands which are needed to hold the gun and the tethers connected to ropes around each of their waists. Cole and Danny lead the way, while I hang a safe distance behind barking out periodic directions. We immediately head west across the back yard and then into the neighbor's property.

"Don't get any bright ideas, boys. I will not hesitate to put an extra hole in either of your heads. My time will be up sometime before the day is out, so don't give me a reason to take one of you with me."

The boys appear to heed my warning as we make it to the edge of the property and begin heading south on Atkinson Street. I reach up and turn off the headlamp in order to minimize our exposure. It's pitch black, so it takes a few moments for my eyes to adjust to the lack of ambient light. After passing a few houses, we come to the intersection with School Street and take a right. The plan is to head west on both School and Taylor before reaching the edge of the forest which surrounds our community. From there we will start turning south through the woods and buy the kids as much time as possible. The brisk pace quickly points out my lack of fitness. I guess it's a little late to start an exercise program.

31

COWAN/GENERAL TAGGERT

IT WAS A nerve-racking drive north, through the eastern edge of town, as we dodged the security cameras. Neil drove the van while Drew utilized the handheld monitor to track security camera operation. While the camera blackouts facilitated our escape, progress was extremely slow due to the time waiting in between. Everyone was packed into the van, and in a state of shock, following Simone's death. Mitch spent the entire trip consoling Simone's mom. She alternated between bouts of hysterical crying to periods of shocked silence. The rest of us remained quiet as we awaited our inevitable capture. I attempted to comfort Marcus along the way, but he just stared out the window. He's struggling with a deep sense of guilt for refusing to forgive Simone prior to her death.

We found an appropriate spot to park, in the northernmost corner of town, where the homes remain uninhabited. Kenji and Drew left cryptic clues on their computers that hinted about a northern escape route. These clues mentioned abandoning the van somewhere in this part of town. Hopefully, this would provide further misdirection for anyone searching for our group. As we piled out of the car, I remember seeing a road sign that read Lincoln Street. It was at this point we entered the woods and have been navigating through the trees ever since.

The going has been slow, but at least the forest provides a sense of coverage. Drew is up ahead leading the group with one handheld monitor, while Mitch is in the back with the other unit. They are intently searching for any sign of search parties or drones. Drew programmed our monitors to pick up tracking signals from any other handheld monitors or soldiers' equipment. He explained to us that both the Environmental and Wildlife Units were ordered to have the trackers enabled on their equipment at all times. They were told this was for safety reasons in the event anyone was injured or lost. Drew believes the real reason is so Headquarters can track any employees that are scheduled to work in the surrounding forest regions. Our hope is to utilize the tracking feature to monitor anyone searching for our group.

As we trudge our way along through the woods, I can just make out the moisture, from my labored breathing, in the minimal light from the stars. Drew and Mitch equipped everyone with cold weather gear, complete with thermal jackets, pants, and boots. These articles, combined with winter gloves and hats, ensure our warmth during the hike west. It's still hard to believe that Simone is no longer with us. Drew overheard Mitch and Arlen discussing the events surrounding her death. Arlen believes the cause of death was a poison released from her tracker. Our group has been confronted with a number of hardships in this territory, but I'm having trouble wrapping my head around trackers containing poison. If Arlen is correct, then we made the right decision escaping from this society. I don't want any part of a community run by maniacs who authorize the release of poison on its citizens.

My relief is short-lived when I start to think about Arlen and what he may be going through at this very moment. I feel a wave of sadness knowing I'll never get to see him again. Even though I only met him a few times, I feel an inexplicable bond between us. It doesn't make sense because I've spent much more time with Mitch, yet the same connection isn't there. We will always be deeply indebted to Arlen for his selfless bravery. If and when we succeed in meeting up with the previous rebels, I vow to keep his memory alive by recounting the sacrifice he made for all of us. Hopefully, I can find some time alone with Mitch to learn more about Arlen.

At least I was able to get a few hours of rest before my presence was required. I try to shake off the last vestiges of sleep, as I make my way to the lab.

"Please tell me you have good news to warrant interrupting my sleep." Sean jumps as I approach him from behind.

"You mentioned that you wanted to be informed when the group started moving again. They left the house a short while ago and began heading west. They are now slowly turning toward the south."

So, our little spy was correct with the direction, just a bit late about their departure time. Perhaps they learned about her spying activities and tried to mislead us with a false date. I look over to Roddy who is monitoring the Law Enforcement Unit's activities.

"Roddy, I need you to organize your units along the southern sections of Ring Road. Our targets are heading in that direction, and I want all of your peripheral security personnel available to intercept them if necessary. I don't want to leave anything to chance along the southern border."

Ring Road is a combination of old highways and newly constructed roads or pathways that surround our territory. It provides a necessary means for our Law Enforcement and Security Units to navigate quickly around our territory. The southern section of Ring Road is comprised of Old Terrace Road, near the town center, and old Route 121 which is located southwest of town. Roddy's units will await our escapees along Route 121, while I have Jim's group follow from the north.

"James, do you read me?"

"Loud and clear, General."

"Our targets are on the move and are currently heading south. I have assigned units to the southern section of Ring Road. I need you to follow from a distance and make sure they can't double back. Await my order to apprehend our targets. I repeat await my order."

"Your directions are clearly understood. We will monitor their progress and ensure they don't escape."

"Sean, I need you to monitor the trackers closely and keep an eye out for anything out of the ordinary. We cannot afford any further malfunctions at this stage."

Hopefully, by tomorrow morning our rebel friends will be in custody, and I will be able to spend the rest of the weekend planning their public trial.

Our trek thus far has been thankfully uneventful once we successfully made it across what Drew termed as Ring Road. He was concerned that we may run into Law Enforcement and Security personnel who utilize this road. He confessed that this crossing would be one of the most dangerous during the early stages of our escape. Drew was pleasantly surprised by the lack of contacts, in the immediate area, during our crossing earlier this evening. The last few hours have been blessedly dull, except for disturbing the occasional animal that was busy either hunting or sleeping.

Sunrise is less than two hours away and Drew estimates we will be about halfway to the cabin by first light. The overwhelming sentiment is that we should hunker down during the day to get some much-needed rest. Drew believes it would be easier for search parties and drones to detect our group during the day than at night. Mitch hopes the diversions will buy us some time and allow us to get some rest. Everyone is not only physically tired but emotionally fatigued as well. For the time being, we keep trudging west in an attempt to put as much distance between us and the enemy as possible. Every step brings us further from capture and closer to freedom.

32

ARLEN/GENERAL TAGGERT

WE HAVE BEEN heading south for well over an hour, and the going has been extremely slow. Trying to negotiate my two captives over and around fallen trees and brush is difficult with the two ropes. My goal is to get as far south as possible before sunrise and then find somewhere to rest and await my pursuers. My prisoners have been surprisingly well-behaved under the circumstances. Cole must be confident that his daddy will come to the rescue soon, but little does he know that I have other plans for him and his friend.

I wish there were a way to contact the kids to find out how they are doing. Mitch and I both agreed that walkie-talkies would be too dangerous, given the chance of search parties eavesdropping on our frequency and discovering our little charade. It was more prudent to abandon any communication between us and simply trust our plan. While I agree with the decision, confirming their escape would ease the growing fatigue I'm currently feeling. With sunrise, less than an hour away, my immediate concern is to find a secluded place to hunker down in order to continue the ruse.

The trees begin to thin out, and my headlamp picks up the outline of a building about a hundred yards up ahead. As we get closer, it appears to be an abandoned farmhouse, with surrounding farmland, that has since become overgrown. It's a two-story farmhouse with the remnants of a barn off to the right. The roof of the house is collapsed, but the top floor appears to be intact as we approach from the backyard. The same can't be said for the barn, which has succumbed to the weather and can be ruled out as a safe haven. As we approach the backdoor of the house, I attempt to examine its condition while keeping my captives in my peripheral vision. The walls, for the most part, appear to be structurally sound, so the house should serve my purpose. Hopefully, the same can be said for the second floor, which would afford me a vantage point to watch for any search parties.

"Okay you two, stand off to the side while I deal with this door."

The boys appear all too eager to get inside, so they obediently move against the back wall. Once we are inside, I reach into my pocket and remove a present for our pursuers. I enable the mechanism and then carefully pull the door closed. Smiling, I turn my attention back to my companions and motion for them to begin walking. The back door leads into a kitchen, which shows the expected water damage from years of exposure to the elements. As we make our way through the kitchen and into the living room, I shine my headlamp on the floor and ceiling. While the ceiling is stained, with the occasional hole, it looks like it may be able to support our weight. Before climbing the stairs to the second floor, I motion for the boys to stand off to the right in the living room. The front door is at the foot of the stairs, so I deposit a second gift using the same method. Satisfied with my traps, I motion for the boys to begin climbing the stairs on our left.

"If I were you guys I would walk along the edges unless you want to end up in the cellar."

Upon reaching the top of the stairs, I can see that parts of the roof and ceiling have caved in, revealing the star-filled sky. We head toward the rooms facing the back of the house, and I select a bedroom which has windows overlooking the north and east. The room just happens to have an old bed with a rusted footboard, which will serve as a perfect spot to fasten my prisoners. I quickly secure one of them to each leg using the tie wraps and then turn off my headlamp as I make my way over to the window facing north.

It takes a few moments for my eyes to adjust to the darkness, but all is quiet at the moment. The fields surrounding the house will work to my advantage since there are very few features to hide behind. The first signs of twilight appear in the east, so I use the opportunity to investigate other approaches to the house. The hallway ends with a window facing west. The minimal light reduces my visibility, but the view shows a large expanse of open flat ground. The likelihood of an assault from this direction is minimal. I enter the bedroom on the left and carefully approach the southern facing window. This window overlooks the long dirt driveway leading to the farmhouse. A small front yard has lost the battle over the years with the encroaching trees and brush. This direction offers countless areas of concealment. Since I cannot be in two places at once, I resign myself to the fact that I will only be able to watch over the northern and eastern directions. I make my way back to the bedroom occupied by my two prisoners.

After briefly checking the field in the back, I grab an old wooden chair and position myself at the eastern window. Amidst all the madness that has been going on over the past few days, it feels good to just catch my breath for a moment. It's hard to believe my life has come down to this one last moment. The journey was not how I would have scripted it from the beginning, but at least I'm going out on my own terms. I can only hope my son was able to make it to somewhere safe, where he can live free and unoppressed. I wistfully imagine that we are sharing this moment of mutual solitude, watching the sky gradually lighten in the east.

My brief respite is interrupted by a sudden sense of foreboding. I slowly approach the other window and peer around the frame. Initially, the field appears undisturbed until a slight movement catches my eye along the right edge of the tree line about fifty yards away. The dark mass, hidden amongst the trees and brush, is soon joined by a few more. From this distance, due to the minimal light, my chances of hitting a target are small. My objective, however, is to buy as much time as possible. Thus, I have the luxury of waiting until my enemy is forced to get closer before making the decision to engage. Every minute they delay their approach works in my favor as twilight ebbs into sunrise. I swiftly move to the eastern window to look for possible activity, where I am rewarded with an undisturbed countryside and the birth of a wondrous sunrise.

Minutes crawl by as the sun makes its appearance on the horizon. Back at the north-facing window I watch the soldiers slowly creeping amongst the trees. I mark an area, where there's a thinning of the scrub and aim my weapon. The group amasses at the edge of the small clearing debating their options. Finally, two soldiers make a daring attempt to cross the small expanse. Without any hesitation, I fire at the center of the first hunched figure and then swiftly move my handgun and fire at the second. The first soldier immediately collapses in a heap, while the second man clutches his right leg and limps toward a thicket of trees. The remaining soldiers open fire on the second floor of the house. If I hadn't started diving after my second shot, a few of their bullets would have hit their mark. As it is, the floor and the bedroom wall are shredded by the automatic gunfire. My captives frantically squirm around in a vain attempt to get loose. After a few moments, the only sounds are the cries and moans of the wounded. I take a quick inventory of myself and determine that I made it through the first volley unscathed. It looks like this old man will get the opportunity to buy a little more time for his friends.

In the aftermath of the initial engagement, I sit in the center of the room and consider my situation. Given that Headquarters is monitoring the kids' trackers, I need to continue to take advantage of this knowledge. If they see all of the trackers in one area, then they will be encouraged to attack the unguarded side of the house. By positioning my prisoners in separate bedrooms on the south side of the house, I may be able to delay future attacks.

The downside is that I will be forced to leave the boys unguarded for periods of time. The benefits outweigh the risks, so I decide to secure the boys in separate bedrooms. Both rooms contain beds, but one is closer to the window than I'd prefer. I use extra tie wraps to ensure that Danny is unable to get loose and signal any soldiers stationed in the front of the house. After rechecking their bonds, I return to the original bedroom to assess my friends outside. Once I establish that everything is quiet, I move to the center of the room and wait.

My plan to capture the rebels alive is becoming less likely, now that they're holed up in an abandoned farmhouse in the southern part of the territory. Maps of the surrounding area indicate that an assault on the house from the east and west will result in further casualties. The approach which promises the highest probability of success is easily the south. Armed with this intelligence, I ordered Jim's troops to stand down while I bring in reinforcements from the south. One of his men was critically wounded, while another suffered a serious leg injury.

"Roddy, I need you to order a squad of troops to approach the farmhouse from the south. The rebels are armed, so have your men get into position and await further direction. I'm still hoping to capture them alive if possible."

"That is affirmative, General. I will muster the appropriate personnel and get them into position. They should arrive at the target location in about thirty minutes."

"Sean, what is the current status of the kids inside the house?"

"General, it looks like they are scattered in rooms on the second floor of the farmhouse. There are two targets in the southeast, two in the southwest and three in the northeast. We have to assume they are all armed. For some reason, they have Bree and Grace stationed in the southeast room, while Cowan and Marcus are located in the southwest. Perhaps the two young ladies are more proficient with weapons?"

Sean snickers after he completes his report. When I don't share his humor, he quickly returns to his monitors. It appears the kids are prepared to go down fighting, which certainly reduces the chance of capturing them alive. Hopefully, we will be able to seize a few of them to use for a public trial.

Approximately thirty minutes later, Roddy verifies that Blue Team is in positon to the south. I already have Green Team awaiting orders to the north. I decide to make one more attempt to attack the house before I'm forced to resort to Plan B. I pick up the radio to initiate the assault.

"Team leaders, I need you to listen up. On my mark, I need you to provide cover fire from both the north and south positions. We need to conduct simultaneous assaults from both directions. Once you gain entry, proceed upstairs to capture the opposition. Shoot to disable whenever possible, but do not put your lives in jeopardy. I would prefer to capture as many rebels alive as possible, but not if it means additional casualties on our side. All teams report in to verify receipt of orders and to acknowledge that you're ready to commence attack."

"Green Team ready, sir."

"Blue Team ready, sir."

"Go on my mark. Good luck and Godspeed. Commence fire in three, two, one!"

Now comes the worst part of being a leader. The feeling of helplessness as you're forced to stand back and let others do your bidding. The monitor shows the seven kids in the house with their vitals appearing on the left side of the screen. Automatic gunfire and communications can be heard over the radio. Suddenly, the heart rates for Bree and Grace drop to zero, while the remaining five increase.

"Sean, what just happened to the two girls in the southeast?"

"I'm running some diagnostics now to determine if the readings are real or if it's yet another glitch in the trackers."

Suddenly a loud explosion, followed by cries of pain, comes in over the radio. Shortly after a second explosion sounds. Orders to pull back are heard from both team leaders, and then the radio is filled with a mixture of random shouts and orders. We all wait anxiously for one of the team leaders to check in.

"Sir, this is Green Leader. Both entries, in the north and south, were booby-trapped with some sort of explosive device. A number of men were critically injured. They need medical attention immediately!"

"Green and Blue leaders, I want you to pull back to a safe location and await a chopper carrying emergency personnel. We will take care of the rebels on our end."

A deafening silence fills the room. The only sound is the static coming over the radio. I turn the volume down and look over at Sean, who wears a shocked expression. After taking a moment to gather my thoughts, I come to the obvious conclusion.

"Did you find out anything further regarding the trackers?"

All diagnostics indicate that the readings are genuine. My best guess is that Bree and Grace were hit by the cover fire at the beginning of the assault."

"We have lost way too many men today. Prepare the remaining five trackers for poison release. Let me know when everything is ready."

I turn and walk away from the monitors to have a moment alone. My desire to have a public trial clouded my judgment and resulted in the pointless deaths of some brave men. Their deaths could have been avoided if I'd only ordered the poison release earlier.

The mayhem finally dies down outside, and I slowly get up from the floor. My body is covered with debris from the gunfire that shredded the upstairs. My presents seemed to have worked, given the two explosions and associated screams. Even though it's the enemy, I take little pride in my actions. I cautiously peer out the window and see no movement. The soldiers are nowhere to be seen. I hurriedly make my way out of the room and check in with Cole. The creaking of the floor boards, cause him to turn his head. His body is likewise covered in rubble, which emphasizes his saucer-like eyes. Under different circumstances I'd laugh, but I need to hurry up and check on Danny's status.

Immediately upon entering the room, it's obvious that something is wrong. The way Danny's head has flopped back against the bed is unnatural. As I approach the bed, I notice the blood pooled around his body. My instincts were correct concerning his position near the front wall of the house. I reach down and touch his neck to verify that he's dead. Now I only have to worry about one prisoner.

Making my way into Cole's room, I crouch down a few feet away with my gun drawn.

"I was just down the hall checking on your buddy Danny. It looks like your daddy's rescue attempt needs a few adjustments. He'll be going back home, but it will be in a body bag."

Cole looks down at my gun and gives me a defeated look as his shoulders slump. Tears begin to well up in his eyes until one finally escapes. As the tears continue, clean streaks appear down his soot-stained cheeks.

"You're a smart kid. I imagine you've guessed how the rest of this all plays out. You know too much, so I can't possibly let them take you alive."

I slowly raise the gun and Cole responds by looking away to his left and closing his eyes. I would expect to be overcome by strong emotions at this point, but I simply feel exhausted. As my finger begins to squeeze the trigger,

Cole's head jerks back in pain. His eyes bolt open and his face creases in distress. I immediately realize what's happening to him.

"Well, it looks like your daddy decided to kill the kids himself. Little does he know that he's killing his own son instead. By the way, Carmen wanted me to tell you to enjoy your time in hell."

At that moment, Cole starts convulsing, and he begins choking behind the tape over his mouth. His eyes suddenly roll back, and his head lolls forward. A quick check of his pulse verifies that the poison did its job.

I decide there are better places to die than in this room, so I head back to my room and pull up the chair and face the east. The sun is rising, and it promises to be a beautiful day. It's gorgeous how the sun splits the clouds and sends a series of beams through the upstairs window. The light resembles a pathway leading up into the sky. Hopefully, this is a portent of the direction I will soon be heading.

"I guess my time has finally come. Good luck kids, take care of my son. I love you all."

Suddenly, a warm patch starts in my left shoulder where the tracker resides. The heat quickly spreads over my left side as the poison disperses. I try to concentrate on the sunlight and imagine the heat is from the beams entering the window. As the heat and the pain intensifies, I close my eyes and envision walking up the pathway.

33

GENERAL TAGGERT/MARCUS

"GENERAL, MEDICAL PERSONNEL are in the process of loading the wounded into one of the helicopters. I have organized a squad to enter the farmhouse to retrieve the rebel bodies and load them into the second helicopter."

"Jim, the bodies are all located on the second floor. There are two bodies in a room located in the southeast, two in the southwest, and three in the northeast. There's a strong likelihood of additional explosive devices, so have your men proceed with extreme caution."

"We will be careful, General."

The radio goes silent, and I replace the handset on the main unit. An overall feeling of fatigue suddenly hits me as I turn my attention to the main monitors.

"Sean, I'm going to head up to my office for a few minutes. Notify me regarding any developments concerning the removal of the rebel bodies or the return of our wounded. I would like to be on-site when the wounded arrive."

As I make my way toward the exit, I notice the subdued atmosphere in the lab. By now, word has circulated concerning the results of the mission. It's difficult to view it as a success when you take into account the loss of life.

Once I get to my office, I find it hard to concentrate on anything as I sit at my desk. My mind keeps replaying the attack and reviewing the critical decisions that were made. I'm relieved when my radio squawks and I hear Sean's voice.

"General, the retrieval unit has safely entered the house and are in the process of clearing the first floor before heading upstairs."

"Thank you, Sean. I'll be right down."

Sean is cycling through the security camera feeds as I approach his terminal. He looks up as I approach with a confused expression on his face.

"The camera feeds appear to be working normally with none of the units experiencing periodic freezing. I will continue to analyze the issue, but it's extremely odd."

Glancing over at the Security Unit's monitors, it appears that life is getting back to normal. Roddy is in the process of redirecting his remaining units to their original positions. The radio diverts my attention as I hear Jim's voice shouting. Something has him flustered because his voice has a nervous, jittery edge to it.

"General, are you there? Can you hear me?"

230

"Jim what's wrong?"

"It's the kids. They aren't here. There's no sign of them. There are only three bodies here. I'm so sorry, General."

"What do you mean there are only three bodies, and what are you apologizing for?"

"It's Cole, sir. He's here. One of the bodies is Cole."

It's as if all the air has been sucked out of my lungs. My body is frozen, and I can only stare at the radio unit in disbelief. Jim continues to ramble on about the bodies, but my mind refuses to process new information. The pieces of the puzzle slowly slide into place as I review the recent events. Somehow, they transplanted the trackers into my son, and whoever else was with him. It must have been while they were at the lab last night. The escape to the south was just a misdirection. It also explains the issues with the security cameras and why they are working now. Somebody tampered with the security software causing the cameras to periodically freeze, and thus allow those bastards to escape. I have moles right here in my headquarters. The thought causes my pulse rate to increase, and I can feel my blood pressure begin to rise.

"General, are you okay. Perhaps you should sit down. You don't look well."

My instincts and training take over, and I realize we are wasting precious time.

"The rebels are still at large. I want their homes and places of work torn apart immediately. Confiscate their belongings and computers in search for any clues which can lead us to their whereabouts. Let's move people!"

* * *

We made it all the way to what was supposed to be a small river on the map called the West River. It was our goal to complete this narrow crossing before sunrise and then find a secluded place to set up camp. Apparently, the snow, melting at the higher altitudes upstream, has caused the river to swell which requires the use of our small inflatable boats. With the sun beginning to rise it was decided to alter our plan and search for a place to camp on the eastern bank of the river. The map showed a small state park located upstream where we found a number of weathered cabins along the river. Most of the cabins had collapsed years ago, but a few suffice our needs as temporary shelter.

It was decided to post sentries, throughout the day, as our group gets some much-needed rest. We all look a little ridiculous wrapped up in our thermal blankets, but Mitch and Drew believe they are essential to avoid being detected by any drones searching overhead. Their thermal sensors are advanced enough to detect a human's heat signature from a surprisingly high altitude. So, here I sit in full thermal attire with a thermal blanket draped over the top of my head and shoulders. Hopefully, the temperature doesn't get much higher this afternoon, or it will be a little uncomfortable. I wash down my daily Apis Pill with a swig of water and examine the remaining pills in the bag. Abby provided each of us with enough pills to last a few months. Mitch and Arlen figured this would be enough to last until we reached our destination.

It doesn't take long for my thoughts to drift to Simone. I recall how furious I became when her spying activities were revealed during our group meeting.

It wasn't just the fact that she was spying on our group, but the betrayal that I felt toward someone I loved. While my friends gradually forgave Simone and welcomed her back into our group, I couldn't summon the compassion. I held on to the false hatred and refused to consider her side of the story. Even though Cowan kept pleading with me to show sympathy, I couldn't bring myself to do it. Now she's gone, and I'm left with an empty spot in my heart, which is amplified by the fact that I never forgave her.

Footsteps, approaching from behind, indicate my watch is over. I stand up and turn to see one of the girls heading in my direction. It's hard to pick out which one, with the thermal blanket similarly draped over her head and shoulders. As she gets closer, I can tell that it's Bree who is taking over my shift.

"Good morning Bree. Did you get any rest?"

"I think I passed out as soon as I laid my head on my backpack. How are you doing?"

"I'm a bit tired, but not bad considering."

"If you ever need to talk, about anything or anyone, we're all here for you."

"I appreciate that Bree."

With that, I turn away and head to my cabin to get some sleep. Mitch, Michele, and Cowan are still fast asleep when I enter the cabin and head over to back corner where I left my gear. You would think, after being up for around twenty-four hours, that I would easily fall asleep, but my mind keeps racing and sleep is elusive. Finally, after tossing and turning for a while, exhaustion wins out, and I can feel my mind surrendering to the inevitable.

The lowered voices of Cowan and Mitch seep into my dreams as I slowly wake up to a confusing reality. It's tough to tell how long I was out, but it doesn't feel like it was long enough. By the way, the sunlight is slanting in from the opposite window, it appears that it's sometime in the afternoon. Not being in an overly sociable mood, I decide to stay in my makeshift bed and attempt to listen to their conversation.

"I'm very worried about Marcus. I think he needs to talk about Simone, but every time I try to broach the subject he quickly dismisses it."

"Your friend needs some time. Like Dr. Timms, he's in shock right now, and his mind is not able to process what has happened. Our brain has a natural defense mechanism, which protects itself during personal tragedy. All you can do is continue to make yourself available and wait."

"I just feel helpless knowing that he's hurting and I'm unable to do anything about it."

Cowan has always been more worried about his friends than himself. This is one of the many traits that makes him the natural leader of our group. Mitch is right about not being ready to discuss Simone. It would be impossible for Cowan to understand how I'm feeling. The only person who would understand is Dr. Timms. I can't imagine the anguish she must be feeling after losing a child at such an early age. Perhaps, in time, we can help each other deal with the tragedy. I put these thoughts aside and return my attention to Cowan's voice

"I keep thinking about Arlen and wondering if he's still alive. I wish there were some way we could communicate with him."

"Arlen and I toyed around with the idea of equipping our groups with communication equipment. In the end, we decided it would only compromise the mission. Arlen was a dear friend, who I grew close to over the years."

"I would love to learn more about Arlen. How did he get involved with the resistance movement and how did he get to know you and my father?"

"I promise to answer all of your questions once we have reached our destination and have a chance to sit back and relax."

"I just feel bad that I was only able to spend a short time with Arlen. The confusing part is, even though I only met him a few times, I feel this strange feeling or connection." There is a short pause before Mitch responds to Cowan's previous statements.

"I think your feelings are totally understandable considering that you have his blood coursing through your veins."

★ ★ ★

I will deal with the death of my son after the group responsible is captured and brought to justice. This singular mindset is what fuels my anger and concentrates my thought processes. I have organized an emergency meeting in the lab to receive updates regarding critical activities and to focus our efforts.

"Roddy, what have your search teams uncovered thus far?"

"General, the kids' homes yielded very little information, but we did find a street map and a topographic map of an area formerly known as Montpelier, VT. This is interesting in light of the information my team was able to extract from two of their computers. I asked Curtis, one of our computer experts, to attend the meeting to explain his findings."

I turn my attention to Curtis who looks like your typical computer geek. He is a waif of a human being, with glasses and a demeanor which screams that he would like to be anywhere else but here.

"Sir, I tried to analyze all the computers which were confiscated. The previous users made every attempt to destroy the units to prevent any data retrieval. I was able to get two of the hard drives to work, however. The drives essentially contained work-related data. It wasn't until I performed searches using locations found in the maps that I was able to possibly verify their intended location. One of the computers contained information associated with Montpelier, VT. which included latitude and longitude coordinates."

"Excellent work gentlemen. Roddy, get your men organized and coordinate search parties. All resources are at your disposal."

"I anticipated your order and have my men getting equipped as we speak. They should be ready to move out very shortly."

"Roddy, why don't you get going and check on the status of your men. Curtis, let me know if you find anything else on the computers."

I turn my attention to Sean, who is the last person left at the table.

"Sean, have you made any progress uncovering the identity of the moles?"

"Not yet sir, but I followed your hunch concerning the earlier security camera issues. Someone embedded a program deep in the software which periodically caused our security camera systems to freeze. The program has since been removed, and we should have no further problems with the system.

I also had a few operators sift through our security camera database and compare footage before and after the blackouts. One of our cameras captured a few frames containing a white van that fit the description of the van which was seen leaving the Apis Corporation building. I supplied Roddy with this information, and he sent a search team up to the northern part of the territory. The abandoned van was found at the western end of Lincoln Street."

"That was some nice detective work, Sean. Why do I get the sense that you are not satisfied?"

"In light of the ruse the group pulled earlier, this recent information fits too neatly together. My gut just tells me that something isn't right. I have an idea on how to use our tracking system to possibly find the location of our rebel group. With your permission, I'd like to pursue it."

"It's imperative that we find the identity of our mole. If you can head up that effort and investigate your idea, then go ahead."

34

KENJI/GENERAL TAGGERT

TWILIGHT IS STARTING to settle around our cabins, causing the temperatures to drop considerably. The thermal clothing will come in handy once again this evening. My muscles are stiff and sore from last night's trek, coupled with a day of inactivity. The rest was sorely needed given the physical and emotional toll our group was subjected to over the past day. As I exit my cabin, I see that everyone is starting to congregate in the center of the camp to plan the river crossing. Mitch has become the unofficial leader of the expedition and has already started organizing our departure.

"Everyone knows who they are paired up with for the river crossing. We'll use six inflatable boats with two riders per boat. I walked down to the river a few minutes ago to scope things out. There's a slight current, so we'll be tethering the boats together for the crossing to avoid getting separated. We will make the crossing just south of the collapsed bridge, where the river narrows slightly."

The group nods at Mitch and then quietly begins to make their way down the trail toward the road leading to the eastern bank of the river. Conversations are whispered as everyone is on full alert of any search parties in the immediate area. At the end of the trail, we turn right and head a short distance to the collapsed bridge. Rusted supports hang down the embankment, which is littered with huge chunks of cement. We all have to carefully watch our footing, but soon we are standing in a small clearing at the edge of the river. Upon arriving at the river bank, we separate into our assigned pairs to await instructions on how to inflate the small rafts. Drew steps into the middle of the group and starts unfolding a small rubber raft.

"After you unfold your raft, lay it flat on the ground with the smooth side facing down. On the rear of the boat, you will find a large, black, circular plug. After you unscrew the plug, reach inside, and you will feel a switch. Just press down on the switch, and the boat will automatically inflate. Make sure to replace the plug after the boat is fully inflated."

"What causes the boat to inflate?"

Drew turns toward Grace and holds the back of the raft up in her direction.

"Inside the rear of the boat is an electric air pump which is powered by a battery. The air pump will inflate the raft to the desired pressure and then immediately shut off."

The groups spread out along the riverbank and soon all the boats are swiftly inflating. As each boat is finished, Mitch and Drew quickly inspect each raft. They then proceed to tie pre-made tethers between them. By now it is dark, but our eyes have grown accustomed to the minimal light. Cowan and Bree negotiate their boat into the water, with Bree getting in first. It's almost comical watching Cowan scramble into the boat and nearly capsize it in the process. Marcus and Grace are next to get in, followed by the rest of the group.

The small, retractable oars work pretty well, and soon Cowan's lead boat reaches the opposite bank of the river. The tethers come in handy as a means to assist the remaining boats ashore. A few minutes later, I reach inside the rear port of my boat to depress the switch, which enables the pump to deflate the boat. As we are waiting for our boats to finish deflating, I hear Bree talking to Cowan off to my right.

"Hey Cowan, we need to be careful when we refold the boats. The back of our boat is pretty hot."

I start to think about the design of the boat. The electric pump must get hot while it inflates and deflates the boat. I reach down to feel the back of our boat, and I'm surprised by how hot it is. I wonder if there is any chance that the rubber could melt. All of a sudden, a thought flashes into my mind.

"Drew, what's the range of the drones that the territory uses?"

He looks over at me with a puzzled look on his face before responding.

"The range of the drones is actually limited by the transmitter. I believe the transmitter has a range of over one hundred miles. The wings of the drone have solar panels mounted on top, which recharge the batteries during the day.

So, as long as the drone remains within the range of its transmitter, I guess it can stay up indefinitely. Why do you ask?"

My stomach begins to roll, as I pointlessly look up at the sky and then turn to address the group.

"Guys, I think we may have a problem. If there are drones up there, then they can certainly detect the heat signature from our boats. We need to get them covered now."

Panic ensues as everyone starts to frantically search for thermal blankets. Within seconds the boats are covered and then paranoia sets in.

"We have to get out of here! We can't just stand around and wait for them to arrive!"

"Carmen, this isn't a time to panic. The chances are very small that a drone was flying overhead in this part of the territory. Any search parties will either be in the southern or northern sections, following the clues we left."

I realize Mitch may be simply trying to set Carmen's mind at ease, but I'm afraid that we need to act now.

"Mitch, we can't be entirely sure where they are searching. They may have already sent out drones to patrol all directions once it was discovered that we weren't the ones escaping to the south."

"Do you think Arlen has already been discovered?"

Mitch turns toward Bree and the stress of the last few days is evident on his face.

"Guys, I have no idea what is happening with Arlen. He bravely sacrificed his life to save all of us. We need to concentrate on the here and now, so his sacrifice won't be in vain."

While Mitch is calming everyone down, I take the opportunity to reach under the blanket to feel along the top surface of our boat. As expected, the surface is warm due to the internal air which was heated by the pump. I notice that everyone is silent and look up to see them all looking in my direction for guidance. I stand up and start saying the first things that come to mind.

"Even though we left clues eluding to a northern escape, we can't be certain the leaders of our territory will be fooled a second time. We have to assume that we have been seen, so the question is where do we go from here. We could re-inflate the boats and head downriver, but we would need to cover the entire boat with a thermal blanket since the pump heats up the air inside the boat. Mitch, how many extra boats do we have?"

"We brought seven boats with us, so we have a spare? How does a spare boat solve our dilemma?"

I consider our inventory of boats and the genesis of an idea begins to form. I scan the expectant eyes of my friends and start to smile.

"Guys I think I may have the answer to our problem."

The search, in the northern sections of the territory, has come up empty thus far today. It's now dark, which means that we have lost the capability to spot the group from the air. My level of frustration is increasing by the minute with every negative sighting. It's as if the rebel group has simply vanished. I'm in the process of scanning some maps and reviewing recent summaries when I notice Sean trying to get my attention. Hopefully, he has some good news to report concerning the identity of our moles. I walk over to his area and see various maps of our territory displayed on his three monitors.

"Good evening, General, I think I may be on to something regarding the present position of the rebel group."

"Well, I certainly could use some positive news. What am I looking at?"

"The map on the left is my original attempt at estimating their present location. I started off by assuming they left the Apis Corporation building around the same time the van was seen exiting the parking lot. I decided to initially disregard the abandoned van location in the northern part of the territory. Assuming the group is escaping on foot, I am estimating their progress at two to four miles per hour. The outer circular band, which surrounds our community, represents the furthest our group could have traveled if they had not stopped to rest for any length of time. The width of the band accounts for the difference in walking speed between two to four miles per hour. The inner band represents the possible progress if our group hid during the daylight hours today."

"Now this is where things start to get interesting. The center monitor shows the recorded movements for all wildlife in our community provided by their trackers. The plot is extremely busy with hundreds of data samples. Keep in mind that our Wildlife Unit has concentrated their tracker implants within a three-mile radius surrounding our community. I wrote a program which filters out stationary and slow-moving data. When I run the program all that's left are sudden movements of any wildlife over the last twenty-four hours. My theory is that animals will get spooked by individuals, such as our escaping rebels, walking through the woods. As you can see the vast majority of the data disappears, and you are left with random data samples. In a few areas, you see small clusters of data, but up here in the north, an interesting pattern of data has developed. If I select this data and connect the dots, so to speak, a distinct line can be drawn heading east to west from a starting point just west of the abandoned van."

"Sean, do you have a time stamp for one of the first pieces of data in that group?"

"All I need to do is zoom in and hold my cursor over a specific reading. The easternmost reading was recorded at 11:53 p.m."

"So, are you telling me the group left the abandoned van and started heading west instead of north?"

"That's what the wildlife trackers appear to indicate. All the data north of the van appears random. Given this location as a probable starting point, I overlaid my original two bands and reduced their radius to account for the delayed starting time of the group. I then extrapolated the direction of the group west until the line intersected with both bands. It's around these two areas that I decided to start my search. I had some drones repositioned in the two areas a few hours ago, and they have been following programmed search patterns ever since."

"The monitor on the right contains some recent data from one of the drones, which was searching the innermost band along the West River. Since it's dark, I'm mainly interested in any thermal detections by the drones. I requested to have the altitude of the drone reduced to two hundred feet to aid with detection. While replaying the data, I found some curious readings which were taken around 8:30 p.m. As you can see on the monitor, the drone picks up random heat signatures from wildlife. The colors displayed on the plot represent different source temperatures, and these are defined by the scale at the bottom of the screen, which normally ranges from 90 to 110 degrees Fahrenheit. The sources coming up, however, are significantly higher. If I pause the data, you can see four sources having temperatures ranging from 120 to 165 degrees Fahrenheit, which is higher than anything living in the forest. There are a few other nearby sources below 110 degrees."

"This is some impressive work, Sean. What do you think those sources are?"

"I'm really not sure, General, which is why I requested to have the drone redirected over these coordinates. I have the live feed, from the drone, being displayed on this monitor. The drone will be flying over the desired coordinates in a few moments."

I'm truly amazed with the progress Sean has made by utilizing the animal trackers and the drones. I find myself glued to the right-hand monitor awaiting the drone to fly over the location of interest. Finally, our wait is rewarded when four distinct contacts appear on the screen starting at the bottom.

"There they are! Hold on, let me bring the contacts back up and freeze the images on the screen."

Sean proceeds to punch a few commands on the keyboard and suddenly four distinct images slowly slide up the screen and then stop. They look like four ovals positioned end to end. One end of each oval appears much hotter than the rest of the surface.

"Where exactly, are these contacts located, and do you have any idea what they are?"

"General, considering that the objects are located in the middle of the West River heading south, I'm willing to bet they aren't cars!"

"Well, it looks like our little rebels made off with a few of our boats. Make sure you keep following them with the drone. I'm going to get Jim's squad over there in a helicopter as soon as possible."

35

JAMES/DREW

AT FIRST I thought General Taggert was just paranoid when I was assigned to gather information concerning a resistance group. It appears that their influence extends beyond a group of kids. The old man was not only involved in the rebel escape plan but probably helped orchestrate the entire affair. I'll bet my life that Mitch and a few other members of Apis Corporation are also involved. Rumor has it that Mitch, along with Michele, are missing and the Security Unit is busy searching for other members.

This whole fiasco should be ending soon, now that the rebels have finally been located. Citizens should realize the territory's security resources are too advanced to entertain escape as a viable option. After General Taggert puts a positive spin on our security success over the past twenty-four hours, rebel hopes will be severely dampened. Anyone currently considering an escape attempt will now realize such an act would be futile.

Looking out the side window of the helicopter, I can barely make out the tops of the trees as they pass by underneath. The rebels did pick a perfect night to make their escape, considering the minimal light provided by the moon. Soon it won't matter after we shine our searchlight on their little flotilla. I turn to the pilot on my left, for an update on our arrival time.

"How long until we arrive at the target location?"

"It should only be a few more minutes. The drone has been supplying updates on the latest rebel position. The boats were last detected about three miles downriver from the initial contact location. The latest coordinates coincide with an area on the western bank, along a bend in the river."

I was hoping to catch them while they were still floating downriver. It looks like we may be forced to finish this search on foot. Hopefully, Mitch will try something stupid and give me a reason to put a bullet in his head. My fantasy is cut short by the pilot's voice.

"We have reached the latest coordinates. Hold on while I turn on the searchlight."

Peering down, I see the occasional flicker of light on the surface of the river. The searchlight suddenly illuminates the river below. As we slowly fly south, the four boats come into view, beached on the western bank along the bend. The four boats appear to be tied together, but there's no sign of any resistance members.

"Take us down as close to the boats as possible, so we can climb down the rope ladder. Start searching west of here until we find evidence of which direction was used to resume their escape."

* * *

Even though we are walking through the woods, I feel exposed. Ever since Kenji pointed out our possible oversight concerning the boats, I feel like a net is slowly closing in around our group. I keep kicking myself for not thinking about the heat radiating from the electric pumps. Hopefully, our latest ploy was unnecessary, and we ended up discarding four of our boats for nothing. After careful consideration, it was concluded to be the safest solution. Taking the boats further downstream would have risked discovery and possibly resulted in our group being trapped in the middle of the river. I look over at Kenji, and it appears his mind is miles away.

"What are you thinking about?"

"Did you just say something Drew?"

"I asked what you were thinking about?"

"I just keep second-guessing my idea to launch four of our boats downriver. I may have wasted four of our assets for nothing. We may regret that decision later when we have a wide river to cross."

"As they say, we will cross that river when it comes."

"That's not exactly what they say, but I appreciate the sentiment."

"We all supported your idea, so I wouldn't waste your time worrying about it. If I would have thought about the heating issue to begin with, we wouldn't have been stuck in that dilemma."

We spend the next several hours walking in silence, with each member lost in their own thoughts. What began as a constant fear of being found, slowly fades to periodic attacks of anxiety. The trepidation is always hovering just below the surface, waiting to surge at the slightest sound coming from the surrounding forest. The mind eventually becomes numb, following hours of this mental torture. The senses are dulled, and the danger is ultimately taken for granted. As we travel deeper into the night, I have to will myself to be vigilant and force myself to concentrate on the monitor.

The handheld monitor has proven to be invaluable since there are no landmarks to validate our direction. The device contains the coordinates of the cabin, and now we are relying strictly on its navigational capabilities to maintain a heading. The tracking feature is running in the background, but thankfully there have been no contacts since last night. This could either mean we are alone, or that our pursuers have discovered their vulnerability and disabled their trackers. Thus, as I lead my friends deeper into the night and the unknown countryside, I attempt to exude confidence. I'm not sure if it's for their benefit or for my own.

My squad has been trudging west for hours and still no sign of the rebels. The six of us are spread out in a line, with approximately one hundred yards between us. The helicopter, which was sent a few miles ahead, has been slowly zigzagging east in an attempt to trap the rebels in between. The pilot has been providing periodic updates, but they are all the same. The rebels have simply vanished once again. Glancing over the treetops, I can see the searchlight making a southward pass up ahead. Even though Headquarters is listening to our live communications, I decide to radio in for any mission updates.

"Headquarters, this is Green Team leader checking in. We will be intersecting with our bird in a few minutes. There has been no sign of the rebels so far. Do you have any mission updates?"

"We have sent a number of drones west of your location to search the area. We have also sent Blue Team to the initial sighting upriver to search for any signs of the rebel group. You are to recon with your helo and continue searching west. We will update you if anything changes."

At least we can get out of this cold and sit down for a while. Up ahead I can see the helicopter landing in a clearing. I motion to my men to begin converging on that location. Within minutes we are all seated in the chopper and rising above the trees. While the helicopter resumes its westward search pattern, I try to concentrate on the terrain below, but my mind is preoccupied with the prospect of another sleepless night ahead.

I'm suddenly awakened by the chirp of the helicopter's radio and then General Taggert's voice.

"Jim, Blue Team has found some footprints heading west, away from the original sighting upriver. We believe the rebel group either split up, or they used some of their boats as a decoy to throw us off their trail. Blue Team is attempting to follow their trail. We are also sending drones up ahead to scan for heat signatures. We will be transmitting new coordinates shortly to resume your search, but in the meantime, begin heading northwest of your location."

"We are on our way, General."

The pilot immediately begins to turn the helicopter in the appropriate direction. I have to admit that the rebel group is demonstrating a great deal of ingenuity. It's too bad it will soon be all for naught.

36

COWAN/JAMES

NO MATTER HOW confident Drew is about his fancy, handheld monitor, I find it hard to believe it will be capable of leading us to the cabin in the dark. He tried to explain how it worked, but I quickly got lost when he started spouting technical words like gyros and accelerometers. Since we crossed the river, everything looks about the same. The fact that we have two monitors, and they're providing the same guidance, does little to increase my optimism. A short time ago Drew announced we were less than a mile away, but all I see are trees in every direction. The stars provide minimal ambient light, so progress is slow as we navigate around fallen trees and other obstacles.

The anxiety level surrounding the group has slowly decreased the further we trudge west. We're hopeful our pursuers will eventually abandon their search as we put more distance between us and our former home. Privately,

Mitch doesn't believe we'll be so lucky. I overheard him talking to Stuart earlier this evening about this very topic. He was confident General Taggert would continue to pursue our group, especially if his son was harmed in any way.

My attention is drawn to some excitement at the front of the line. Drew appears to be pointing at something up ahead. As I continue forward, I can barely make out a dark outline through the trees. It's essentially the lack of light, which distinguishes the image from the surrounding forest. The structure begins to take shape as we approach until the details of a small cabin emerge through the trees. The interior is dark, and there doesn't appear to be any activity around the building. I'm not sure if I expected a welcoming committee, but the absence of a rebel lookout raises some obvious questions. By the looks on my friends' faces, I'm not the only person experiencing a rush of anxiety.

"Where is everyone? What are we going to do now?"

Carmen voices what I imagine everyone is thinking. Mitch wastes no time to seize control before the situation gets out of hand.

"Let's not panic until we investigate around and inside the cabin. Cowan and Marcus, you take the north side of the cabin, while Neil and I take the southern side. We will meet around back. The rest of you stay here until we return."

We emerge from the trees into a small clearing containing high grass and scattered undergrowth. Marcus and I reach the front of the cabin, which consists of a wooden door flanked by two small windows. Wooden shutters cover the window openings, and they appear to be fastened shut. I carefully reach up and tug on one of the shutters, but it won't budge. Apparently, someone has nailed the shutters closed to protect the inside of the cabin from the weather. As we make our way along the side of the cabin, our passage is hindered by encroaching trees and brush. A lone window faces the north, and it too has shutters fastened in place. Nearing the corner of the cabin, I can hear a small stream running along the rear of the building. Finally, we make our way around to join Mitch and Neil standing at the bank of the stream. Mitch wastes no time outlining our next course of action.

"Well, at least from the outside, the place appears deserted. Let's collect the others and search the inside of the cabin. Hopefully, they left us a note saying they'll be back in fifteen minutes."

Mitch displays a sarcastic smirk, following his last statement, and immediately turns away toward the front of the cabin. Upon arriving at the entrance, Mitch turns and mounts the lone step leading to the front door. Without hesitating, he grasps the door handle and attempts to push it open. The door opens slightly but immediately gets stuck. Apparently, the wood has warped over time from the inclement weather. Mitch lowers his shoulder and drives forward into the door. The wood groans against the frame, but easily opens the rest of the way. I hold my breath awaiting an attack by some hidden assailant.

My squad is getting some much-needed rest, in an abandoned school building, just west of the river where the rebels were initially detected. Our pilot landed the helicopter out behind the school, and he's presently snoring off to my right. I should be taking advantage of the short respite, but my mind keeps going over the events of the past few days. Sean has sent a number of drones out, to canvas the countryside, west of our location. Hopefully, it will just be a matter of time before we receive a positive sighting. The second helicopter has already headed back to base for recharging. We have enough charge in our helicopter, for another three to four hours of flying time, if the drones come up empty. The plan is to coordinate search missions with the second helicopter until the rebels are found. A third helicopter is being serviced, but it won't be operational until later today. My radio chirps and I reach for it in anticipation.

"Attention Green Team, the drones have detected a heat signature in an abandoned structure approximately twenty-five miles southwest of your location. I will have the coordinates sent to your helicopter along with real-time updates. General Taggert will provide you with mission plans once your unit is airborne."

"Thanks for the update Sean. We will be on our way momentarily."

My concern was unwarranted when it turned out that Mitch had barged in on an empty cabin. After a cursory search of the interior, Mitch reappeared in the doorway and gave the all clear signal.

The twelve of us are now huddled inside, with battery-powered lamps, trying to figure out what to do next. The cabin looks like it has been abandoned for a while, which doesn't bode well for our current situation. It's comprised of a single room with a fireplace located on the west wall. A small sink, containing a hand pump for a well, sits just to the left of the window which faces north. To the right of the window is a shelf containing a few cups and plates. The only furniture in the room is a wooden table with two matching chairs. A large, frayed area rug covers the floor in the center of the room. Marcus is over by the south-facing wall, where there are two shelves with various items. One of the objects, which he is looking at, appears to be a ceramic football helmet. He turns around and looks over at me with a smile.

"Hey Cowan, what football team is this?"

I begin walking over and note that it's a white helmet with some sort of large, blue, four-legged animal on the side. The image looks familiar, but it doesn't immediately come to mind. I try to visualize the magazines Marcus used to give me to review. Suddenly, the answer pops into my head.

"I believe that is a Buffalo Bills helmet!"

"Very good my friend. I see all my teaching hasn't gone to waste."

He gives a brief smile and turns his attention back to the items on the shelves. It's good to see him smile again. I hear Bree and Kenji discussing something off to my right. They are looking at some objects just to the right of the window. There appears to be a small piece of paper, and a U-shaped metal object nailed to the wall.

"Kenji, what's this metal thing on the wall?"

"That is called a horseshoe. They were nailed to the bottom of the horse's hooves for protection. This piece of paper is interesting."

Kenji removes the paper from the wall and begins to examine it more closely.

"This is an old, one-dollar bill. It's what people would use to buy things. The year on the bill is 2025, and it's circled in red. I'm not sure what this message means that's printed in red lettering. It says, 'Break in Case of Emergency' across the front."

"Well, I would say this certainly qualifies as an emergency!"

A few of us look over at Bree and chuckle, but the emotion is forced. I can sense tension starting to fill the air around the room. We finally arrived at our destination, only to discover the cabin to be abandoned. Even if we've been able to escape the territory the question is where to go from here? I look around the room and sense the others are dealing with their own emotional turmoil. The silence is finally broken by Carmen's voice.

"What kind of clue is that? That thing is made out of paper. How could you break a bill anyway?"

Kenji looks toward Carmen and smiles.

"It's an old expression for spending the money to get change."

"Wait a second, did you just say break a bill? C'mon, it couldn't be that easy."

Marcus immediately grabs the football helmet off the shelf and shakes it. Something rattles around inside the ceramic helmet. Without any hesitation, he drops it onto the wooden floor where it shatters, causing pieces of ceramic to fly in every direction. In the center of the mess is a folded piece of paper, a key, and a small figurine. Marcus bends down to pick up the articles.

"This looks like a turtle. Don't tell me we have another clue to solve."

He starts to unfold the piece of paper and begins to read what is written inside.

"Here's a surprise! It looks like we have yet another puzzle to solve. The paper reads, 'It is Erie how close a Bill's fan is to the Great Wall.' What's with these people? Can't they just come right out and tell us what to do?"

Kenji walks over to Marcus and holds out his hand.

"Can I have a look at the paper? I think the rebels, who left these clues, were just being cautious. They didn't want the wrong people figuring out where they went. They were probably hoping the present rebel network would have additional information to help solve the clues."

"Kenji is mostly correct. The main priority of the rebel network is to keep the location of the previous groups secret. Regretfully, we don't have any additional information, however. Arlen and I were just given the location of this cabin. It was our understanding there would be someone here to provide further direction."

After Mitch finishes speaking, he proceeds to look over Kenji's shoulder as the pair attempt to figure out the riddle. Kenji eventually turns toward Marcus, who's standing a few feet away fiddling with the turtle figurine.

"What was that helmet called again? Something Bills?

"It was the Buffalo Bills. They were a professional football team years ago."

"That's interesting because the word 'Erie' is spelled wrong and capitalized. I wonder if the clue is hinting at Lake Erie. If I remember correctly, Buffalo, New York is near Lake Erie. Hey Drew, can you pull up a map of Buffalo and its surrounding area on your monitor?"

Both Drew and Mitch begin punching buttons on their monitors as the rest of us start to gather around the two monitors. On my way over to Drew's monitor, I feel the floor give beneath my feet. I make a mental note to check this out later. It's probably just a few loose floorboards, but we can't risk having one of us crash through the floor and break an ankle.

"You're right Kenji. Buffalo is located on the eastern shore of Lake Erie. Now we're getting somewhere. Let's assume we have the correct area. What did they mean about the 'Great Wall?'"

Mitch shakes his head looking as perplexed as the rest of us.

"I don't remember a wall being built in that area. There's nothing around there except Rochester, to the east, and Niagara Falls and Lake Ontario to the North."

Silence descends upon the room as everyone struggles to decipher the clues.

"Mitch, what if the wall wasn't man-made? What if the wall consisted of water?"

"Kenji, you are a genius! The clue must be indicating Niagara Falls. I'll bet our next objective is somewhere near Niagara Falls."

Everyone starts hugging Kenji and slapping him on the back, as there's a distinct sense of relief inside the cabin. Finally, it's Abby who asks the obvious question.

"How far away is Niagara Falls from here?"

Drew looks at her with a somber look on his face.

"I just punched in both coordinates to set my monitor. It estimates a little over three-hundred and fifty miles from here."

The temporary euphoria is sucked out of the building as reality hits everyone at once. We've only walked forty-five miles, so the prospect of hiking that far seems impossible. While everyone is pondering the impossible, I decide to busy myself by checking out the loose flooring. I pick up one corner of the rug and fold it back to access the floor. I'm amazed to discover that the source of the problem is a trap door beneath the rug.

"Hey, guys check this out. It looks like our rebel friends decided to build a cellar underneath the cabin."

Neil helps me fold the rug away from the door. I grab a recessed handle near the top of the door and pull. The door lifts easily, exposing an opening with a ladder heading down. I lean over and flick on my headlamp which illuminates a passageway starting at the base of the ladder.

"On second thought, there appears to be a passageway at the bottom. Hey Marcus, it looks dark down there. Do you want to volunteer to go down first?"

Marcus gives me the one-fingered salute and shakes his head. I return a smile as I lower myself through the opening and onto the top rung. There's a total of six rungs leading down to the floor of the passageway. The ceiling is less than six feet high, so I'd have to hunch over to use the tunnel, which appears to head off to the west. The tunnel is lined with gray-colored blocks which are connected by a series of wires. The ends of the wires are coiled up and connected to a box having a switch and a dial on its face. My instincts tell me that what I'm looking at is dangerous.

"Hey Mitch, could you come down here and take a look at something?"

I hear footsteps above, and then a boot appears coming down through the opening.

"Did you find a treasure chest down here?"

Mitch's face appears, and his jaw drops immediately.

"Cowan, don't touch anything. This tunnel is lined with C-4, which is a plastic explosive. The box hanging on the wall must be the detonator. Apparently, our rebel friends were concerned with this place being discovered and wanted a way to cover their tracks. It looks like the detonator also has a dial, which can be set to delay activation. Let's leave everything like we found it and join everyone upstairs."

Mitch and I carefully make our way up the ladder and replace the trapdoor. As expected, everyone isn't too thrilled to hear about the explosives stacked under our feet. Drew, however, is immediately intrigued by the tunnel.

"So, Cowan, you're sure the tunnel heads off to the west? Do you have any idea how long the tunnel runs?"

"My headlamp only illuminated about thirty feet, so it was impossible to tell how long it goes, but it appeared to keep going straight."

"I'm going outside to see if I can find where the tunnel comes out. It wouldn't hurt to have another escape route in case Taggert's men find this cabin."

"There's no way I'm going down into a tunnel surrounded by explosives!"

Drew smiles at Carmen, and gives her shoulder a squeeze, as he turns toward the door. He gives the handle a hard tug and takes one step when a loud crack is heard outside. Drew is immediately thrown back into the cabin, with the monitor flying out of his hand. He lands on his back and begins clutching at the right side of his chest. A large, dark patch begins to bloom under his hands. It takes a few seconds before I realize it's blood. My brain has trouble processing that Drew has been shot. Evidently, I'm not the only one to react slowly, but in no time pandemonium ensues inside the cabin.

37

JAMES/KENJI

"WHO TOOK THAT shot without my order?"

"He had a gun in his hand, so I didn't want to take a chance."

"I want everyone to stand down. Keep your eyes focused on any exit locations and report any movement immediately. Is that clear?"

That's all I need is a bunch of trigger-happy soldiers in the middle of this dark forest. I'll be lucky to make it back alive at this rate. At least we have the rebels trapped in the cabin. My scouts verified that there is only one exit and I have all sides surrounded. It will only be a matter of time before the rebels are in custody. I should report in to update the situation.

"Base, this is Green Leader. We have the cabin surrounded."

"Jim, did I hear a gunshot?"

I was hoping the general would have been away from the radio during the initial encounter. Doesn't the man get any sleep?

"One of the young recruits got a little overzealous. The situation is under control."

"I expect you to keep your men in line. If you are unable to fulfill this responsibility, then I will find someone else who can. Keep us updated on the situation."

The communication is promptly terminated, and I'm left holding the handset to my mouth. I clip the handset to my belt and send a piercing stare in the direction of the reckless recruit. I'll deal with him later, but for the time being, I need to carefully appraise our current situation."

Dr. Timms immediately started treating Drew following the shooting. She was successful in slowing the flow of blood, but I could tell the gravity of the situation when she walked away to brief the group. She said the exit wound is lower on Drew's back, which indicates the bullet must have deflected off of a rib. His right lung is collapsed, and he has internal bleeding in his chest cavity. The consequence is that his breathing will become increasingly labored and his heart function will be impeded soon. She estimated that he has less than an hour to live.

The rest of the group were immediately evacuated into the tunnel to avoid having someone else get shot. I'm presently standing at the top of the ladder waiting for Mitch to finish talking with Drew. Eventually, he grabs Drew's hand and says a few final words before motioning me over. He takes a deep breath and regards me with bloodshot eyes before speaking.

"Kenji, I'm so sorry this has happened. Take a few moments with your friend. I'll be down with the others making final preparations. Please make it brief, because I don't know how much time we have left."

With a solemn nod, he heads over to the opening in the floor and proceeds down the ladder. I look down at my best friend, who is laying on his back in obvious pain. His face is extremely pale and bathed in sweat. He looks up and smiles, as I fight to keep my emotions in check. I look up at the ceiling in a vain attempt to hold back my tears.

"Hey Bud, that's what I get for always being the first one out the door."

He starts laughing which induces a coughing fit. When I look down the tears start streaming down my face. My vision is blurred, but I can see blood trickling out the corner of his mouth. It's difficult to imagine this will be the last time I talk to him. I want to pick the perfect words to say, but I feel rushed, and my thoughts are all jumbled. It's impossible to condense a lifetime of memories into a few short minutes.

"I'm going to miss our long conversations about everything. You were the only one who understood why I had my nose in a book all the time."

"All that research is being put to good use now. These guys need that amazing brain of yours. Don't be afraid to use it. You better get going. The soldiers could storm this place at any moment."

He holds up his hand, and I grab it with mine. We lock eyes, and for a moment the room fades, and it's just the two of us alone. Drew breaks the bond by releasing his grip. I lower his right arm to the floor and give his hand one last squeeze.

"Goodbye Drew, I will miss you."

"Goodbye Kenji, make me proud."

I slowly stand and make my way to the opening in the floor. As I lower myself halfway down, I reach back to grab the end of the rug and pull it even with the top of the trapdoor. Our goal is to conceal the opening just long enough after the front door is breached. Before closing the door, I take one last look at Drew who is stretched out to the right of the front door, which is slightly ajar.

The cabin remains dark and quiet as pale light begins to lighten the eastern horizon. Our stealth advantage will soon be lost if we don't move in soon. We have successfully deployed men near the windows on each side of the house. No conversations and only a few noises are heard coming from the interior.

"Jim, there's movement at the front door."

I look at the front door and see what looks like a white towel being waved up and down.

"Well, it looks like our rebels have finally decided to give up."

I look over at the two men crouched behind the fallen tree with me.

"You two cover me from behind as we make our way across the clearing. I will take cover to the left of the door, while you guys go to the right. Let me inform the rest of our men about our plans."

"Men, this is Green Leader. Everyone hold your positions. We are going to make an assault on the front door."

I look at the cabin and see the towel still waving. After a quick nod, I vault over the tree and start running across the clearing. A few seconds later, I slam my back against the front wall of the cabin. As I catch my breath, I look over at the two men on the other side of the door. The towel continues to bob up and down just a few feet away.

"We have you surrounded. I'm going to walk through the door. If you show any signs of resistance, my men are instructed to eliminate everyone inside."

A hoarse voice answers from just inside the door.

"We surrender. It's safe to enter."

The voice must be coming from the rebel who was shot. He sounds extremely weak and near death.

"We can have medical attention here in no time. I'm coming in now."

I slowly turn toward the front door, which is opened slightly. The interior of the cabin is dark, so I flick on my headlamp. As I push the door open, I can see two legs off to the left. My light reveals a young male with bloody bandages across his chest. A pool of dried blood encircles his torso on the floor. I don't immediately see anyone else around him. As I turn to the left, I see a stick fastened through an eye-hook on the door frame. The towel, which is fastened to the end, gently waves in the wind. Alarms start to go off in my head as I train my headlamp back on the prone figure. I notice two wires leading from the right side of his body to a rug in the middle of the floor. My attention is drawn back by the voice of the young man.

"Is your name James Moeller?"

I look down at the young boy and nod.

A smile spreads across his face.

"Mitch asked me to give you a message."

38

MITCH/GENERAL TAGGERT

AFTER LEAVING THE tunnel, we've been heading north in an effort to confuse our pursuers. The tunnel surfaced just west of the stream running behind the cabin. I note the lightening sky off to the east, which increases the urgency of finding a place to camp. We're about a mile north of the cabin, and I'd like to put a little more distance behind us before finding a place to hide.

Suddenly, a huge explosion occurs to our south. I quickly look back to see orange light and smoke above the treetops. I wonder if Drew was able to trigger the detonator, or if the explosion was initiated by the timer. Looking down at my watch, I see that there are still fifteen minutes before the timer is set to go off. Apparently, Drew was able to deliver my message personally. Hopefully, my friend James was there to receive it. I should feel some retribution that our hasty plan worked, but it's difficult to find anything positive at the moment.

Drew's injuries were mortal, and movement was out of the question, so the two of us concocted the plan. He was the one who came up with the detonator idea. I hated to agree with him, but it did serve a number of purposes. We rigged up a white flag, attached to a string, which he could engage at the appropriate time. It was a despicable ruse, but there's no room for compassion when your friends' lives are at stake. There was some dissension when I presented our plan to the group, but in the end, everyone agreed. Now I've lost yet another friend and have the deaths of how many others on my conscience. I've always been a competitive person, but I never imagined ruthless being one of my traits. Yet that's how I feel as the group stands looking south at the glow above the tree line.

Carmen's sobbing breaks the silence, and I look over to see the girls huddled in a circle. Kenji is off by himself, near the front of the line, staring off to the south. Reality is probably seeping in that his best friend is finally gone. As I walk forward, I look at the group scattered around and wonder how many more won't make it to the end. Just thinking about the senseless loss of life begins to stoke the anger burning inside. Upon reaching Kenji, I put my arm around his shoulder and look toward the fire glowing above the trees.

"Your friend was extremely brave you know. I'm not sure what I would have done in his position."

"He was always quiet and hated confrontation. I guess he was tougher than I thought."

"You guys are all pretty tough. You're going to have to be if we're going to see this thing through."

★ ★ ★

"General I have lost contact with Green Team. The last transmission was a few minutes ago, just before their assault on the cabin."

"Perhaps they turned their radios off during the attack? Give it a few more minutes and then try to re-establish comms."

As if on cue, the radio chirps, and we both turn our attention to the voice on the other end.

"Headquarters, this is Green Wing. There was a loud explosion out here, and I can see an orange glow above the trees. Did you happen to catch it over the radio?"

"That's a negative Kurt. How close was the explosion?"

"I set my bird down in a clearing about five hundred yards away from the cabin. The explosion seemed to come from that direction."

"Kurt, take your bird up and investigate the area around the cabin. Keep your radio on so we can hear the live feed."

The sound of the rotors beginning to turn can be heard over the radio. In a few moments, we can hear the helicopter taking off.

"General there's definitely something burning off to the south. I'll be at the cabin location in a few seconds."

Sean and I concentrate on the radio. I'm trying to think of what could have caused an explosion. Did Jim's team get carried away?

"On my god, General, the cabin is gone! I repeat the cabin is gone!"

"What do you mean it's gone? What do you see?"

"There's nothing left of the building. There's just a big crater with sections of the cabin burning. A few bodies are scattered on the ground, but none of them appear to be moving. I'm going to set the chopper down as close to the building as possible."

The room is silent as everyone, in the vicinity of the radio, attempts to digest what they just heard. I come to the realization that I can't stay in this room a moment longer. I need to get out in the field and see the destruction firsthand.

"Roddy, radio ahead and have the second helicopter ready to leave in five minutes. I want to be out at that site as soon as possible."

Within thirty minutes our helicopter is approaching the location of the cabin. I can just make out the smoke rising above the trees up ahead. As we make our first pass over the site, I see that Kurt has already moved a few of the bodies away from the smoldering cabin. I signal the pilot to take us down, and he begins to circle over a location near the first helicopter. The medical team, seated in the back, prepare to disembark as soon as we land. By the looks of the scene below, I'm afraid medical attention will not be required.

As soon as we touch down, I make my way over to Kurt who has just finished moving another body. Soot and gore cover his clothing, and the shock of recent events are etched on his face.

"Did you find any survivors?"

"I'm afraid not, General. I was able to remove four bodies from the periphery. The fire was too hot to get at any remaining victims. I can see the remains of one other near the front entrance."

I shake my head as I survey the wreckage and the surrounding area. The heat, from the glowing embers, is evident even from a distance away. Kurt's face and arms are red from first degree burns.

"Why don't you take a break and get some medical attention for your burns? The medical team can take it from here."

Kurt nods and heads toward the medical personnel stationed near the second helicopter. I attempt to get closer to the blast area, but the heat is too intense. The lack of rebel bodies, even with the presence of the crater and the pile of burning rubble, is perplexing. We won't be able to search the area until the fire burns out and cools, but something tells me the search will only create more questions. I wonder if Sean can detect anything with the drones.

"Sean, this General Taggert, can you see anything with any of the drones?"

"Negative sir, the fire is too hot to get close, and the smoke is too thick to get any useful visuals. Did you find any survivors?"

"It looks like the only survivor from the blast is the pilot. We believe the other six men are dead including Jim."

"I'm sorry to hear that, General. Is there anything we can do from here?"

"I'd like you to keep a few drones searching this area. We also need to search the surrounding area in case the rebels escaped. My guess is they continued west, but I need you and your team to narrow down the possibilities."

"We'll get right on it sir."

Following my conversation with Sean, I attempt to gather my thoughts, as I walk around the remains of the cabin. A blast of this magnitude would require a significant amount of explosive material. Where did this material come from and who brought it here? Jim's team only carries enough to gain entry into buildings, and I can't imagine why the rebels would haul that much material all the way out to this location. It seems we keep uncovering more questions than answers. My frustration just keeps mounting along with the body count of good men. I look up at the sun, which is partially obscured by the smoke, and hope that it's dawning the final day of this manhunt.

39

COWAN/GENERAL TAGGERT

THE DAYS FOLLOWING our escape from the cabin have smeared together, to the extent that it's tough to distinguish one from another. We've mainly hiked during the dark, and the similar terrain has created an eerie feeling of walking in place. The monitors and an old compass provide the only assurance that we are progressing to our destination.

The better part of those first few nights was spent heading north to provide separation from our pursuers. Mitch has assumed Drew's place at the head of the column, with Kenji manning the second monitor at the rear. Toward the end of the second night, it was decided to start looping to the southwest toward our final destination. During our trek, Kenji has been providing a geography lesson to the rest of the group. Even Mitch and the rest of the Apis folks have learned a few things from our little genius. I think the geography discussions have provided Kenji a much-needed distraction from being consumed by his best friend's death. Drew's attack and his selfless sacrifice affected us all, but it hit Kenji extremely hard. He seems to be handling it as well as can be expected. Dealing with loss has been a common theme for just about everyone in our group. This has forced each member to not only become physically stronger over the course of our trek but emotionally hardened as well. Hopefully, these transformations will be useful during the remainder of our escape. Kenji estimates a few more days before we reach the Niagara Falls area. The group has rounded into shape after covering close to 350 miles of countryside.

Our first major river crossing was upstream of the Hudson River. Any bridges spanning this river were manned by soldiers, which forced us to find a secluded spot to cross with our remaining boats. I led the initial group of six across the river and then paddled back across with the tethered boats. The thermal blankets were utilized to mask the heat signatures of the boats. While anxiety levels were high, the crossings were completed without any apparent detection. Since then, the terrain has been free of major rivers, which has significantly reduced the chance of being detected by drones. This, and the fact that our route has taken us north of any patrolled roads has aided our progress to this point.

The landscape has slowly transformed from predominantly forest to mainly urban surroundings. The abandoned roads ease our progress, but they don't provide the concealment required to move about during the day. The size of some buildings has been amazing to see over the past few days. Just last night we passed by a few buildings which were almost twenty floors high.

Mitch said they were abandoned apartment buildings, where people used to live. It's tough to imagine that the population of our former community could live inside those buildings. Mitch was amused by my friends' reaction when we first saw the buildings. He said there were much higher buildings a few miles south in the city of Rochester.

The group has currently set up camp in a narrow strip of woods just north of Route 104. The sun has been up for about an hour, and a few of us are preparing to scout our next river crossing just west of our location. I have been told that it's Wednesday, May 9th, but the morning air feels like early April. I decide to walk over to the eastern edge of the woods to check out the city of Rochester off to the south. Upon reaching a clearing, I turn to the south where I'm greeted by an incredible view. The rising sun is shimmering off random windows on each of the buildings. Even though the buildings are far off, it's clear they are the highest I've ever seen. Most of the windows have been damaged over the years, but the buildings are still standing. After taking in the view for a few more minutes, I decide to make my way back to camp. Marcus and Kenji have completed their preparations and are standing off to the side awaiting my return.

"Guys, you need to see those buildings off to the south. You wouldn't believe how high they are."

"Cowan, they're even bigger where we're going."

I look at Kenji in disbelief, but he just nods and heads off in the direction of the river. It only takes us a few minutes to reach the edge of the woods. We hunker down behind a few bushes and peer off toward the river that cuts across our path. The river slowly meanders from north to south before passing beneath a bridge off to our left. Kenji looks down at his monitor and hits a few buttons.

"It says here that we are looking at the Genesee River and that's the Veterans Memorial Bridge."

Marcus and I turn to look up at the bridge, which towers over the tops of the trees.

"I can't see the top of the bridge from here, due to its height. There could be guards stationed up there, and we have no way of knowing without hiking further upstream for a better angle."

Marcus nods and begins scanning the opposite bank of the river. There's a similar strip of woods on the other side. The sun has cleared the trees behind us and is currently bathing the western bank with its rays. Various shades of green are captured by the early morning light, creating an image fit for a painting.

"What the heck was that?"

I turn toward Marcus and see that he's concentrating on a section of the far bank off to our right. I start scanning the area but don't see anything out of the ordinary.

"What did you see over there?"

"I'm not sure, but I could've sworn there was a reflection on the other side."

The three of us remain stationary behind our cover, carefully searching the far bank for anything peculiar. This time it's Kenji who notices something.

"I just saw it too Marcus. It was a double reflection a short distance apart. My best guess is that it was the sun reflecting off a pair of binoculars."

"Do you think they are guarding the bridge from the woods?"

Kenji looks over at me and nods.

"Perhaps they're trying a different tactic. They probably figure that having soldiers guarding the bridges out in the open hasn't worked. We see them in plenty of time to simply head further away to cross the river."

Kenji's explanation makes sense and rules out using this bridge to get across. We will have to hike further upstream and cross the river in the dark. Hopefully, the combination of the darkness on our side of the river and the sun at our backs has made it impossible to detect the three of us. We need to carefully move away from the edge of the woods and return to camp with our discovery. So much for having a restful sleep today. I'll be lucky to get any rest knowing the enemy is so close.

It's a rainy Wednesday morning which fits my mood perfectly, given that it's day thirteen of the rebel manhunt. I'm heading to our daily status meeting with low expectations that anything positive will result. Since the cabin explosion, our search teams have uncovered only a few signs of the rebel advancement. It didn't come as a shock to learn that there was an escape tunnel beneath the cabin, which the rebels attempted to conceal with explosives. Their rigged explosion claimed the lives of six men, which has only hardened my resolve to bring the group to justice. It wasn't until late last week that one of my search teams found evidence that a group of individuals had recently used an abandoned barn as shelter. The clues appeared to be a few days old, but they substantiated our assumption that the rebels are heading west. The trail has gone cold following the discovery, but we have instituted a few ideas, which will hopefully result in a positive sighting. It is with these thoughts in mind that I enter the lab and head toward the bank of monitors which serve as our meeting area.

"Morning Sean, Roddy."

"Good morning General."

"Roddy, are there any further sightings or signs of the rebels?"

By the look in Roddy's eyes, it's obvious he has nothing positive to report.

"As you know, we are trying to funnel the rebels into our traps as they head west. If you look up at this monitor, you'll see we have selectively left a few bridges standing and seemingly unguarded. A number of concealed teams have been stationed at each bridge. We are also patrolling the rivers with drones in the event the rebels choose to cross away from the bridges."

Looking up at the monitors I can see Sean's handiwork with respect to extrapolating the group's progress. A series of circular bands radiate outward from the last assumed location of the rebels, which was the abandoned barn. These bands are shown ranging from red to green in order to signify the likelihood of the rebel group appearing at that location. The green band, which shows the highest probability stretches from Lake Ontario, through Rochester, New York, and south through Ithaca, New York.

"If you were to hazard a guess, where do you think our rebels are right now?"

Sean clears his throat and begins typing on the computer. The display zooms in on the area of the map displaying Rochester, New York.

"If we follow the assumption that our group is maintaining a westward direction, then it would put them somewhere in the highlighted arc between Lake Ontario and Route 290. They will probably stay away from major roads, so I'd concentrate my resources in less populated areas."

"That sounds logical and is in accordance with their behavior for the most part. You have my approval to concentrate the majority of our units in those regions. I still want to maintain some men and equipment in secondary areas of interest. As we have experienced firsthand, this group is full of surprises. We have to be prepared for some unorthodox strategies on their part."

Both men nod in agreement, but I sense a lingering tension in the air.

"Do either of you have anything else to report?"

Sean immediately glances over at Roddy, and they both hesitate before Sean responds.

"Well sir, we have had a few more incidents of graffiti in town. It appears the perpetrators are getting more daring."

"Sean, what exactly do you mean by daring?"

"Let me show you a few examples of what we found. As you know, there were a few instances of the number seven being painted on walls around town. We believe this is the rebel's way to pay tribute to the seven kids who escaped.

The following pictures were taken by our security forces over the past two days."

Pictures begin flashing up on the center monitor. With each picture my blood pressure rises and my pulse quickens. Sean was spot on when he described the culprits as being daring. The pictures show sevens on the hoods of military vehicles, on the fuselage of a helicopter, and even on the side of a security camera. The last photograph causes my jaw to drop and my pressure to go through the roof. The picture appears to be taken by one of our security cameras, and it shows seven masked individuals forming a seven in the back, parking lot of the Apis Corporation building.

"How the hell were they able to orchestrate that picture without our security forces being able to arrive in time?"

"We wondered the same thing until we accessed the security programs for the cameras and discovered the code had been altered once again. Rebel moles were able to temporarily disable any cameras in the areas of the graffiti."

"We need to identify the moles in our midst immediately. The rebels are making us look like idiots. They will only gain confidence and support the longer we allow this to continue. Either you find the identity of our moles or I will find someone else who will."

I abruptly turn and storm away toward the lab exit. Any personnel in my path quickly scurry out of the way. My blood is still boiling as I reach the second floor and head into my office. I walk over to the window overlooking the lab and scan the workers below. Everyone appears to be busy at work, but who among them are the moles. I need to find a way to flush them out before they reek even more havoc.

My mind is still preoccupied with capturing moles, as I open the rear door of the Headquarters building, leading to the back parking lot. I start heading toward my company car but decide to take the short walk home instead. The rain, from earlier in the day, has stopped and the sky is clear. It's late in the day, and the sun has dipped below the trees off to the west. As I walk toward the setting sun, I am reminded of the rebels who are somewhere off in that direction. My thoughts are quickly drawn to my son, and the painful memories threaten to rise to the surface. I make a conscious effort to keep my feelings in check, while I watch the sky slowly turn various shades of orange. It's amazing the things we take for granted, like the beauty of a sunset, or the health of your family. My wife used to preach this all the time until cancer ironically took her life when Cole was just a baby. Cole would have turned out differently if cancer had chosen his father instead.

I attempt to shake my mood as I head west on the narrow section of South Street. Hopefully, a stiff drink will settle my nerves and provide some much-needed sleep. Eventually, the gables of my house rise above the bushes on my right, as I approach the corner of South Street. Crossing the deserted street, I notice the two chairs on the wrap-around porch. An image of Cole and I, reclining with drinks in our hands, comes to mind. Sometimes we would just sit quietly without saying a word.

A gust of wind disturbs the bittersweet memory and blows a few leaves onto the porch. My attention is drawn to my front door, which displays a dark shape. In the fading, light the diagonal marking appears to be blood. Suddenly, I realize the substance is red paint, and the symbol transforms into a giant seven. The paint appears to be wet, which means the perpetrator may still be in the vicinity. I rush down the steps and run to the corner of the street, where it's possible to see in both directions. As expected, there's no sign of my little artist. I reach down to my belt to grab my radio. My stiff drink will have to wait. First, a few heads need to roll.

40

KENJI

IT'S EARLY IN the morning on Saturday, May 12ᵗʰ, and our group has finally reached the city of Niagara Falls. The sun isn't due to rise for a couple of hours, but the moon provides enough light as we carefully negotiate the streets. The past few days have gone relatively smooth, since our close call with the soldiers back at the Genesee River. Troop activity has increased, as we near the Niagara Falls River. We can see a helicopter with a searchlight scanning the river less than a half mile to our west. As we proceed down Niagara Street a subtle glow of light fringes the buildings near the end. An ominous rumble grows in volume the closer we get to the river. Mitch said the sound is being produced by Niagara Falls. He explained there are falls on the United States side and then a larger waterfall connecting the United States and Canada. I find it hard to believe a waterfall could create such noise, but the truth remains that the volume increases as we head west.

Mitch slows our pace as we near the end of the street. We hug the side of a building and carefully peer around the corner where we determine the source of the light. Portable lights have been placed at the eastern end of a long bridge. Parked across the bridge is an army jeep flanked by three soldiers. Mitch motions for the group to back up as he turns to face everyone.

"The long bridge over there is Rainbow Bridge, which connects the United States to Canada. Apparently, General Taggert wants to make sure nobody leaves the country."

"Let them think that we are leaving. What we need to find is an information center to help us figure out where to go next."

"That's an excellent idea Kenji. My monitor shows a Niagara Falls Visitors' Center about a block away from here. Everyone follow me and try to stay in the shadows to avoid being seen."

The group follows Mitch as he heads down Rainbow Boulevard toward our destination. After a block, he takes a right and begins to walk slowly west toward the Niagara River. The lights, positioned on Rainbow Bridge, illuminate the edge of a towering cube-shaped building on our right. Mitch stops at the end of the building and carefully looks around the edge.

"The Visitors' Center is diagonally off to our left. We need to be careful, as we cross the street because we will be exposed to the soldiers stationed on the bridge. Everyone stay down and quickly follow me when I determine the coast is clear."

About a minute later, Mitch signals for everyone to follow. Our group quickly scurries across the road while the soldiers are facing the opposite direction. The Visitors' Center is comprised of a series of buildings nestled in a wooded area. A number of walking paths meander through the park connecting the buildings. The park overlooks the Niagara River and provides views of both sets of falls and Rainbow Bridge. The main building is located right on Prospect Street, and it's here that we begin our investigation into where to go next.

The inside of the building is dark, but the moon affords enough light to navigate around. The interior is comprised of a large room with a series of displays mounted on the walls, which recount the history of Niagara Falls.

"We need to be extremely careful using our headlamps in here. Any soldiers patrolling the streets will be able to see the lights unless we hood them with our hands and hold them close to the walls. Let's separate into small groups and search for any clues."

Following Mitch's directions, everyone quickly pairs up and begins to search the interior of the room. Marcus and I head to the nearest wall to begin our investigation. I remove my headlamp and cup my hands around it, so only a narrow beam illuminates a small portion of the wall. Marcus copies my technique before scanning his section of the display. It appears that the periphery of the room is set up in chronological order. Our section starts at the year 2020 and describes what was done to combat the erosion caused by the powerful forces brought on by the cascading water. The results of a study, measuring the rates of recession for the rim of the falls, are provided. The results claim that the Niagara Falls has eroded over seven miles in the last twelve thousand years. That's an average of three feet per year. A water diversion project was started in 2021 to reduce the erosion rate and to provide additional hydroelectric power to the surrounding area. The project was completed in 2023 and reduced the erosion rate to less than a foot per decade. Subsequent expansion efforts were pursued, which reduced the rate even further. I'm deeply engrossed in the information when I hear Marcus' voice to my right.

"Hey Kenji, what was the date on the dollar bill we found in the cabin?"

I reach into my pocket to retrieve the bill, focusing my lamp on the front face.

"The year is 2025, why do you ask?"

"Come over here. There was a project that was started on that year. I haven't read the details, but I wonder if there is a connection."

I move over next to Marcus and train my lamp on the display. The title is 'Scenic Tunnel Experience', and it describes a joint project between the United States and Canada in 2025. The goal was to dig a tunnel between the United States and Canada behind Horseshoe Falls. An electric tram, powered by the falls, would be constructed to transport visitors from one end of the tunnel to the other. Scenic spots would be built behind the falls to provide visitors with unique views of the falls. Restaurants and other facilities would gradually be added along the length of the tunnel. Suddenly, a connection is made in my head to a name mentioned in an earlier paragraph.

"Marcus, I think you found the answer!"

"How can that be Kenji? It says here that the construction project was stopped due to the lack of United States' funding."

Marcus has a point, but it seems that the pieces fit too well to result in a dead end. While we discuss the merits of his discovery the rest of the group begins to make their way over to our location. Mitch and Dr. Timms are the first to arrive.

"Did you two find something over here?"

I turn toward Mitch who has a hopeful expression on his face.

"This wall summarizes a tunnel project between the United States and Canada which was started in 2025. This year just happens to match the date circled on our dollar bill. The tunnel was located behind Horseshoe Falls."

I hold up the horseshoe to emphasize my point.

"That's excellent news guys! Why do you two still look skeptical?"

Marcus turns to Dr. Timms and points to a large timeline painted on the wall showing major milestones for the project.

"This timeline shows that the project was stopped in 2027 due to lack of funding on the part of the United States."

Everyone stares at the wall and ponders the information just presented.

"This has to mean something. Why would the previous rebels leave these clues if they ultimately lead to a dead end? It just doesn't make sense."

Bree walks over to a map, which shows the location of the project in reference to the Niagara Falls area. After studying the map for a few moments, she points to a particular location.

"It looks like this small island, called Goat Island, connects to one side of Horseshoe Falls at a spot called Terrapin Point. The map shows two small bridges which access the island not too far from here."

Everyone turns to look at the spot on the map where Bree is holding her finger. I can hear Marcus mumbling something next to me.

"Terrapin, Terrapin, where have I heard that name before? I know, it's the mascot for Maryland! It's a turtle!"

We all look at Marcus who is holding a small turtle figurine up in the air. All the clues point to the tunnel as our next destination. Now that the mystery has been solved let's hope the tunnel is there.

The group quickly collects their things and heads back to the front entrance. Mitch scans the street outside for any activity. It's almost 5:15 a.m. which means that sunrise is in about forty-five minutes. He leads us out the door, and to the right, in the direction of the Pedestrian Bridge that connects to Goat Island. A path, lined with trees, offers some cover as we quickly make our way to the bridge. At the end of the path, we veer into the woods in order to survey the entrance to the bridge. There doesn't appear to be any soldiers guarding the bridge, but it could be a trap similar to previous river crossings. After a few minutes scanning the entrance, Mitch motions to the rest of us to gather around.

"There doesn't seem to be any soldiers guarding the bridge, but I'm not totally sure. It is now twilight, and the sun will be rising in about a half hour, so we really need to get moving. What do you guys think?"

Mitch scans our faces, but everyone appears afraid to comment. Ultimately, all eyes turn in my direction.

"It sort of makes sense that the soldiers would leave this bridge unguarded. If we go with the assumption that General Taggert believes the tunnel is unfinished, then the bridge only leads to a dead end. If it turns out to be a dead end, then we will have to find a place on the island to hideout and figure out where to go from here."

Heads begin to nod following my explanation, and then the group patiently awaits Mitch's decision.

"I agree with Kenji's assessment. We have come too far to turn around. All the clues point to the tunnel crossing. You guys know the drill. Keep down and follow me across."

As we make our way across the bridge, you can hear the water flowing underneath. I can see the rapids as the river travels over the remaining distance before reaching the precipice of the falls. My body is tense as I await the inevitable gunshot from a hidden enemy position. The short expanse seems endless until we ultimately reach the far end of the bridge and take refuge in a tiny copse of trees. Everyone is breathing heavy from the exertion of the run, combined with the fear of being discovered.

Up ahead is an intersection with crumbling roads leading in all directions. A small sign leans at an angle indicating points of interest. The group cautiously moves into the open and heads toward the sign. An arrow, with the name Terrapin Point, angles slightly down and to the right. Mitch immediately turns in that direction and begins walking along the tree line. I try to picture the map of Goat Island in my head as we make our way alongside the weather-beaten road. If my memory serves correctly, the small island is ovular in shape with Terrapin Point at one of the ends.

Eventually, we come to a parking lot on our left with a number of buildings off to the right. The growing rumble and the increasing mist from Horseshoe Falls confirm we are headed in the right direction. Looking off to the right, I can see the lights on Rainbow Bridge less than a half mile away. I look up to scan the sky, but the helicopter is nowhere in sight. Apparently, they figure nobody would be crazy enough to cross the river this close to the falls. Hopefully, the helicopter is one less thing to worry about at this point. Finally, the trees thin out and the road opens up to a direct view of Horseshoe Falls. Between the roar of the falls and their sheer size, my senses are overwhelmed. As I scan the faces of my friends, it appears that everyone is experiencing the same reaction.

A grassy peninsula stands between our group and a small building which stands at the start of Horseshoe Falls. A pathway leads from the main road to the entrance of the building. The ground is covered with large birds that are too busy hunting for food, to be concerned about our groups' sudden appearance. Mitch pauses for a few seconds, to survey the immediate area, before heading down the pathway to the building. As our group hurries down the path, I can see more of Rainbow Bridge come into view on our right. Suddenly the birds begin to take flight in a flurry of activity, swirling in the air above our group. The birds start forming a makeshift formation as they head over the falls. Within seconds a huge searchlight starts scanning the peninsula, its beam illuminating the last few members of our party. Immediately, everyone starts sprinting toward the building before the light is swept back over our group. The entrance contains double doors with the majority of the glass panes either cracked or missing. Cowan is the first the reach the doors, which thankfully open on his first attempt. Our group begins to pile into the building as the light sweeps back over the open field. As soon as the door closes behind me, the searchlight flashes across the building entrance.

The building is comprised of a small foyer leading to a ticket window. There is an elevator off to the right along with a staircase leading down. Mitch wastes no time leading us down the stairs. We continue down four flights of stairs before emerging into a small room. Other than the elevator, the room has a single exit consisting of a double door. Above the doors is a sign stating, 'Welcome to the Scenic Tunnel Experience.'" Mitch walks up to the right-hand door and pulls on the handle, but this time the door is locked. He turns toward Marcus, who proceeds to reach into his pocket for the key we found at the cabin. Marcus steps forward and inserts the key into the lock. The group holds their collective breath as the key turns and produces an audible click. Marcus pulls the handle, and the door opens, exposing a dark tunnel on the other side. A loud rumble emanates from further down the tunnel, and the air feels moist, as a noticeable draft escapes through the door. We take turns peering through the door and then at each other, unsure of what to do next. Mitch finally reaches up and turns on his headlamp.

"Guys, I'm afraid we are going to have company very soon. Let's hope our rebel friends know more than we do, or this is going to be a short trip."

Without another word, Mitch disappears through the door. One by one the rest of us turn on our headlamps and follow him to our fate.

41

GENERAL TAGGERT/MARCUS

T HERE'S NOTHING LIKE a strong cup of coffee to clear your head and get the day going. I usually try to enjoy my first cup while sitting on my porch enjoying the sunrise. It's one of the few times during the day that I can enjoy a little peace and quiet. These moments of solitude have become less frequent since the rebels made their escape. I glance back at my freshly painted front door, as thoughts of rebels invade my morning solace. I attempt to clear my mind while taking a sip of coffee, but now there's a bitter tinge to the flavor. So much for my temporary respite from the daily stress and aggravation. As if to confirm my thoughts, the radio chirps on the table next to my chair. With a heavy sigh, I reach over to pick up the unit.

"General, are you there?"

Apparently, Sean has already started his day. I came close to firing his ass, along with Roddy's, when I discovered the graffiti on my door, but common sense prevailed the next morning. I came to the realization that they are two of a few trusted individuals at Headquarters. With moles still roaming around, I couldn't afford to part with their services.

"I was enjoying a peaceful moment on my porch. What is it Sean?"

"General, we just received a report, from our lookouts on Rainbow Bridge, that a group was spotted near Niagara Falls."

"Where exactly was this sighting and how many individuals did they observe?"

I'm already up and out of my chair and on my way into the house. It looks like my day has started earlier than expected. I try to keep my emotions in check after having my hopes dashed a number of times over the past couple of weeks.

"The soldier said he definitely saw a few individuals running across the western end of Goat Island. They disappeared into a small building located near Horseshoe Falls. His group has continued to watch the building, and they are certain that nobody has exited. They radioed nearby personnel to head over to the island to check out the situation and to report any findings."

"Sean, instruct the recon team to surround the building from a safe distance. We should all be well aware by now what this group is capable of doing. I'm heading into Headquarters now to discuss the situation. Contact Roddy and have him meet us in the lab. In the meantime, have your team research the Niagara Falls area in an attempt to figure out why our rebels chose that location. Also, arrange for a helicopter to be ready. I want to personally coordinate the assault on the building."

My thoughts are focused on the rebel plans, while I make my way through the doors of the lab. A sense of déjà vu seeps into my thoughts, seeing Sean and Roddy stationed near the monitors. The two gentlemen nod, as I approach, and then return their attention to a map of the Niagara Falls area. Sean zooms in on a small island, which is located between the American Falls and the Canadian Falls.

"What did your team find out about this area?"

"There wasn't much recent information in our archives. We had to go back sixty years to find anything pertinent. Evidently, in 2025 the United States and Canada started the construction of a tunnel behind Horseshoe Falls. The project, however, was canceled by the United States in 2027. Perhaps our rebel friends stumbled upon some old research and mistakenly concluded that this was a way to escape."

"You are certain that the tunnel was never finished?"

"Everything we found on the subject states the tunnel construction was stopped due to insufficient funding on the part of the United States. If the group in that building are our fugitives, then they will soon discover their escape has reached a dead end."

"Good work, men. I'm heading out there now. It looks like it will take a few hours to get there. Call in reinforcements to surround the area and have them wait until I arrive. Let our rebels stew in the darkness for a while. Perhaps they will be anxious to give themselves up by the time I land."

★ ★ ★

Thus far, the trek through the tunnel has been both amazing and frightening. In some places, there's a ledge connected to the tunnel, leading directly to the backside of the falls. A few of us ventured out on the ledge to get closer to the falls. The sound was deafening, and the footing was slick. Sections of the ceiling, near the opening, had caved in and large fragments of rock were strewn across the opening. Kenji explained that the erosion rate must be back to normal, now that the water diversion projects have been abandoned since the eruption. He said that pretty soon this tunnel would be gone as a result of the erosion.

We are presently about halfway through the tunnel, and our progress has slowed. The diameter of the tunnel has dramatically reduced. We are forced to crawl on our hands and knees to continue our forward progress. The tunnel itself is showing definite signs of erosion. The ceiling is dripping in spots forming large puddles along the base of the tunnel. Our group is forced to crawl through frigid water as we make our way along. The diameter of the tunnel continues to shrink, along with my confidence of the tunnel ever leading us to safety.

Suddenly, what sounds like gunshots echo from behind, followed by a loud bang. Everyone stops to listen, but the roar of the water above drowns out any further noise. I can hear Mitch talking from a few positions ahead.

"It sounds like the door to the building has been breached. It looks like our only hope is to continue forward."

The pace of our advance quickens, with the threat of soldiers approaching from behind. After a few minutes, my dwindling hopes begin to increase when I notice that the tunnel appears to be getting bigger. Peering around Cowan, I see people up ahead disappearing over the edge of the tunnel. When I finally reach the edge, I'm rewarded to find that it opens up into a large space with a large section of the tunnel continuing on the other side. I carefully crab walk down the slope and join a few of my friends standing on the floor. Off to the right, a few holes are cut through the rock showing the backside of the waterfall. It feels good to stretch after being hunched over in the tunnel. Once the rest of our crew has successfully navigated the slope, leading to the room, Mitch addresses the group.

"Everyone, take a few minutes to catch your breath, but we have to get moving quickly. I'm afraid we have unwittingly exposed the nature of this tunnel to our enemy. I wish there were something we could do to stop them."

"Do you think that this would help?"

Everyone turns toward Cowan. He has his backpack off and is in the process of reaching inside. He pulls out a gray brick of material, followed by a timer and some wire.

"I found this in the tunnel under the cabin. I figured it just might come in handy."

Mitch rushes over to inspect the materials. He shakes his head, gets up, and gives Cowan a bear-hug.

"Cowan, you little sneak. You are a chip off the old block. Hopefully, this is enough to suit our purposes. Come on and help me install this stuff above the roof of the tunnel we just exited."

Mitch and Cowan hurry up the slope and begin mounting the explosives above the opening. The rest of us watch helplessly from below as they do their best to conceal everything. A few minutes later they clamor down wearing matching looks of distress.

"It has taken us about twenty-five minutes to reach this point. I set the timer for thirty-five minutes, to hopefully give us enough time to reach the end and get out, but still trap our pursuers when the explosion occurs. So, let's move it!"

The group doesn't need any additional incentive to get moving. We quickly scamper up the far slope and through the connecting tunnel. The second-half of the tunnel is much wider, which facilitates our progress. The Canadian side apparently planned similar viewing attractions, as evidenced by a few large rooms and ledges cut out behind the falls. Our group quickly passes these features in our haste to reach the end of the tunnel.

It takes our group less than twenty minutes to arrive at what appears to be an exit door. Mitch holds up his hand to signal our group to stop and then holds a finger to his lips. He then proceeds to shine his headlamp on the door. The light illuminates an object which appears to be taped to the center of the door. The object appears to be a paper maple leaf leaning on its side. Mitch reaches out and removes the leaf from the door and then turns around. He holds the leaf up to the light and begins to examine both sides.

"It just appears to be a simple, red maple leaf. I can't find any writing on it."

He proceeds to pass the leaf to Cowan, who gives it a cursory glance before passing it along. The leaf starts making its way around the rest of the group.

"Since we have less than fifteen minutes before the timer expires, I propose we get out of here and then try to figure out the significance of the leaf later."

"I think I know what the leaf was trying to tell us. We need to turn right once we exit this building."

Everyone turns to listen to Kenji's opinion regarding the leaf.

"What makes you say that?"

Kenji turns toward Bree and holds up the maple leaf. He then turns the leaf on its side.

"I think the leaf was telling us which way to go!"

Mitch starts laughing, which becomes contagious given the stress everyone is under.

"Kenji, I've said it before, and I'll say it again. You are a genius. Let's get out of here and then I'll gladly try your theory concerning the leaf."

Mitch carefully places his left ear up against the door while covering his right ear. The rest of us patiently wait for an all-clear signal. Finally, Mitch reaches out and slowly pushes the bar on the door. He inches the door open, while visibly bracing himself for an attack from the other side. The group lets out a collective breath after he successfully passes through the doorway. The rest of us follow his lead and find ourselves in a room similar to the one on the United States' side of the tunnel. There's a staircase off to the right, and we waste no time heading in that direction. We quietly make our way up the stairs, stopping periodically to listen for any sounds above.

Eventually, we reach the top of the last flight of stairs, which opens into the lobby. Just past the elevator, on our right, is a ticket window. Diagonally in front of our group is the entrance to the lobby from the outside. Sunlight slants in through the double doors and the windows that line the outside walls. When I focus my attention on the entrance doors, I notice another red maple leaf attached to the left door. This time the leaf is leaning on its left side. Carmen apparently notices the same thing because she's the first to comment.

"Hey genius, that leaf points to the left. So, which direction is it going to be?"

"Both, actually."

"How are we supposed to do that?"

Kenji patiently turns to Carmen and holds up his leaf.

"First, we head to the right, and then we take our first left."

Everyone smiles, except for Carmen, who just shakes her head. Mitch motions for the group to stay back, while he cautiously approaches the front doors. After peering out the doors, he removes the leaf and then peeks out each window before returning to the stairs.

"As far as I can tell there's nobody waiting outside, but they could just be hiding behind something waiting for our group to emerge. We obviously can't just stand around here, so follow me and stay down."

Mitch then turns around and heads across the room to the exit. The rest of us mimic his motion by hunching our bodies over in an attempt to create as small a target as possible.

"Okay everyone here's the plan. We're going to head straight out the door and cross the walkway. Let's meet behind the building over there. I'd like to keep this building between us and the island across the way. Stay down and hopefully nobody sees us leaving this building. After we've safely crossed, we'll follow Kenji's hunch."

Our exit from the building seems to go undetected. As we carefully skirt from behind the buildings, there's a sound of an approaching vehicle. Everyone hastily takes cover just in time to avoid being seen by the occupants of a jeep. The jeep screeches to a halt and three soldiers jump out and find separate cover. They appear to be focused on the building we left just minutes before. Stuart is the first to break the tension.

"Well, it looks like we escaped from the tunnel just in time. It seems Taggert's men are taking no chances."

"It doesn't appear that we were spotted, so let's get away from here before any more soldiers arrive. We also need to be as far away as possible when the explosion occurs."

No sooner does Mitch finish his statement, that a muffled explosion emanates from the building entrance. A surge of water bursts into the air and then the middle of the horseshoe begins to collapse. This continues for a short time before the center of the rim slowly begins to level off.

"I guess we used enough explosives. I doubt anyone will be using the tunnel anytime soon."

Mitch claps Cowan on the back in response.

"Nice job burying our tracks. Now let's move it before more company shows up."

Everyone gets up and hurries after Mitch as he begins winding his way behind the buildings and through the sparse trees. We continue heading north along Niagara Parkway until the trees are intersected by a road. Mitch stops and turns to face the group.

"My monitor says this is Murray Street. What do you think Kenji?"

"Since this is our first left, I say we head uphill to the left."

"Unless someone has a better idea, I vote left."

Judging the lack of response to be agreement, Mitch begins to lead us up the hill. The trees quickly begin to thin, and large buildings loom on either side of the road. Before we get a chance to start second guessing our decision, I see Cowan point over to something on the opposite side of the road. Peeking just over the top of the hill is a sign with a large red maple leaf.

42

GENERAL TAGGERT/MITCH

AS THE HELICOPTER hurtles westward, my mind attempts to make sense of the drama that has unfolded up ahead. My flight has been spent coordinating the personnel and resources outside the building containing the rebels. Earlier in the flight, I ordered soldiers to surround the building on the Canadian side of the falls. Even though Sean was certain the tunnel was incomplete, I wasn't about to take any chances. So far, there have been no reports of any rebels emerging from either building.

My latest conversation with Headquarters contained some sobering news. Evidently, the first soldiers to arrive at the building took it upon themselves to conduct an early assault. This was apparently initiated before orders to surround the building and stand-down were received. The individuals have yet to reemerge from the building. During our recent discussion, Sean reported an apparent explosion which occurred somewhere in the tunnel, near the center of Horseshoe Falls. Sean believes the rebels must have encountered the end of the construction and attempted to blast a hole through to the Canadian side. The fact the explosion was seen from land, indicates the tunnel was breached and is most certainly underwater.

While it should be a relief to finally have this crisis over, I can't shake the sudden feeling of emptiness. Perhaps it's the realization my son is dead and there may not be a person alive to answer for his death. Maybe it's the rising body count resulting from this escape attempt. Either way, there has certainly been no winners over the past two weeks. These are the thoughts occupying my mind as the falls come into view.

My helicopter finally touches down on the western end of Goat Island, safely away from the building used by the rebels. I am immediately met by the commanding officer, as I jump down from the helicopter. We hurry away from the prop wash and don't stop until we are standing behind a jeep about two hundred feet from the building entrance. I turn to the commanding officer for an update on the situation.

"What's the latest intel? Are we ready to go in?"

"As you know there was an explosion earlier near the center of the falls. The behavior of the water after the explosion seemed to indicate the tunnel had been breached. We're prepared to move in on your command."

"I want to converge on both buildings at the same time. Your men need to be extremely cautious of traps or any further explosives. This group has already left a few presents which have claimed the lives of good men."

The soldiers methodically close in on all sides. The first group carefully inspects the front entrance before opening the doors and entering the building. They are soon followed by a few more men. About a minute later, a soldier appears in the doorway and waves us over. As I cover the remaining distance, I can see the sober look on the soldier's face.

"What's wrong son?"

The young man struggles to make eye contact as he searches for the right words.

"Sir, I'm afraid there are no survivors. The water level is up to the top of the stairway connected to the first floor. We just received word over the radio that the same can be said for the building on the other side of the tunnel."

Without replying, I maneuver myself through the front door and head over to the stairwell. A group of soldiers move aside as I approach the stairs, their faces downcast. The lobby is lit by the morning sun, but headlamps provide the necessary lighting for the back stairwell. As described earlier, the water level has risen just below the top step. Various debris and detritus float on the surface, but there's no sign of any soldiers or rebels. I'm not sure what I expected to see or feel, perhaps a sense of closure after the past two weeks. Other than an understandable sense of sorrow for the soldiers who were lost, my sentiments regarding the rebels appear to remain unchanged. After a few moments of reflection, I turn away and head toward the exit. I can feel the troubled gazes of my fellow soldiers tracking my exit from the building.

Once outside I make my way to the left and find a location overlooking the falls. I can see soldiers milling around the building on the Canadian side. I slowly reach for my radio and bring it to my mouth.

"Sean, Roddy, are you there?

After a few seconds, the sound of Sean's voice responds.

"What's the status, sir?"

"We've just entered the building only to find the water level up to the top of the stairs. There's no sign of any survivors. I've been notified the same can be said for the building on the other side."

"Well, I guess that's it, General. The rebels must have been trapped and took a chance at opening the blocked tunnel. Their explosives must have breached the surface causing the tunnel to flood."

As Sean is providing his conclusion, I find myself searching the opposite bank of the river. The sixth sense, which has proven invaluable in the past, refuses to settle down.

"Your explanation makes sense, but something just doesn't seem right. After weeks of avoiding capture, why would the rebels place themselves in a situation where they could be easily trapped."

"You kept saying they would eventually make a mistake. You kept the pressure on and funneled them to this area. You can take some solace in the fact you finally achieved the upper hand and defeated the rebels."

"Sean, I find it hard to feel victorious at the moment. I just can't shake the feeling that we haven't seen or heard the last from this group."

My arm drops to my side, and the radio falls from my grasp. The tension of the last few weeks begins to recede, leaving behind a total sense of exhaustion. I place both hands on the low wall and attempt to lose myself in the cascading falls.

The building, with the red maple leaf out front, turned out to be a two-story restaurant. Our group quickly canvassed the interior of the building to ensure it was safe. The remainder of the day has been spent resting and taking turns monitoring the area around the restaurant. Michele and I have just started our shift downstairs. It's just after midnight, and neither of us have been able to get much rest today. The fatigue and emotional stress are evident in her eyes as she scans the deserted street outside.

"Michele, I can handle our shift alone. Why don't you try to get some sleep? You look like you're about to collapse any second."

"Mitch, I appreciate the offer, but I'm afraid sleep won't be an option for a while. I can't stop thinking about Simone and everything she must have been going through. I just wish I would have picked up on things sooner."

I reach over to grasp her hand, which feels dangerously cold. At least she has started talking about her daughter. Perhaps, the initial stage of shock is beginning to fade. She briefly looks over, before returning her attention to the street. She needs time to cope with the loss of her daughter. While our experiences, over the years, have rendered us accustomed to the loss of life, nothing can prepare a parent for the loss of a child. The pain will subside, but the memories and sadness will always flow just below the surface.

Our moment of reflection is interrupted by knocking coming from the rear of the building. I immediately grab my gun and bolt out of my chair. Michele gets up, and I motion for her to stay back. I slowly cross the small dining room and head to the back hallway leading to the restrooms. The hallway ends in a door which leads to the alley behind the building. As we enter the hallway, the knocking is repeated.

"Michele, warn the others we have visitors at the back door. I want them to be prepared in case an assault occurs."

"I'm not leaving you alone down here."

As if to emphasize her point, she levels her gun at the back door. I let out a sigh in resignation and turn to make my way to the back door. As I place my left foot down just before the door, the floorboards creak. My body tenses as I await the gunshot through the wooden door. The tension is broken by a calm voice.

"We are rebel friends, and we're here to escort you to your final destination. Please put down your weapons, so nobody gets hurt."

"How can we be sure you're not the enemy?"

A few moments pass and I begin to worry that the front door is unguarded. A scraping sound begins at the base of the door. Michele bends down to retrieve a piece of paper. I turn on my headlamp, which illuminates a dollar bill. Michele turns the bill over revealing the words 'Break in Case of

Emergency' written across the front. The year 2025 is circled in red. My pulse quickens as I stare at the bill.

"Does that allay your fears?"

I look back toward the door and then at Michele, trying to decide our next move. The voice continues, but with a more sarcastic tone.

"I would have brought a Buffalo Bills helmet, but it wouldn't fit under the door."

Michele smiles, and I can feel a weight suddenly lifted from my shoulders.

43

COWAN

I STILL CAN'T believe we are on our way to the settlement of the previous resistance groups. Our vans have been driving north for over two hours. We passed the city of Toronto an hour ago, and have been driving on Route 400 since. There are six of us in each van, along with a few of our new friends. Bree has her head on my left shoulder, and the sound of heavy breathing indicates she has fallen asleep once again. Marcus is on her left staring out his window, apparently sharing my difficulty with falling asleep.

My thoughts drift back to the initial meeting with the rebels at the restaurant. At first, I was convinced, it was a ploy by General Taggert to capture our group. As Derek, who was the unofficial spokesman for our newest friends, described the cabin and its contents, I began to lower my guard. They were impressed at the skill of our group to decipher all the clues without the help of additional information. They had our group under surveillance during the day in order to verify our identity. A group of them had been camped out next door listening to hidden microphones and viewing hidden cameras. For obvious reasons, they had to be certain of our intentions before making contact. At one point Kenji asked them how they knew we had arrived at the restaurant. Derek smiled and asked him for the ceramic turtle he had obtained from the cabin. Kenji retrieved the turtle and handed it over to him. He turned the figurine over and explained that a tracking device had been embedded inside. Apparently, the rebels had been tracking us since we left the cabin.

As a matter of fact, our progress is being tracked at this very moment. So, here I sit, finding it impossible to sleep, as I anticipate meeting my father for the first time. Eventually, we pass through a populated area with numerous cars pushed to the side of the road. I wonder if there are bodies still inside some of the vehicles. Before my imagination has a chance to get away from me, I turn my attention to the interior of the van. Mitch is sitting in front of us between Dr. Timms and Grace. He has very little room since both shoulders are busy supporting sleeping individuals. If it weren't for Mitch, we probably wouldn't have made it to this point. He was always calm under pressure, which kept everyone believing we had a chance of successfully reaching our destination. As if reading my mind, Mitch slowly turns his head and looks back. Dr. Timms rolls off his shoulder and leans against the window to her right. Mitch glances over at Bree and then appears to rummage around in his jacket for something. He then turns around and reaches back over the seat. In his right hand are two envelopes.

"I was told to hold on to these until the appropriate time."

I reach forward and take the two envelopes. I turn on the reading lamp above my seat and notice one envelope has my name on the front and the other has Bree's. Bree lifts her head from my shoulder and turns her attention to the two envelopes. After handing over her envelope, I find myself staring at my name. Finally, after gathering enough courage, I break the seal and pull out the paper folded inside and begin reading.

Cowan,

I made Mitch promise he would wait until you were out of harm's way before giving you this letter. The fact you are reading this means my mission was successful. I wish I could have spent more time with you, but I'm grateful I was able to witness firsthand the man you have become. I'm proud of you, and I know your father will feel the same. Please give my son a hug for me and send him my love. Also, please continue to take care of your sister Bree. Mitch just found out recently, and he thought a family member should present the great news. I will hopefully be looking down and watching the rebellion grow.

Love,
Arlen

My heart is still racing as I reread the bottom of the letter. I look to my left to see Bree's startled expression. Apparently, her letter contained the same bombshell. Without speaking, we throw our arms around each other. My emotions, which I had kept in check to this point, suddenly spill over. I can sense movement behind Bree followed by Marcus' voice.

"What the heck is up with you two?"

The letter, which I have clutched in my right hand, is pulled free. After a few moments, I hear him gasp.

"Damn, I knew there was something up with you guys. Suddenly everything makes sense."

One by one, the rest of the van turns around to see what all the commotion is about. Letters are passed around, followed by congratulations and hugs. Eventually, the excitement calms down, and everyone settles back for the remainder of the trip. The constant hum of the tires finally lulls me to sleep.

It must be close to sunrise when my eyes finally open. In the twilight, I can make out trees on either side of our van. The van is bouncing up and down due to rugged terrain. We have left the paved road and are currently moving along a dirt trail littered with ruts. The condition of the track forces the van to slow down. We creep along at a slow pace for the better part of an hour. By this time the sun has started peeking over the trees as we make our way around a sharp bend in the road. The driver pulls off to the left shoulder and brings the van to a long-awaited stop. The front doors open and our new friends motion for us to get out of the van. They begin walking over to the edge of the road which overlooks a valley.

A small settlement has been established in the valley, along a small winding river. Rustic log cabins have been built in neat rows surrounded by well-maintained fields. A few people can be seen walking around and performing various tasks. The tableau below us, coupled with the sun rising above the trees, provides an air of peace and tranquility. Derek, who has spent the entire trip in the front passenger seat of our van, turns toward our group.

"Welcome to the rebel settlement. This is your new home."

It must have been the combination of the beautiful landscape and the trials of our long trek which brought out the groups' emotional response. Suddenly, everyone starts hugging, laughing, and acting like a bunch of kids. Our new friends have no choice, but to join the spectacle. Finally, with everyone emotionally spent, Mitch asks the question on everyone's mind.

"Derek, where are we?"

"I guess it's safe to tell you now. We are currently in the heart of what was called Algonquin Provincial Park in Canada. Early on we searched for a place that was secluded, provided for all of our needs, yet was close enough to be accessible to future rebels. This land has served us very well. So, what do you say we go down and get you guys settled."

I hesitate and take one last look at my new home before I feel Bree's hand pulling me toward the van. As we start down the last phase of our long journey, my anxiety begins to increase as I prepare to meet my father for the first time. I imagine Bree must have similar feelings, which must be heightened since she has only had a few hours to prepare.

The van continues down winding trails, as it makes its way down the hillside. The trail begins to level off as we finally reach the canyon floor. The trees become sparse on either side of our vehicle, where we emerge from the forest and enter the outer reaches of the settlement. The dirt road leads to a small bridge spanning the narrow river. On the opposite bank of the river, the road continues down what appears to be the main street in the settlement. The wide dirt street runs between identical log cabins, set in the midst of large plots of land. As we drive slowly down the main drag, curious citizens periodically emerge from their homes. The road continues until it's joined by a smaller perpendicular path containing additional buildings on either side. A larger building faces the end of the road with a small dirt parking lot in the front. Our van crosses the smaller road and pulls into the small clearing. The second van pulls alongside, and then everyone begins to get out of both vehicles.

My heart begins to race, and my mouth gets dry, as I realize the moment has arrived. I reach down to grab Bree's hand only to find it moist with sweat. The side door of the van slides open on my right side, but I continue to lock eyes with my sister.

"Cowan, I haven't been this scared since we left the territory."

I look into her eyes and smile, suddenly aware my feelings are different now that I know she's my sister.

"Don't worry. Your big brother will take care of you now."

She smiles, but her eyes glisten, and a lone tear escapes down the right side of her face.

"I hate to interrupt this touching moment, but I'm all cramped up over here."

We both look over at Marcus, and this time it's Bree who punches him in the right shoulder. The exchange has lightened the mood and reduced our anxiety. The three of us join the rest of the group outside of the van.

The front door of the building opens and out strides an imposing figure followed by a few other citizens. The man proceeds to walk down the steps and toward the group of us in the parking area. He's tall and broad-shouldered, but what causes him to stand apart is his fiery, red hair which falls to his shoulders. His eyes are locked on mine, and as he gets closer, the blue color becomes obvious. He continues to walk directly toward me, before stopping directly in front and stretching out his arms.

"Son, you can't imagine how long I've dreamed of this moment."

I glance over at Bree, and she gives a subtle nod. Without missing a beat, we both turn toward him and reply at the same time.

"Father, it's great to finally meet you!"

The look on his face is priceless. The two of us waste no time to rush into his outstretched arms for the long-awaited embrace.

As the three of us embrace, I observe the rest of our group celebrating with their newfound neighbors. Images of our trek flash through my mind as I hug my family, hesitant to let go. A long journey has finally come to an end, but something inside me wonders if it's not just the beginning of a new one.

TO THE READER

If you enjoyed this book, please leave a review. Reviews are the best way to help self-published writers get noticed.

I would also like to get your opinion about the book and find out what you'd like to see in upcoming books in this series. So, please contact me either by e-mail or by visiting my website.

childrenofapis@gmail.com

www.childrenofapis.com

Thank you for taking the time to read my book, and I look forward to hearing from you.

ACKNOWLEDGMENTS

First of all, I'd like to thank all my beta readers and editors, Al, Mike, Jordan, Norm, Jian, and Ruth, who took the time out of their busy schedules to help out a first-time author. The numerous changes and critiques helped polish the original story and were provided in a manner that didn't douse my enthusiasm.

I'd like to thank Vann Baker, Elegant Book Design, for his professional cover design. Thank you for being so patient and flexible during the initial layout process.

To my daughters, Shannon and Shaelyn, and my step-children, Baylee and Ian, who provided the much-needed young-adult perspective. In the words of my daughter Shae, "Dad you really killed it." Apparently, in young adult lingo, it means that I did a really good job.

Most of all, I need to send a special thanks to my best friend and wife, Ruth. When she came up with the crazy idea, in August of 2015, that I should write a book, it was met with laughter. When I finally composed myself, a seed of an idea was planted. Over the course of 2016, the idea blossomed into the journey which you just completed. Hopefully, you enjoyed reading the adventure as much as I enjoyed writing it.

ABOUT THE AUTHOR

 John Raposa lives in Bristol, Rhode Island with his wife, Ruth. He has two children, Shannon and Shaelyn, and two step-children, Baylee and Ian. Children of Apis: Rebel Blood is his first self-published novel. When he isn't keeping his wife awake with the clicking of the keyboard, he works as an electrical engineer in Newport, R.I. His hobbies include, softball, running, spinning, and writing. He is currently working on the next book in the Children of Apis series.

www.ingramcontent.com/pod-product-compliance
Lightning Source LLC
Chambersburg PA
CBHW060517180626
46817CB00002B/389